The Door that Faced West

an Early Western

Alan M. Clark

IFD Publishing
P.O. Box 40776, Eugene, Oregon 97404 U.S.A.
www.ifdpublishing.com

Originally published by Lazy Fascist Press.

This is a work of fiction. Although the novel is inspired by real events and actual human lives, the characters have been created for the sake of this story
and are either products of the author's imagination or are used fictitiously. Any
resemblance to actual events or locales or persons, living or dead, is entirely
coincidental.

Acknowledgments

Thanks to Cameron Pierce, Kirsten Alene, Eric Witchey, Jill Bauman, Susan Stockell, Randy Fox, Paul Groendes, Owl Goingback, Pigg, Frank Freemon, David Conover, Hans Von Wirth, Dieter Annecke, Dirk Bützer, Laurie Ewing McNichols, Rena Mason, Ross E. Lockhart, Molly Tanzer, and Melody Kees Clark.

Special thanks to Rose Prescott for horse sense.

Author's Note

This is my third novel of historical fiction. When choosing subject matter from history, I'm drawn to the lives of people who were compelled by circumstance to make decisions they believed were in their own best interest, but which had terrible consequences. Our inability to see the future, coupled with a desire to solve our problems quickly, often gets us into trouble.

The Door that Faced West is inspired by the murderous Harpe brothers, Wiley and Micajah, of early American history. I've changed the names of some of the principal characters and some place names. For purposes of storytelling, I have not adhered strictly to the history as we know it, and where needed, I created scenarios out of whole cloth to further the plot.

The story takes place in the American South as the eighteenth century fades and the nineteenth century begins. At the time, the new states of Tennessee and Kentucky were part of the western frontier. Law and order had only a weak grip in the wilderness of the new states, consequently brutality and sudden death were common-place. With poor communication between isolated settlements, the frontier was an area where unscrupulous men frequently got away with terrible crimes.

The story in *The Door that Faced West* unfolds from the point of view of one of the Harpe brothers' wives. Sadie Rice is the sixteen-year-old daughter of a minister. She falls in with the brothers because they appear to be the sort of tough men who will help her survive in the wilderness of the early American frontier. Even as the violent nature of the two brothers is revealed, she sticks with them. With her decisions, she becomes complicit in the most horrendous crimes.

What we know of the woman from history is that she traveled the wilderness trails with the Harpes and was witness to terrible violence. When she was finally separated from the brothers, she remarried, settled down, had children, and lived out her life in an unremarkable, seemingly normal fashion. That is virtually all history tells us about her.

I wanted to know what sort of emotional gymnastics were necessary for her to live with herself. Having come from what people of the time considered a good, spiritual background, why would she endure the hardships of life on the trail with the horrible Harpes? How could she go on with a peaceful life after witnessing and benefitting from their most terrible deeds? What of regret, guilt, and shame did she experience or was she secretly filled with glee for what she'd seen and done? The possibility exists that she felt both extremes.

I wrote *The Door that Faced West* to explore through character and story development the emotional evolution of one who found herself in such circumstances. While writing, I discovered a hell of an adventure.

—Alan M. Clark
Eugene, Oregon

The Door that Faced West

an Early Western

Alan M. Clark

Publishing

Eugene, Oregon

1
Misgivings
Russellville, Kentucky
1835

Sadie Rice Early had struggled to love her fellow human beings, including family, since the start of her seventeenth year, three and a half decades ago. Experience had given her a hatred of living souls that prevented her from succeeding until her daughter, Minerva, gave birth to Timothy.

Although Sadie had an affection for the boy from the moment she set eyes on him when he was an infant, their true love for one another emerged on Timothy's fifth birthday. She, the boy's parents, and Timothy were celebrating with a picnic in a beautiful green glade on their property along a curve of Wootens Creek. The young boy had opened his presents. While pleased with the dark brown walnut bear his father, Doyle Tenbrook, had whittled and the blue cotton shirts Minerva had made for him, he was most delighted by what Sadie gave him; a small silver ring engraved with the letters TRT.

"Those are your initials," Sadie told him. "I give you the ring because you have something of mine and I have something of yours."

Minerva had a troubled look, but she smiled, as did Doyle.

The obvious question formed in Timothy's eyes and he lifted his tiny eyebrows in wonder.

"Your middle name is my maiden name," Sadie continued, "the name I went by before I married. We share the name Rice."

In that instant, Timothy gave a smile to his grandmother that created the bond between them. Something about the look in his bright green eyes had captured her heart. Sadie set aside the misgivings she normally held toward her fellow human beings, and within a short time she gratefully came to love him more than life itself.

At present, Timothy was eight years old, and Sadie couldn't do without him. She found that they had an uncanny ability to communicate without words. A nod or the slightest facial expression or gesture of limb shared between them seemed to convey what required a full, vocal conversation for others. They delighted to speak to one another secretly in that way, across a room perhaps, while others present remained unaware of their communication. At the heart of each of their wordless conversations was the expression that they shared not only experiences, but a similar response to the experiences, that they were allies who understood each other intuitively in a wide world full of misunderstanding, and that they appreciated and loved one another. The practice had drawn them close in a manner she had not experienced with anyone, save Bett Roberts, her best friend when she was a child.

Sitting with the family for breakfast as the sun came up on a warm summer morning, Sadie kept her eyes on Timothy. Minerva set a steaming-hot bowl of grits before him and one before Sadie, then returned to the kitchen. Timothy watched his mother go, then glanced at his father, who was breaking the beeswax seal on a fresh jar of crabapple preserves. Sadie knew the boy was making sure his parents weren't watching before turning up his nose at his grits. As she expected, he made the face while looking straight at her across the dining room table. Sadie allowed a slight smile. Minerva returned from the kitchen, set a porcelain bowl of grits before Doyle, one at her own place setting, and sat to join the family for breakfast.

Sadie considered the lumpy white porridge. Although she'd known much hunger in life, and therefore ate anything edible placed before her, she lifted one side of her lip to let Timothy know she agreed with his assessment of the food.

He usually said, "Hominy grits did you get, Grandma?" Instead, he merely smiled and suppressed a giggle as the joke now went without saying.

Sadie dutifully lifted a spoonful to her mouth, pausing to wait for him. He smiled, then widened his eyes, flared his nostrils, lifted a fork of the food to his mouth, and took a bite. Chewing, he made a soft pig-snorting sound.

Doyle rapped the tabletop to get the boy's attention and gave him a stern look, but not one without a touch of good humor. When Timothy glanced at his mother, she was slowly shaking her head.

Sadie had gotten her grandson's message, though, especially since he'd expressed the sentiment at the breakfast table in words on two other occasions. "Anything that has to be treated with lye to become edible," he'd say in a pompous, preaching tone, "isn't meant to be eaten by man."

His parents thought his words funny the first time. The second time, he'd added, "Hominy is hardly better than the feed corn we give the pigs." When Timothy followed that with a loud raspberry, he'd been told his comments about the food were no longer welcome.

At present, Sadie tilted her head and showed Timothy a sympathetic smile, then dug into her grits as if the porridge were the best food in the world. He smiled grimly and nodded his head for her. He ate all his grits and then licked the bowl.

Sadie's heart swelled with pride.

~ ~ ~

In the evening, as Sadie joined the family for dinner, she noted that an unease had taken hold of Timothy since breakfast. He wasn't a child given to sadness or worry, but he was clearly brooding about something. Although he took his place at the table with the rest of the family, he seemed far away. His feelings remained hidden behind a stony face, and his eyes were downcast. He refused food and mumbled something about having a stomachache.

"All the more reason to eat your vegetables, young man," Minerva said.

"Leave him be, sweetheart" Doyle said. "I can see he's not himself."

Timothy remained strangely quiet. Even when ill, he was normally demonstrative. Sadie recognized something of herself in her grandson's current bearing, something she realized in that moment was an unflattering quality in herself. In addition to his emotional withdrawal, he was guarded in the things he said in response to his father's smalltalk, as if afraid that if he opened up too much, a secret might get out.

"I thought we should take the afternoon Thursday to go fishing," Doyle said to Timothy.

"Huh?" Timothy grunted, his thoughts seemingly far away.

"Pig says, 'Huh?'" his father said. "Pull his tail, he says, 'Uh-huh.'"

Meant as a humorous way to discourage his son from responding in grunts, Doyle's expression usually got a smile from Timothy.

When the boy didn't respond, Minerva placed a hand on his forehead. He tried to shrug her off, but she was insistent. "No fever," she said after a moment, then frowned. "I'm sorry you're not feeling well."

Although he might be suffering a belly ache, Sadie suspected he also endured a sore conscience. Although surrounded by those he loved, Timothy seemed particularly ill-at-ease. She knew well the experience of being uncomfortable around family. Shamefully, she found herself becoming angry with him, and hoping he would hurry up and get over whatever bothered him so she wouldn't have to find out about it. Despite her reluctance to know about his troubles, her love for the boy compelled her to watch him closely.

He ate nothing that night, a small amount of scrambled eggs for breakfast the following morning, and had little to eat at midday. He'd always had a confident and steady gaze, but as he went about his work, helping his father tend the plants in the fields and make repairs to the tobacco barn, his eyes darted with wary glances. In response to his father's jokes, Timothy's laughter was forced and his smile a brittle thing, where before the expression had been large, toothy, and joyful. At dinner, he ate only a biscuit and asked to be excused from the table.

"If he isn't better the day after tomorrow, we should call on the doctor," Minerva said. Doyle nodded his agreement.

Sadie believed that she alone suspected the boy suffered more than a physical ailment.

Although Timothy's hunger had returned the next day, his good humor had not. Sadie decided to draw him out and try to help, despite an unaccountable trepidation about discovering what lay behind his troubled green eyes.

Knowing Timothy loved nothing so much as pie, she baked one, and while the sweet-smelling pastry cooled, she sought him in the barn where he busied himself mucking out the horse stalls. "When you're finished, come enjoy a slice of elderberry pie with your old grandma."

"Yes, ma'am," he said without displaying his customary enthusiasm for the treat.

After several hours passed without Timothy appearing in the kitchen for his slice, Sadie left the cold pie wrapped in a cloth on the kitchen table and went in search of the boy. She found him sitting on the old, wooden bridge over Wootens Creek, his feet dangling over the edge and a glum look on his face as he watched the brilliant green and blue damselflies flit about on the rocks below. Seeing her coming, he bowed his head in shame.

"I know you know," he said as she stepped onto the bridge and leaned on its weathered railing. Timothy had yet to look up.

"What do I know?" she asked quietly.

"That me and Whorley stole his mother's pies, the ones she baked for the charity picnic at the church. You know what he's like." Tears spilled down Timothy's tanned cheeks.

"Whorley and I," Sadie corrected. She allowed silence as she thought of Whorley Emmons. With a chill intuition, she understood Timothy's association with the rapscallion. Although nothing but trouble, Whorley's commanding and reckless character was attractive for one seeking adventure. When young, Sadie had known his type intimately. She thought briefly of Wiley and Micajah Harpe. The comparison was hardly fair. The Harpe brothers had been such savage—

No—she would not dwell on it—not now.

Damn it, why was life so hard? Why did she have to watch the boy become guarded and unhappy as he slowly and inevitably lost his innocence? Although she wanted to return to the house and allow her grandson to work his problems out for himself, she had a responsibility to help him. Sadie steadied her trembling hand before placing it on Timothy's shoulder.

"He made me do it," the boy said miserably. "I stole the key to Mrs. Emmons's pie safe while he drew her away, making trouble out back. Later, while she went to the privy, we took the pies to the woods."

Timothy broke down crying. Sadie knelt to comfort him despite the pain in her arthritic knees. She would stay because she loved Timothy and he needed her, but every part of her insisted that she flee.

"I told him, I don't want any of the pie 'cause it's wrong. He said, you might as well go on and eat some, since I'm gonna get punished for it, not you. I won't tell nobody you was in on it."

Timothy sobbed. "I ate so much, I was sick for two days."

Sadie felt ill as she listened.

"I went to Mrs. Emmons and told her. She said she knew Whorley got good boys into trouble sometimes and she forgave me. That made it worse! I confessed in prayer, but I don't feel better. How can I make it right when I knew it was wrong?"

Sadie had spent much of her life asking herself the same question concerning the year she'd spent with the Harpes. She didn't want to remember—*not now*—yet the memories came anyway: The metallic odor of human blood and offal, a man's corpse sunk in a river, its gutted belly burdened with heavy stones, and the balling of an infant cut short against the hard trunk of a tree.

No, there was no answer for the boy's question! He was a fool to think that confession would do him any good. If he knew what she'd done in her life, he wouldn't think his petty crime so horrible.

Timothy's expression told Sadie that he saw her distress—and was that a hint of contempt in his eyes? For the first time she got a glimpse of Micajah Harpe's features in the boy's face.

In that instant she had to be rid of Timothy. Sadie shoved him hard enough that he fell and struck his head on the railing. She stumbled back in horror at her own actions, tripped and fell to the ground just past the end of the bridge.

She didn't want to see how badly Timothy had been harmed. With the dread sounds of the boy finding his feet and walking toward her, Sadie curled up defensively on the ground. He was a mere silhouette against the sky as he loomed over her, and she feared he might strike her.

Instead, he bent down to help her up. Sadie saw the blood running down his forehead as she stood.

The bright red on his face was horrible enough, but the blood smeared on the rough wood of the bridge railing touched something much deeper; a memory of running over uneven ground with one foot bare and her young lungs aching with each panicked breath. Sadie shut out the recollection before it was too late.

"Are you hurt, Grandma?" Timothy asked without anger. "Did you trip?"

He'd given her the benefit of the doubt. He must have thought she'd pushed him as a consequence of losing her balance.

My shame crafted the contempt and placed it in his eye!

Timothy had forgotten his problems concerning the theft of pies in the face of possible danger to his grandmother. He truly held no scorn for her.

What's wrong with me?

Despite the boy's words and actions, her bad feelings toward him persisted. Seeing the worried look on his face, she knew he'd tragically misread her character. For that, she hated him all the more.

Sadie had a perverse desire to tell him all about her past. The truth would horrify him and he'd never love her again. The cruelty of the idea was startling. She'd never had such pitiless feelings toward the boy before.

How could she think and feel such things, when she loved him so?

Timothy still waited for her answer.

"No," she said, hiding her feelings. "I'm not harmed."

Sadie had to get away before she did something worse to Timothy. She shook herself loose from the boy and hurried toward the house. A glance back showed him watching after her, a troubled look on his face.

Sadie cleaned up the kitchen and retired to her room. She drew the window curtains and lay on her bed for the rest of the day and the night. Although she expected to rise the next day feeling better, she found herself still stricken with horror and grief over her reaction to Timothy. Sadie spent the following day hiding under the bedclothes. Nothing Minerva or Doyle said or did would rouse her from her bed.

They kept Timothy away from her, telling him that she needed her rest. Sadie was glad. She didn't understand the source of her anger, and feared unleashing the darkness in her heart upon the boy.

During the years of raising Minerva, Sadie had reached within many times for the affection needed to be a good mother, and found nothing. Minerva had turned to her father for emotional guidance, and Sadie was left feeling hollow and without purpose. She didn't know how she'd endured the loneliness until Timothy had come along. Life had begun anew with his arrival. Turning from his problems in concern for hers, as he did on the bridge, that was *her* Timothy.

Now in her fifties, with her health beginning to fail, Sadie found that Timothy's presence in her life was all that mattered. He deserved much better from her. To give that to him, she had no choice but to endure the pain of looking again at herself.

2
Flight
Tippens, North Carolina
July 15, 1800

"She ain't here," Mr. Roberts said. "Took up with scoundrels, same as carried off her sister, ten years ago. Good riddance I say."

Sadie had never spoken to Bett's stepfather before. By his accent, English or Scottish, she suspected he hadn't spent the bulk of his life in North Carolina, and by his language she presumed he was a rather rough man.

What he said didn't make sense—did it? Bett had gotten a reputation in the last couple of years for getting into trouble. Rumor had it that she'd been caught smoking cigars and laughing with young men while without a chaperone. Sadie had never asked her about the rumors. Bett wouldn't run off with scoundrels, though, would she?

Sadie stared at Mr. Roberts, not knowing what to do. He leaned on his cane, the one she had heard plenty about from Bett. While the walking stick was meant to help him cope with a war injury, a ball still lodged in his lower leg, the stout wooden staff was also the weapon he most often wielded against Bett.

"You find her, tell her she should pay what's owed."

Again, Sadie didn't understand what Mr. Roberts was talking about.

"Have you no notion where she might have gone?" she asked.

"Likely she's over in The Cut." Without further ado, Mr. Roberts shut the door of his cabin.

Sadie found herself alone again in the night. She pulled her shawl more tightly about her shoulders.

Although a shocking idea that Bett might have fled to The Cut, the suggestion made sense in a way, considering what she'd always said about taking refuge where family wouldn't follow. Sadie had heard the squalid hamlet was a cluster of rough dwellings below Blackburn Bluff, about five miles away. Church-going folks said The Cut was a lawless place where whites and Indians "carried on."

Since Sadie's father, Reverend Rice, would be looking for her and she needed an ally, she didn't have much choice but to continue the search for her friend. Although Sadie found the prospect of looking for Bett in The Cut frightening, she didn't think the Reverend would look for her there. To get to Blackburn Bluff, Sadie would have to move west, crossing planted fields belonging to several farms, and make her way through a forested area along Vitner Creek. She'd always had good night vision, and the gibbous moon, currently high in the starry, clear sky, would provide her with illumination.

She turned to face the Big Dipper in the west, hurried across the rutted road in front of the Roberts home, and entered the shadowy woods. As she moved between the dark tree trunks, among the sounds of crickets and the soft yellow flashes of the lightning bugs, Sadie knew she'd have to hurry if she didn't want to be knocking on strangers' doors in The Cut in the middle of the night. Had Bett taken up with some man, an Indian, perhaps? Sadie couldn't imagine what that might be like.

She had taken to the woods to avoid the danger of being spotted on the road, by either Reverend Rice or someone willing to report to him. As the forest grew denser, her concern for her safety returned with a memory: She'd overheard Mr. Parches tell her father that red wolves had recently taken a toll on local livestock, and that farmers had been hunting the predators.

With an abrupt feeling of naked vulnerability, Sadie's flesh crawled with goosebumps. She flinched as sounds from the forest told her imagination that she was being stalked. Twigs snapping became misplaced stealthy footsteps, and the sounds of tree limbs groaning as they rubbed together in the wind were the low growls of a savage beast crouched to spring. Trying to take even breaths, Sadie held down her rising panic and concentrated on placing her footsteps quietly.

Coming to the first planted field she would have to cross, she began to breathe more easily. Then, moving between rows of tobacco plants, she realized that her sense of relief was premature; if she were seen or heard moving through the night across a farmer's property, she might be greeted with rifle fire.

She'd moved fifty yards into the field when a dog began to bark and her panic rose again. As several more canine voices joined the first, she crouched behind a plant and listened, her senses suddenly much keener. A commotion of snarling toward the west resolved itself into a pack of dogs in pursuit. They moved south at a right angle to her course, however, and she decided they were occupied with other prey, perhaps red wolves. Sadie rose and continued, increasing her pace, still moving westward.

Keeping an ear on the activity of the dogs, Sadie stumbled through a melon patch, breaking and slipping in the fruit as she went, then entered another planted field.

The dogs seemed to have cornered something. Shouting emerged from the direction the pack had taken, and Sadie knew that men had joined the hunt. To her relief, they still didn't follow her.

Sadie negotiated more fields and plots than she cared to count. No doubt passing through property belonging to several farmers, she crossed four roads, and climbed over eight split rail fences. Finally, she dodged her way through orchards full of low-hanging branches that plucked at her in the dark, and reached the edge of the forest again. Before passing beneath the dark canopy of trees, she checked the position of the Big Dipper and then continued west. As she entered the forest, a distant gunshot—perhaps a fatal shot to some poor red wolf—echoed in the night.

Sadie moved through the trees at an even pace for another half hour, maintaining awareness of the position of the Big Dipper when possible through the small gaps in the foliage overhead. To prevent her imagination getting the better of her, Sadie tried to ignore the sounds of the darkened forest, and didn't hear the animals stalking her until almost too late.

She turned to see two red wolves running crouched in the brush to her right. With more swiftness than she'd have thought possible, she pivoted left and grabbed a low tree branch. Sadie hadn't climbed a tree in a couple of years, but she scrambled up without a thought, her mind racing, her limbs flush with a shocking energy. She swung up onto the branch and drew her tingling legs and feet up as the wolves lunged for them. A scream struggled to emerge. Sadie gasped for air and the cry died in her throat. She climbed higher. The frustrated beasts clawed and leapt at the tree, making a futile effort to clamber up after her, their eyes occasionally flashing a demonic blue-green in the moonlight.

The sack of food hanging from her right shoulder slipped off. She caught the cloth strap and kept it from falling. Preparing to run away from home, she'd wanted to take something along to eat. The easiest for her to carry were some hoecakes and tallow candles. She'd grabbed a handful of the cakes and six of the skinny candles and stuffed them in the sack. Of course, the smell of the tallow attracted the wolves.

She imagined having to spend the night in the tree, and knew that eventually she would become sleepy. At first she thought sleep in the tree was impossible without falling to a certain death. Then she noticed a configuration of four limbs that would hold her securely. She climbed to that perch and tried to relax.

Strangely, she felt less unease in the presence of wolves than she did at home with her own father. Many believed the predators a manifestation of demonic power in the world. Although she found them frightening, she didn't believe they were evil. Simple and straightforward, they were merely hungry and wanted to survive, and she could not begrudge them their savage behavior in a brutal world.

Sadie had come to believe that if evil existed—such as her father's need to be cruel—the wickedness was the exclusive territory of Man. Within her mind, Sadie had left him long ago, having rejected him as a parent, as a teacher, and as an example. She didn't believe what he taught of discipline or the spirit. She did not believe in his religion or God.

At present, feeling safe in her perch in the tree, if a little uncomfortable, she watched the lightning bugs. With time, the sound of the crickets faded into the background and she heard the wolves' breathing. The rhythm slowed with time, each breath longer, deeper, as if the animals were falling asleep. With the peaceful sound, she felt at ease, away from her father. As exhaustion crept up on her, so did a half-formed thought: Even if her father found her, hidden in the dark, the wolves would provide her protection of a sort. The wolves did not lay siege, but stood guard, she told herself. With friends of that sort, the night no longer held any threat.

Sadie pulled her shawl more tightly against the slight chill in the air and closed her eyes.

3
Blackburn Bluff

At dawn Sadie became aware of the stirring of the wolves on the ground below. She saw them staring into the distance toward the East. Looking in the same direction, she saw nothing at first, then hounds came into view through the trees, a couple hundred yards away.

The wolves were definitely aware of them. They paced, growling deep in their throats, while the dogs began to bark in hysterical fits. The wolves looked up at Sadie, clearly unwilling to leave her. Despite her earlier notion of them as protectors, she knew they would devour her, given the chance.

At present, she could see men with rifles following the hounds—another hunting party.

Sadie gulped several fearful breaths, then tried to calm herself and think, but she saw no way out of her predicament.

The hounds would track the wolves to the tree and the hunters would find her. They'd save her from the wolves, only to turn her over to her father.

At least the wolves could get away. Sadie turned to them. "Run," she said. They lifted their gaze to her again. "Run away," she said.

The big one tilted his head as if considering her words. He looked at the smaller one, then they both took flight, running northwest through the trees. The hounds heard or saw the wolves. Baying, the dogs chased the predators, drawing the hunting party away from Sadie's hiding place.

The wolves had protected her after all.

When they were far enough away that she could no longer hear them, she climbed out of the tree and moved southwest for a while. Then, taking her position from the golden glow of the rising sun, Sadie resumed her westward course.

She heard several dogs barking even before Blackburn Bluff came into sight. As she drew closer and saw the rock face in the distance, she moved cautiously for fear the dogs might attack. Unmolested, she arrived at a broad, muddy path that ran between hovels at the base of the bluff. The dogs, five mongrels of varying size and color, were all tied. Each lunged at her when she went by, but their tethers brought them up short.

She looked doubtfully at the dwellings on either side of the path. Most were the crude wattle and daub structures the Indians favored. Others, under an overhanging rock of the bluff, were simple shacks made of rough-hewn saplings strapped together with poplar bark rope, perhaps unfinished wattle and daub. She detected the faint odor of rotting flesh under the strong smell of slops and woodsmoke that permeated the area.

Shuttered windows here and there had opened a crack as she made her way through the community. She went unchallenged, and decided she must not appear threatening. Still, the inhabitants weren't going to help her find Bett without first being asked. She'd have to start knocking on doors and talking to strangers. At the thought, her heart leapt in her chest. How would she be received? If a male Indian answered the door, might he drag her inside and rape her?

No, she thought, looking at the position of the sun and deciding that the time was close to eight o'clock in the morning. *The men will be about their business outside the home. If anyone answers, she'll be a woman.*

Sadie picked a hovel to approach and was moving forward, carefully stepping around piles of horse manure in the muddy track and swatting away flies, when she heard the creaking of a wooden hinge. Looking up, she saw Bett standing in the doorway of a wattle and daub structure a stone's throw away on the left side of the path, a surprised yet mischievous smile on her face.

"Come quickly," Bett said, "before you wake the dead."

Quaking with excitement and relief, Sadie hurried across the deeply rutted path, fouling her boots to the ankle with mud. She smiled as Bett held the crude door open for her. Upon entering the dark interior, however, her joyful expression withdrew quickly. The smell of unwashed bodies and bodily waste within was potent. She had certainly had her share of experiences with such odors, but never so overpowering. Sadie became lightheaded and stumbled in the darkness. Bett caught and steadied her.

"How do you happen to be here?" she whispered.

Still unable to see much in the darkened room, Sadie concluded that Bett spoke quietly because someone slept nearby.

"Father would have killed me if I'd stayed," Sadie whispered when she'd caught her breath.

"Yes," Bett said, as if the statement went without saying.

"I spoke to Mr. Roberts. He said you might be here. How long have you been?"

"Four days."

Bett Roberts, born Bett Woods, was eighteen years old, two years older than Sadie. She had blue eyes in a round, pretty face, glossy dark brown hair, and pale skin with plenty of freckles. Their friendship began when they were small, Sadie eight years old and Bett ten, while attending Mrs. Evory's Dame School for girls.

Sadie and Bett took a similar route between home and school, twice a day. Conversations with Bett strayed into rather mature subjects at times. Sadie frequently found their discussions uncomfortable. They were also the most interesting and exciting she'd ever had.

With time, and the appearance and healing of numerous and similar scrapes, cuts, bruises, limping gaits, tender shoulders, arms, backs, hips, and abdomens between them, their haunted eyes met in an understanding that they both suffered the same sort of brutality in their respective homes. Their friendship continued after they left school. When Sadie was thirteen years old and Bett fifteen, they began to talk about the abuse, and Bett had made a suggestion: "I think we should run away to the frontier."

Sadie's eyes had grown large and her mouth had dropped open. With few settlements along the rivers west of the Appalachian Mountain range, the wilderness in the new states of Tennessee and Kentucky was vast and peopled with savage Indians and white criminals who had fled prosecution in the East. For Bett to suggest such a thing, she was either foolish or brave.

"I could never do that," Sadie had said, shaking her head. She *did* think of running away to the frontier, however, especially on the day her father dunked her left arm into a hot rendering pot as punishment for what he considered an inappropriate smile. The more she thought about Bett's suggestion, the more sense it made. At present, Sadie thought her friend's idea might be the only solution to her predicament. Even Reverend Rice would be discouraged from searching for his daughter among the wilds.

She wondered if Bett still considered fleeing to the frontier. Her father might not be quite the threat to her that the Reverend was to Sadie. If she did travel into the wilderness, she should be a part of a larger group for protection.

"I hope you don't mind me coming to you," Sadie said, "I had nowhere else to go. I have no one else. If Father finds me—"

25

"I understand, and I'm glad you came," her friend said, hugging Sadie.

Bett released her, bent to pick something up, and moved to a crude fireplace. With small tongs, she uncovered the banked coals, lifted a hot, orange fragment and used the ember to light a small oil lamp. The burning oil smoked, adding an acrid odor to the foul atmosphere. Sadie coughed as Bett turned to face her with another smile.

"Is someone ill?" Sadie asked.

"No, just asleep."

Who would still sleep at this hour?

As if hearing Sadie's thought, Bett swung the lamp so its metal reflector aimed light toward the corner of the room where a man's form stirred in a rope bed.

Sadie's mouth dropped open. Was her friend married to the man?

"You should see your face," Bett said.

"I'm sorry to impose."

The man in the bed turned onto his back and opened one eye that caught a glint of the lamplight. The greenish-blue hue that reflected back reminded Sadie of what shone from a canine eye in the dark. The gleam gave the man's gaze a fiendish glare that sent a chill and a shiver through her.

"No imposition, lass," he said, his voice higher pitched than she expected.

He seemed to have something of the sing-song accent she'd noted in Mr. Roberts' speech, Scottish perhaps. Sadie didn't like the voice at all. She glanced toward the door. "I should leave you to—"

"Nonsense," Bett said, putting her arm around Sadie. The embrace gave little comfort.

The man sat up in the bed and swung his feet to the dirt floor. He smacked his full lips crudely while looking down, and rubbed his head of wild hair, which Sadie thought was much the color of the fur of red wolves. He was a small man dressed only in his inexpressibles.

So why, she asked herself, *do I find him frightening?*

Out of courtesy, she tried to turn away. "I should go. Perhaps—"

"You said you had nowhere to go." Bett turned her and looked her in the eye. "Your father will be looking for you."

Sadie had more reasons and excuses for leaving, but kept herself from expressing them. Her imagination was running away with her. She truly had only one thing to fear and Bett had named it. The reminder changed everything.

"Wiley, she's afraid," Bett said to the man. "This is Sadie. Please put her at ease."

He looked up, rubbed sleep out of his dark eyes. With his lean, nearly hairless face, small nose, and narrow jaw, he looked a bit devious and weaselly. Even so, Sadie found something appealing about his features. He patted the straw mattress beside him. "Come sit, pretty lass."

"I couldn't sit there," she said, turning back to Bett, "on your *marriage* bed."

Wiley chuckled and shook his head.

"No," Bett said, her smile lopsided. "Oh, you are still so young, Sadie."

"What goes on," a deep voice bellowed from somewhere else within the dwelling. "Come to me, woman."

"I must go to him," Bett said. "Wiley will treat you well. Don't be frightened."

Sadie wanted to ask who called for Bett, but after her blunder about the marriage bed, she was too embarrassed.

Bett set the lamp on a small table beside the bed, then drew back a piece of hanging cloth to reveal a doorway. She disappeared through the opening and Sadie was alone with Wiley.

"Sadie means princess," Wiley said.

Sadie had heard that from her teacher, Mr. Quinton Evory. To hear the same from one she'd thought rather coarse was a delightful surprise.

"Please, Princess Sadie, do me the honor of sitting here." He patted the lumpy mattress again. "I won't bite you."

Sadie's father would beat her to unconsciousness if he knew she sat on a man's bed. But then, if she were to truly leave her old life behind, what he thought didn't matter. The life Reverend Rice deemed proper for her, one with regular beatings, would lead to an early grave.

If she was to get away from her father, she must trust Bett, for Sadie had no other ally. Despite Wiley's unseemly ways, Bett would not have left Sadie with him if he were dangerous. Still, her imagination overwrought from recent experiences, she hesitated.

Wiley held out his left hand, palm upward. His expression betrayed no cunning.

Bett is brave, Sadie thought. *I must borrow her courage.*

Without looking at the half-naked man, Sadie moved cautiously toward Wiley, despite the impression that he would indeed bite her. She sat on the edge of the bed two feet away from him.

"Would you like a drink?" he asked. "I have cider that'll put you at ease." He pulled a bottle from under the bed, removed the cork, and poured some of the contents into two dirty mugs on the table beside the lamp. He lifted one and offered the drink to Sadie.

Out of courtesy, she took it. The smell of alcohol rose to her nose. "Is it strong water?"

"Not very strong," Wiley said, a smell of sleep on his breath. "No more so than the vile syllabub served to women and young children at celebrations. Still, it should help."

"I have never taken a drink, even syllabub."

"Well, there is a first time for all things."

As Sadie sat with the strange man, in the disgusting hovel, in the vile little town, she realized just how many things she'd never done before and how frightening was the prospect of doing them *now*. To help quell her unease, she took a deep draught of the cider, and then quickly took another.

4
Scars

Wiley had taken the cider away from Sadie after her second gulp. Even so, she had quickly become somewhat confused and disoriented. While she counseled herself to be wary, she had a sense of separation from herself and her experiences that was strangely pleasant and relaxing.

Wiley watched her and tried to catch her eye a few times. Sadie found his manner disquieting, yet his behavior concerned her only distantly, as did the silence between them.

Sadie swayed a bit and sat back on the bed, leaning against the rough wall to steady herself. She tried not to look at Wiley or think about what he might do.

Hoping Bett would rejoin her again soon, she wondered again if her friend had any plans to leave Tippens. Mr. Roberts didn't seem interested in coming for his stepdaughter, so Bett might not have plans to flee. Sadie definitely needed to get far away from her own father, but she didn't want to do it alone. Lost in thought, she flinched when Wiley spoke.

"I can see you're a young lass who knows herself," he said.

She believed that quite the contrary was true.

He took her left hand and caressed its mottled skin. Sadie was embarrassed that he'd become aware of her burn scar. She wanted to withdraw her hand, yet she didn't want to offend him.

Wiley pushed her hair out of her eyes and looked at her face. Sadie glanced at him timidly. His expression was open, and she saw no threat.

"Your scars tell me someone mistreats you," he said.

"My father," Sadie said.

"He's a hard man?"

The word, *hard*, wasn't enough to describe Reverend Rice. Sadie thought of the beating he'd given her older sister, Virginia, for secretly writing to a Catholic fellow. Since Virginia had influenza at the time, Sadie supposed her father had easily told himself that her sister's death wasn't his fault. No one questioned what happened.

Thinking of her sister's death always made her wonder about her mother's fate. She had gone missing five years ago, and no one had heard from her since. Sadie's father would say that his wife had wandered off, but no one truly knew what had become of her, except perhaps the reverend himself, and no one was willing to question him about her either.

And then there was what happened yesterday between Sadie and her father. Reverend Rice had given her a job to do—to make six dozen tallow candles for the church before he got home in the evening—yet she'd found she didn't have enough fat to complete the task and there was no time to get more. While she worked, she kept glancing at the clock above the fireplace mantle and at the door that led outside, fearfully anticipating his arrival and his reaction. Although the clock told her that over an hour would pass before he came home, the door to the cabin opened early.

Reverend Rice, dressed in the black of his calling, stepped inside, a cruel suspicion darkening his eyes and mouth as he stared at her. She knew the frightened look on her face would feed his distrust, and she struggled to calm herself, smooth her features, and still her quaking gut and trembling limbs. He wasn't expected until five o'clock, but Sadie couldn't ask why he'd come home early.

No, Reverend Rice would be the one with questions that would quickly turn to accusations. He approached slowly, his black footsteps measured and deliberate. Without taking her eyes off his face, while maintaining awareness of the location of his hands in her peripheral vision, Sadie backed away from the trough of hot tallow, feeling behind her to prevent upsetting the dipping frame and spoiling her candles.

"After your malingering yesterday, I thought to look in on you today," he said, his nostrils flaring and upper lip curling in anger. He was a large man with hair and beard as dark as lamp black and deep-set eyes not much brighter. With only his collar white, at certain angles he appeared to be solid shadow.

"You know some take ill with the wool," she said, her voice cracking feebly. "I did my best with the carding, despite my cough and eyes nearly swollen shut. I got the better half of it done, and worked late into the night to finish."

"You forgive yourself easily." Unnaturally still, his lips barely moved with his words. "Good thing I came. Those—" he said, gesturing at the candles "—are but tapers. No good for the church. They won't pay."

Sadie backed into the corner where the logs that formed the walls of the cabin met and overlapped. Her head bumped into the wall, breaking free a small piece of the clay and horse hair chinking from between the logs above and to her right. The hairy chunk fell to the puncheon floor, leaving a small opening, and letting in a thin beam of warm afternoon sunlight that struck her father in the face.

His left eye blazed fiercely red in the beam. As he moved slightly to get out of its glare, the Reverend gritted his teeth and balled his fists. Sadie braced herself for a physical blow, but he made a visible effort to relax, unclenching both hands and jaw, all while keeping his black eyes on her.

Sadie knew his calm wouldn't last.

He closed his eyes and seemed to pray, his mouth moving silently.

Sadie glanced left along the wall to the door, wanting to make a dash for it, but she was too afraid. He'd only come after her.

Thankfully, her gaze returned to him a moment before he opened his eyes. "I know what takes your mind from your chores, child."

Sadie was confused as he unbuttoned his breeches, and shocked when he reached inside them.

"You're a daydreamer, and I know what occupies your fond hope. All girls dream of holding sway over a man, and there's truly only one thing for it."

To Sadie's horror, he pulled out his manhood, which was bruised and scoured raw, a pattern of scabs appearing along its length.

"Your mother was the same," he said, eying her as if gauging her reaction.

Sadie turned away. "Please, Father…" she wept. She sat on the floor, hugged her knees to her chest and pulled her skirts tightly around her ankles and buttocks. At more than twice her weight and much stronger, if he intended to molest her with that miserable organ, there was little she could do to prevent him. Then again, if he abused her that way, perhaps he would not also beat her. She truly didn't know which would be worse.

He remained still, however, and Sadie realized he had no intention of using his wounded member. No, he saw sexual desire as merely a temptation of the flesh, born of evil. He practiced self-flagellation as penance for lustful thoughts. Seeing the condition of his manhood, Sadie presumed he must also abuse the organ to further blunt his desire.

"After your mother had her way and left me with you, life has been nothing but an endless trial."

Two, Sadie reminded herself, *she left you with* two *daughters*. Reverend Rice had not spoken of Virginia since her death.

"Father," she said, "I never…I *have* never—"

"Don't *lie* to me," he cried. "This is what you dream of. Look at it. This would be your familiar. It's a miserable worm that passes corruption of the flesh and that of the spirit."

When, against her better judgement, Sadie glanced at his penis once more, the organ seemed to have grown larger. Several of the scabs had cracked open and seeped bright red blood.

As her eyes widened in terror and disgust, he seemed to notice her expression and he looked down. His penis was half erect, there in his hand. His rage boiled over.

"You would use your beguiling face to *tempt* your *father!*" he bellowed, advancing on her.

Sadie screamed and tried to crawl inside herself, for she had nowhere else to hide.

He grabbed her by the hair and dragged her to the tallow trough. She flailed, trying unsuccessfully to grab onto anything that might help stop her forward progress across the puncheon floor. Reverend Rice held her shoulders with his right arm, while using his left to push her face toward the hot yellow fat as he also bent forward. She gripped the sides of the trough and pushed back with all her might, the edges of the thin metal digging into her palms.

"I'll make sure that face will *never* tempt a man again," he shouted in her ear.

As they fought, the trough tipped dangerously. He pressed her chest against its hot metal side and shifted his right arm to hug and steady the trough. The top of the apron and the cloth of her shift protected her breasts for a moment, but then the heat came through. Sadie cried out with the pain.

Nothing would stop him. She would lose the battle and her face would burn. She couldn't think of it. The horror was too much, the price too great. She had to give in, let the worst happen, and then begin to heal again. What choice did she have? *Just don't think about it and let go*, she told herself.

Still, screaming, she fought the inevitable.

Then voices, male and female, came from outside. The male voice hailed the house from beyond the door. "…Reverend Rice. Mrs. Vickery has requested your presence. Please come before it's too late."

Sadie's father became still, and let go suddenly. Sadie barely kept the hot tallow from spilling. Reverend Rice stood up, and stepped back. She rolled away from the trough to one side and lay weeping on the floor.

Her father took several deep breaths and straightened his clothing. "Compose yourself, young woman." Though out of breath, he said the words rather casually. "We have guests."

Sadie scrambled up the ladder to the loft as he walked to the threshold, opened the door, and spoke to the man and woman on the other side. Finally, the Reverend turned to look up at the darkened loft. "Mrs. Vickery has taken a turn for the worse. I must go, but I'll be back before our appointment at the church. Finish your work."

After his departure, Sadie threw off her apron and swept the tears from her eyes. She loaded food into a cloth sack, and gathered a few belongings into a leather pack. She pulled on her shawl, hung the sack over one shoulder, the pack over the other, and fled through the door.

Before going far, she would have to find Bett. Sadie had walked a half mile to the Roberts' cabin only to find that her friend had run away as well.

She didn't know how she felt about those with whom Bett had taken refuge. Sadie was more at ease with Wiley at present, but she maintained some trepidations about the fellow.

In answer to his question about Reverend Rice being a hard man, Sadie shrugged and said dismally, "He's a minister, a man of God."

"That gives some men leave to do as they please." Wiley looked down, shook his head slowly. "You poor girl. It's not right."

Sadie looked at him squarely for a moment. How could such a rough man have more sympathy than all others in Tippens save Bett? The townsfolk had seen her scars and bruises. Those who attended her father's church had seen them with regularity, and yet she had not heard a single caring word from any of them.

5
Finding a Man

Sadie's dream of finding a man was simple and naive. The fellow for whom Sadie would have tender feelings might love her simply because her existence made him happy. He would be the sort of man who would provide her with a kindness from time to time without asking for anything in return. Such a thing might be a small gift, perhaps one of no value to anyone but Sadie, a warm gesture or caring expression, something sweet to eat, a bouquet of fragrant and colorful flowers or a delicate caress along the side of her neck. She would, of course, want to find ways to show kindness to him as well. He might be something like Quinton Evory, yet more handsome, more complete.

Mrs. Evory had stepped down as the mistress of the Dame School in the same year that Sadie's sister, Virginia, died. Sadie was twelve years old at the time. Mrs. Evory's son, Mr. Quinton Evory, took up the position. He was a hero of the battle of Lounds Mill during the war. Folks said he'd once been handsome. In a later battle he'd been struck by a volley of British grapeshot, and sustained grievous wounds. Mr. Evory was virtually blind from disfiguring injuries to his face and had lost portions of the lower half of his body. Confined to a wheeled wicker chair, he couldn't work the fields as did most men of the community. He was an excellent teacher, however. Despite his loss of vision, he was able to perform his demonstrations by touch and memory.

Although addressing him respectfully as Mr. Evory aloud, in the privacy of her own thoughts, Sadie delighted to know him as Quinton. She had never known a man to show such kindness to others. He wasn't an angry man, even when impatient. The children weren't expected to understand him the first time he said something, and when a student had difficulty with a specific idea or technique, he provided the child with brief individual tutoring that usually helped.

Sadie needed help with the counterclockwise spinning of flax. "Remember to dip your hand in the water bowl to keep the fibers moist," he'd say or, "don't be afraid to use a little spit if you need to." His deep voice was gently insistent, and Sadie developed a small crush on Quinton as he guided her hand in holding the fiber "just so." She was sad to leave the school in her twelfth year, and still thought fondly of her time with Quinton. She decided she'd be lucky to grow up and marry such a man.

After church a couple of months ago, while talking to Bett about finding a mate, Sadie had told her friend, "I try not to imagine what my love will look like, what his manner might be, or what occupation he might hold."

"How do you know what you want, then?" Bett asked.

"Doesn't matter what I want. I'm not a particularly deserving soul."

Bett balked. "That's your father talking."

"Perhaps. Yet I fear having a picture so fixed in my mind that I won't recognize my love when finally we meet. It seems that leaving my hopes and desires shapeless makes them more possible." Even as the words left her mouth, she knew that her unwillingness to imagine her mate had more to do with a fear that she might see a man as cruel as her father. If she did not picture such a man, Sadie thought, she had a better chance to meet someone different, someone capable of love.

Bett had laughed. "He's bullied you so badly, your dreams are stunted. Excuse me for saying so, but the Reverend is piss proud. He struts around telling people how to live their lives, and folks listen to him only because they believe he leads an upstanding life. If they knew what we know, the church would be empty on a Sunday. If he wasn't the lickspittle of our Town Fathers, your bruises would tell the tale for you and he'd be nothing."

Sadie was frightened by Bett's language, and turned away to hide her reaction.

Bett followed her, trying to maintain eye contact. "I didn't mean to upset you, talking ill of your father. I have the same anger for him that I have for Stepfather."

Sadie had heard Bett also speak of her stepfather in crude terms. That had bothered Sadie at first. Reverend Rice was, indeed, a bully and a lickspittle. She knew that if she weren't deathly afraid of him, she'd find her friend's statements satisfying.

"I wish I could say horrible things about him too," Sadie said with a shy smile.

Bett grinned. "And one day you will, when you have the love and protection of that *shapeless man* you dream about."

Childish sentimental assumptions about marriage had given way in that instant to more practical concerns. Sadie had not considered that becoming a man's wife would provide protection from her father, but a strange thought came into her head: A man always protects his property against the abuses of another. The dream of finding a man to love didn't change. Her approach did change, however. First she must find a man who would want to possess her and then she would hope they fell in love. She'd told herself that the new approach would not diminish the likelihood of finding love.

Was Wiley a candidate for love? Was he her *shapeless man*, as Bett had put it? Sadie chose not to look at the question too closely.

"Another sip?" he asked, offering the bottle.

Sadie had another swallow of the cider, then asked, "How did Bett come to know you?"

"That is a tale Bett should tell," Wiley said, smiling pleasantly. "You are too polite to ask about me, so I will happily present myself to you." He sat back against the wall with her. The angles of his sharp face were no longer devious. "I travel with my older brother. Some call him Big Harpe and me Little Harpe. Of course, I am only smaller by comparison. You'll see when you meet my brother. We are adventurers of great boldness. You see us now in humble circumstances. Such are the ups and downs of the adventuring life that we currently find ourselves wanting. But our spirits rally quickly and we will shortly move on to our next campaign, one that is sure to carry us to riches again. We head for the frontier soon, despite the dangers—nay, glad for them! We are veteran fighting men who endured against great odds in the war. The opportunities in the land to the west are boundless for those with the pluck to seek wealth and defend our own."

A noble bearing had emerged from his features as he spoke. Sadie sat so close to Wiley, their hips touched. The only other man she had sat so near was Quinton. Seemingly against her will, she found herself similarly drawn to Wiley.

He clearly noticed, since he was bold enough to reach out and touch her face gently, his fingers exploring several small scars. Wiley was perhaps thirty years old, an unkempt fellow, unwashed and possessed of a heady odor, yet not unattractive. His caresses were delightful, and she felt herself blush. He bent toward Sadie to deliver a delicate kiss on her lips. His breath wasn't as strong as before.

Then his hand found her abdomen. Instead of being alarmed, Sadie found his touch arousing.

"You don't flinch from a bit of canoodling," he said. "If I had my guess, though, I'd say you're not a woman yet."

She knew his manner should concern her, but with the increasing intoxication and the warmth of his touch, her conscience drowsed.

He nuzzled her neck and ear. Despite the rough stubble on his chin, he was gentle. Sadie relished the simple pleasure of tender human contact.

When Wiley slipped his hand down to grip her crotch, Sadie's sense of decency finally awoke from its lethargy. She tried to push away from him, even as she gasped with pleasure at his touch.

"Did your father?" he asked, his hand still between her legs.

"No," Sadie said breathlessly, her eyes wide. She knew what he was asking. She didn't want to talk to Wiley about that. She needed to get away, but his touch felt so good there wasn't much fight in her, and he seemed to know that.

"Don't be afraid." He massaged her through her skirts. "A little firky-toodle never hurt anyone."

"But I—" Sadie began, arching her back.

"No, you don't," Wiley said.

"Bett will—" she started.

"—not come in without a warning," he finished for her.

He'd found a spot she'd used to give herself pleasure, and his fingers knew what to do. Sadie quaked with an intense and previously unknown satisfaction.

When he was done, she wanted more. She embraced him fully and kissed his mouth.

"I will make a woman of you," he said. "Then you'll have a new confidence and know your own worth."

In his words, Sadie heard she was desirable. Although passionate feeling was quickly eclipsing rational thought, her mind made a quick reckoning. Wiley was smaller than many men, but if he claimed her as his own, perhaps he would protect her. She could well imagine that what he said about his bravery in a fight was true and therefore he'd be capable of protecting her from her father. Sadie doubted that Wiley was the man she would fall in love with, yet when he reached to touch her under her skirts, she willingly spread her legs for him.

6
Decision

"Up, up!" came a woman's voice as the door to the outside opened. "Everyone up!" she cried between heaving breaths.

Sadie was not fully aware that she was awake yet. Wiley stirred beside her and sat up in the bed. Seeing him, and remembering what they'd done together, a wave of shame washed over Sadie, but then she was mercifully distracted.

The woman, plain and unkempt, about five feet tall, maybe twenty-five or thirty years old, stopped long enough to give Sadie a glaring look, then strode swiftly across the small room and went through the doorway hidden behind the hanging fabric.

"You keep that up, Suesanna," Wiley called after her, "and Micajah will put you *down*."

"Cease, or you'll wake him," came Bett's voice from the other room.

"Who?" Sadie asked. She pulled the bedclothes up to her neck as she squinted at the daylight shining in around the door that had been left opened.

"My brother," he said.

"Who is she?"

"Micajah's wife."

Sadie gave up. Perhaps she'd understand when she was more awake.

The deep voice Sadie had heard the night before roared, and the sounds of a struggle followed.

"You must listen," Suesanna said, desperation in her tone. "I—" Her voice cut off with the sounds of further tumult.

"Micajah!" Bett said, "she *must* have a reason."

Sadie heard the sounds of a fist striking flesh and her friend crying out in pain. She tried to get up to help Bett. As she reached for her blouse and skirt, Wiley stopped her with an iron grip on her wrist. He looked her in the eye and shook his head.

Sadie was concerned that she'd fled one brutal man only to take refuge with two more. Wiley released the wrist, however.

"They found the pig carcass in Cooks Creek!" Suesanna shouted. "They're coming! We have to flee."

"You *woke* me!" bellowed the voice Sadie presumed belonged to Micajah.

"Please, forgive me," Suesanna said. "They're coming for you, twenty men. Samuelson was with me when a man came to the door and told him to assemble with the militia for a raid on The Cut. He said, 'The Harpes been at it again, a pig this time, sunk with stones.'"

Sadie didn't understand much of what the woman said. She did get the impression she'd left one dangerous environment for another. Her impulse was to run, but she was near naked under the bedclothes, and she still needed to trust Bett. Her friend wouldn't have come to The Cut, wouldn't stay with these people, if the situation was worse than her own home. "It won't take too long for them to rally," Suesanna continued, "I ran the whole way. *They'll* be on horseback."

Out of the other room erupted the largest man Sadie had ever seen. His great bulk broke one side of the flimsy doorframe. His large masonry block of a head sprouted a riot of auburn hair that came far down on his forehead. A short stubble of reddish whiskers bristled from his square lower face, and a mottled burn scar, that rumpled up his brow and much of his left cheek, gave him a fearsome permanent scowl.

As he straightened his broad back and stood fully erect, Sadie drew back in fright, for he was completely naked. While his head and arms were bronzed and reddened from long exposure to the sun, his hirsute chest and abdomen were white as a fish's belly, and tapered down to what hung between his legs; the third and smallest adult penis Sadie had seen in her life. He reeked of sweat and sleep.

Whatever he may have lacked in manhood, he made up for in sheer menace, as he bounded about the tiny room on legs stout as cabin logs, swinging arms so heavily muscled they appeared to have braided ropes just beneath the skin. Clutching at his face as if he could pull the sleepiness out of his head, he knocked over a stack of wood and kindling, and crushed a fireplace stool under his right foot.

"Buckskins," he shouted. Bett stood in the broken doorway, a fresh pink bruise on her freckled cheek, holding out sweat-stained leather clothing.

Micajah turned to rip them from her grasp, but his angry eyes met

Sadie's, and he stopped dead in his tracks. The room went silent for a moment, and the menace dropped from the big man's gaze. In that instant, he looked to Sadie like a giant little boy fascinated by some bright bauble.

Then Wiley got up and broke their eye contact as he stepped between them. He moved to dress himself in similar leathers, and Micajah turned away to don his own clothing. The big man pulled on breechcloth and leggins, then turned to Wiley. "This is your doing," he said, his mouth and eyes drawn into a fierce frown.

Wiley glanced up, trying unsuccessfully to look untroubled by Big Harpes's anger. "Cannie wee prick snuck up while I wasn't looking," he said, shrugging and continuing to dress. "Then he was gone before I got my legs under me. I tried to go after him, but he was a fast little pish spot."

After him for what, Sadie wondered. *Must have something to do with the pig carcass.* The words of the men raised too many questions, ones she thought would be unwelcome. She let the questions go as she reached for her brown wool stockings. Chagrined at the thought that Micajah might see her legs, she moved fast. He didn't look her way.

"Should've waited till you had one of us to stand watch." Micajah shook his head in disgust. "And what'd we get, ten pound of dried pork?"

"Aye, 'bout that."

"You know the rules."

"Aye."

Wrapping a broad black belt, decorated with red and yellow beads, around his waist several times and tying it, Micajah nodded his head as if an argument with his brother had been settled. He reached under the bed and retrieved numerous pistols, two broad knives in sheaths and a large stone tomahawk. He handed one of the knives and four of the firearms to Wiley, then tucked the other knife, the stone tomahawk and four pistols into his own belt.

Sadie had never seen men with so many weapons. Why would the brothers dress like Indians and arm themselves so? The sight disturbed her. She'd seen men who dressed that way before, known as longhunters, who regularly entered the wilderness to the west to hunt and trap. Many who took that calling disappeared into the West, never to be seen again. Perhaps the adventures of which Wiley spoke concerned hunting and trapping. That would account for all the weapons.

Something at the edge of memory troubled her. She'd remember if she tried, but couldn't concentrate as she hurried to prepare herself to leave.

Suesanna and Bett hastily gathered belongings into packs and prepared bedrolls, the older sister directing the younger. Wiley took two shot pouches, a brass powder flask, and a powder horn off a peg on the wall behind him. He swung one of the pouches and the powder horn to his brother. Micajah caught them and hung them by their straps over his shoulder. Wiley did the same with his, then turned to Suesanna. "Spare flints?" he asked.

"Bestowed," she answered with a tight smile, handing him a leather pack and then another to Micajah. The men stood and retrieved rifles that leaned into the corner by the door.

Sadie had barely dressed before she was ushered out of the cabin. She tied her woolen shawl around her waist, picked up her small pack, and exited the cabin. Once outside, Suesanna gave her another leather pack to carry.

Getting her wits about her as she stood in overcast daylight, Sadie's memory troubled her no longer as she realized that Mr. Roberts had been telling the truth. Bett had told her something about the Harpes over a year ago. Known as Big and Little Harpe, they were citizens of North Carolina, loyalists to the British Crown, and notorious for their brutality against American patriots during the Revolutionary War. The brothers were part of a raiding party of mostly Cherokee Indians that sacked the Woods's family farm in 1781. Bett had not been born yet, and her sister, Suesanna, was still a small child. Bett's father, Jeremiah Woods, wounded Wiley Harpe during the raid. In 1790, in an act of revenge, the Harpes returned to the Woods home, killed Bett's father, and abducted her sister, Suesanna, when she was fourteen years old. Mr. Roberts had later married the widowed Mrs. Woods, becoming Bett's stepfather.

"Have you ever heard what became of your sister?" Sadie had asked Bett the day she told the story.

"She's married to one of the Harpes, the big one, I think," Bett said, shrugging. "Rumor has it she got pregnant and did what she had to. No doubt they treat her better than Mr. Roberts would."

Sadie nodded although she didn't understand. Trading one bad situation for another didn't sound like a good idea. However, she wasn't willing to think about what pains she'd endure to get away from her father. But that was then, and at present, Sadie had a choice to make.

Had she fallen in with murderous criminals or were their misdeeds merely a product of the brutal war that raged, and thankfully ended, before Sadie was born? Was the problem with the pig carcass a misunderstanding? Should she go with them? What of her safety if she did go?

If Suesanna was married to the big one, then what was Bett doing with the big man last night?

As she watched the two men, her friend, and her friend's sister preparing to leave The Cut, Sadie couldn't decide whether to go with them or run away.

Suesanna headed toward two mangy horses in a muddy paddock, but Wiley stopped her. "Leave them. We'll move faster and quieter without them and leave less to track."

As they waited for Suesanna to rejoin them and the men were shouldering their packs, Sadie looked to Bett, hoping for answers to her unspoken questions. As Sadie hesitated, she could see that her friend presumed she'd follow. The answer in Bett's eyes was clear enough: *What other choice do you have?*

Sadie thought about her father's anger for only a moment and then agreed.

7
The Trail

The brothers and Suesanna moved rapidly and quietly through The Cut, staying out of the mud. Apparently they knew the way well. All three of them wore moccasins. Sadie and Bett struggled to keep up, their boots with hard soles making a racket by comparison. Micajah stopped and looked at Sadie's feet, an angry expression on his face, then he looked at his brother. Wiley shrugged and moved on, and they all followed.

"Where are we going?" Sadie asked. Micajah hushed her with such ferocity, she knew he feared the militia might hear them any moment. She tried to walk more quietly.

Leaving the path that ran through The Cut, the party turned onto a well-traveled road. As they moved, no one said a word. Suesanna and the men continually turned to look and listen for signs of the militia. Twice Micajah stopped walking, held up his hand, whispered sharply, "Be still," and closed his eyes for a moment. Finally, seeming satisfied each time, he signaled for everyone to continue forward.

Suesanna eyed Sadie uncomfortably as they moved along, her unabashed gaze lingering though Sadie stared right back at her. The woman was five years older than her sister, Bett, but looked at least ten years her senior. She wasn't a handsome woman, having a rawboned and somewhat stooped frame, thinning brown hair, hollow cheeks, and a weak chin. Her skin was coarsened from long exposure to sun and weather. Whatever life she'd led with the Harpe brothers had been hard on her. Because her eyes were deep-set and hard, her brow had a masculine appearance. Her expressions were wary and reserved. Suesanna's resentment toward Sadie was clear to see, yet the cause wasn't. Sadie gave Bett a questioning look, while nodding toward Suesanna. Bett shrugged and shook her head, rolling her eyes.

The sky had darkened some as they walked. Because of the overcast, Sadie couldn't tell if the diminishing light were due to weather or dusk descending. For all she knew, with her need for more sleep after the night spent in the tree, she'd slept through a day and night and dawn had come again.

Half a mile up the road, Micajah turned onto a small path that ran into the forest. Everyone followed, and once they were among the trees, the men slowed their pace. As the forest became thicker and the trees taller, Sadie knew they moved away from Tippens into virgin wilderness. With frequent changes in the course of their path and the increasingly dense canopy of green above, however, she couldn't tell where they were going.

At least on the narrow forest trail, Sadie didn't have to endure Suesanna's stares. So singleminded were the men leading the way, that frequently they were out of sight beyond turns in the trail. Sadie kept her eyes on Bett, who was ahead of her and behind Suesanna. Occasionally, Sadie lost sight of Bett and feared taking a wrong turn and becoming lost. Bett came back for her three times and insisted that they run to catch up. The first time she came back, she whispered, "We're headed west, into the frontier of Tennessee." Her smile was large, but troubled.

"That's what we wanted," Sadie said, although not absolutely certain that was what she desired. "Our plan!"

Bett nodded. She put her finger across her lips to remind Sadie to remain quiet.

The second time she came back, Bett said, "Do whatever they ask you to do. Where we're going, you'll want them to fight for you."

Sadie understood, though she had many questions, each fighting to be answered first. Again, Bett crossed her lips with a finger.

The third time, Bett said nothing at first. She grabbed Sadie by the wrist and yanked her forward. Sadie stumbled, but kept her feet, and gave her friend a pained look. "You must move faster," Bett said with a frown.

Micajah waited for them on a platform of rock beside a small creek, his arms folded across his chest. "That's enough!" he said. Grabbing Sadie in his hands, he lifted her and placed her in a seated position on a rock prominence. So used to holding her tongue to prevent worsening her father's anger, she managed to suppress the scream that tried to escape her throat. Micajah pulled the bows loose from her laces and tore her boots off. He inspected the soles of her feet.

"Sit and take off your boots," Wiley said to Bett, and she sat to do as he told her.

"Old shirt," Micajah said, holding out a hand to Suesanna, palm upward.

Moving slowly, she rummaged around in her pack and pulled out a filthy, sweat-stained buckskin garment. She seemed reluctant to turn the shirt over to him, and again glared at Sadie.

Micajah took a large knife from his belt and cut the garment into four multi-lobed pieces. Each piece, he folded over several times. Then he fashioned two of them into makeshift moccasins on Sadie's feet. He finished by cutting the lobes that extended up her legs into strips that he tied together around her ankles. As the process was repeated for Bett, Sadie tried out her new shoes. Stones beneath her poked her soles painfully when she stood, but the moccasins were securely fastened to her feet.

"The stones are like insults," Wiley said. "Don't take offense and you won't gather pain."

Sadie didn't know what to make of his statement until they resumed their trek. At first, with the torment of her feet, she suppressed exclamations, and could see that Bett endured similar discomfort. With time, Sadie learned to relax the muscles in her feet. Her weight spread out more evenly with each step, and she avoided much of the pain.

The sky cleared, and Sadie determined that the time was mid-afternoon. As they progressed, the party stopped only to drink from available water sources: Several small hillside springs and a couple of creeks.

Scooping water from a creek, Suesanna stood and leaned backward with a moan. Her loose clothing parted slightly and her belly stood out. Suesanna was pregnant. Seeing that, Sadie had a begrudging respect for Suesanna—the woman's endurance was remarkable.

Night was falling. Sadie and Bett were dragging their feet from exhaustion by the time they arrived at a small, mossy sink hole, forty feet deep and sixty feet across at its broadest. The party made their way to the bottom where a trickle of a stream emerged from one wall, cut across the boulder-strewn floor, and disappeared into the wall on the other side. They all paused to scoop water from the stream and refresh themselves.

The air in the sink hole was cooler than the summer air above. Sadie set down her packs, and pulled her shawl from her hips up to cover her shoulders. Her limbs felt heavy and her feet were sore. Suesanna built a small fire while the men relaxed. Bett sat, rubbing her feet. Sadie slid down to the ground to lean against her friend and relax for a moment.

When Suesanna saw Sadie on the ground, she whispered viciously, "Up, up!"

Sadie decided to ignore her, but Suesanna stood and moved toward her menacingly.

"Get up, girl," she commanded.

Sadie got up quickly.

"Unroll the blankets and get the men something to drink." Suesanna tossed her a bedroll.

Sadie caught the bundle and set about to do the woman's bidding. Once the blankets were spread, she thought about getting the men a drink. No doubt, Suesanna meant something besides water. All day, Sadie had heard the sound of glass containers clinking together in the heavy pack Suesanna had given her to carry. Inside, she found what she was looking for. She gave two bottles full of amber liquid to the men. They accepted the drink without comment, uncorked the bottles, and drank.

Bett sat on one of the spread bedrolls. Sadie stood nervously beside her for a time until Bett tugged on her. Sadie sat cautiously.

Suesanna struck sparks into a piece of charcloth and then coaxed them into flame with her breath. Once the fire was going well, she shared out portions of dried pork.

"You savor that pig," Micajah said to no one in particular. "Must be fine fare, considering what it cost us."

"If you'd spend more time helping to keep us fed," Wiley said, "I wouldn't have to take such risks. Your need is as great as your frame, but isn't matched by your effort."

"Risk isn't the half of it, brother," Micajah said. "If you'd've killed that boy, we wouldn't be hounded the way we are."

"I have brought trouble upon us, brother, and for that I'm sorry."

Sadie asked herself if she'd heard Micajah correctly. *Did he* want *Wiley to kill a boy?* With her exhaustion, she didn't trust herself to sort out the meaning of his words. She was hungry, and the pork tasted good. When she was done eating, her eyelids became heavy and she leaned more heavily on Bett.

As she began to doze off, she heard Micajah commanding Suesanna to make proper moccasins for Sadie and Bett. Sadie couldn't see the older sister's face, yet was certain she wasn't pleased.

~ ~ ~

Sadie awoke to find Wiley grabbing her crotch again. Then she realized he clutched at her while mounting Bett right next to her. Although Sadie thought she must be dreaming, she quickly knew that wasn't so. He groaned, prodded, and poked until he got his fingers inside her.

What would Bett think, Sadie wondered, *if she knew he was touching me while...?*

She wouldn't like it any more than I do.

She wanted to push Wiley away, but she remembered Bett's words:

"Do whatever they ask you to do. Where we're going, you'll want them to fight for you."

Wiley turned his head toward her, and she quickly closed her eyes, pretending to sleep.

I want this to be a dream, Sadie told herself, and did her best to return to sleep. Unable to doze off, she remained still until Wiley's rhythmic thrusts changed to a writhing and he struggled to stifle his own moans. Finally, he pulled his fingers out of her and rolled off Bett. He lay right beside Sadie, facing Bett.

Sadie was puzzled to find herself angry with her friend, even though Wiley was the one slighting her. Then the answer came: *I'm jealous.*

She had assumed Wiley had chosen her. Sadie hugged herself within her shawl and wept silently.

Wiley's breathing deepened and the sink hole became quiet except for the sounds of insects.

Eventually Sadie's tears dried, and she began to plan for the future. Although she tried not to think of the dangers ahead in the frontier, she knew her life was at stake and resolved to do whatever was necessary to regain Wiley's favor and perhaps that of Micajah. Hopefully, her actions would not hurt Bett too much. Her friend *did* have Micajah, even though she was in competition with her own sister for Big Harpe's affections.

What did Sadie have to offer, she wondered, and how was that any better than what Bett had? Sadie tried to examine her own attributes. She couldn't easily guess whether a man might find them more desirable than those of her friend. She was smaller than Bett and Suesanna. Sadie was much prettier than the older sister, and perhaps not as handsome as the younger. Her hair, while not quite flaxen, appeared golden in sunlight. Her hips weren't as broad as Bett's, yet her bosom was ample by comparison. Her breasts were smaller than Suesanna's, but the older woman was pregnant and would lose some of her advantage with time. Both Sadie and Bett were educated and smart. Although Suesanna probably didn't have the same education, the older woman's knowledge of the Harpes' ways was perhaps more important. Suesanna's manner was coarse and unpleasant. Bett was angry, having been treated unfairly by the man who took her father's place. She was also brave in ways that Sadie wasn't. Sadie believed herself to be generous, honest, willing, and capable, although perhaps not as driven as Bett.

Sadie would have to keep up with her friend, and even surpass Bett's efforts to contribute to the wellbeing of the whole party. She'd start by offering as much as she could, learning about the party's needs while on the trail, and striving to become more useful than the other women. She would curry favor from the men whenever and wherever she could.

Bett might become jealous, but Sadie could only hope that the one friendship she had wouldn't suffer too much.

Given time, she would have a clearer view of her standing within the party.

Sadie set aside her fears, and let go of the day.

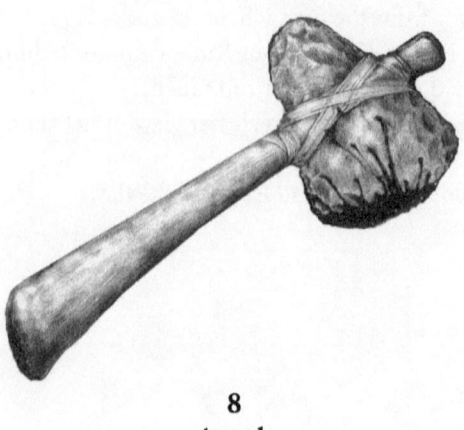

8
Attack

The second night on the trail, all were exhausted as they set up camp at the base of a rocky outcrop below a ridge. Sadie could see that even Wiley was dragging his feet, and hoped she might sleep through the night without being molested. At dusk, they ate a small meal of dried pork, along with some mushrooms and greens Suesanna had gathered along the trail. They all turned in as night descended, wrapping themselves in blankets against a slight chill in the air. Bett slept with her sister and Big Harpe; Sadie fell asleep with her head on Wiley's shoulder.

Sadie was awakened in the night by a grip around her neck. Unable to cry out, she was dragged backward, away from Wiley. She saw that he was roused from sleep, yet he was slow to react. Although she feared she'd end up facing a wolf, Sadie tried to turn toward her attacker, to twist out of the grip. But instead of teeth, she felt buckskin against her throat.

She heard a heavy object strike flesh behind and to her left, and she was released. Sadie rolled away toward Wiley and turned to look back. The full moon high above provided illumination. Micajah rushed toward a tall Indian who had a tomahawk embedded in his left cheek. They fought in a terrible embrace not ten feet away from her, each struggling to throw the other to the ground. The Indian's right hand was missing, though the arm wasn't bleeding. Sadie recognized the weapon in the Indian's face as Micajah's tomahawk.

Sadie followed Wiley as he scrambled backwards out of the blankets, her foot kicking a knife which lay upon the ground next to the bedding.

Then Wiley was up, and he moved toward the men.

Spitting out teeth, the Indian broke free from Micajah, pulled a war hammer from his belt, and swung on Wiley's jaw. The smaller man

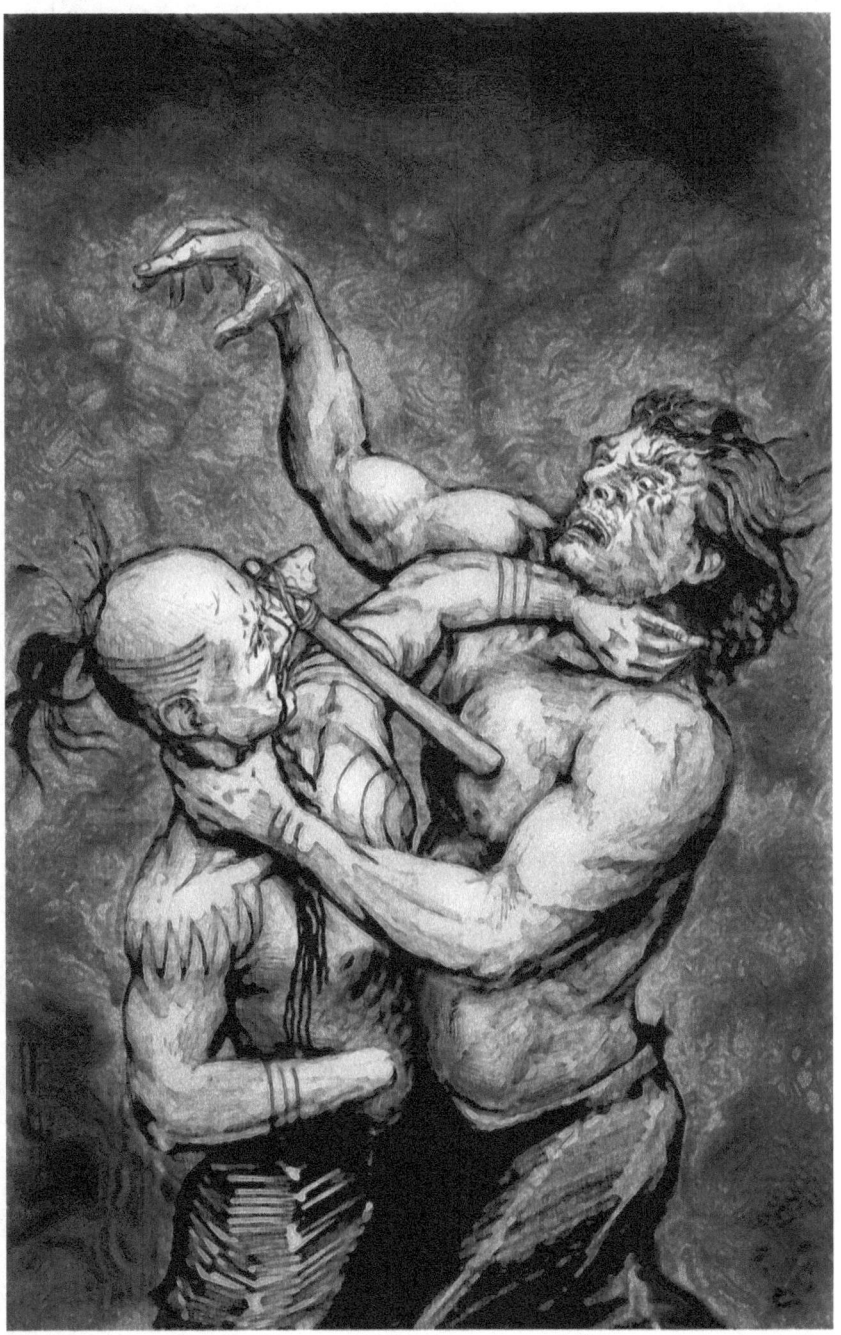

pulled his head back and danced out of the way. Micajah hooked the arm holding the hammer, grabbed the hand, and twisted until the Indian let go of the weapon. The Indian twisted around and struck Micajah a great blow to the face with the nub of his right arm. Big Harpe stumbled back and the Indian grabbed him. Wiley moved in with a knife. The Indian turned Micajah toward the smaller man's blade. As the big man received a slash from his brother's knife across his side, he managed to throw his opponent off to his left. The Indian struck the ground and rolled. The tomahawk broke away from his face, and as he stood, a rush of blood poured from his cheek and his jaw hung at a horrible angle. He staggered, and Wiley advanced on him. The younger Harpe made two quick slashes at the man's throat. The Indian reached for his neck as he stumbled back. He turned hate-filled eyes upon Wiley, then fell and became still. Sadie gulped breath, suppressing a rising panic and desire to scream. Suesanna hugged Bett protectively.

"He was quiet," Micajah said, shaking his head and gasping for breath. He sat in the dirt and explored his bleeding side with his fingers.

Sadie felt moisture on her face and brushed at it. Her hand came away bloody. "Am I harmed?" she asked, her voice cracking.

"No—his blood," Micajah said, shaking his head quickly.

Big Harpe's face was partly shadowed. He looked her in the eye, his gaze lingering with an expression of concern and relief. *Thank you,* she mouthed silently to him. Micajah nodded and turned away. No one else was aware of the exchange.

"Is it Kegg?" Suesanna asked.

"Aye," Wiley said. He examined the Indian's facial wound, then turned to his brother, his eyes wide. "Did you *throw* your weapon?"

"Aye," Micajah said.

"You might have killed her!" Wiley glanced at Sadie. She couldn't read his expression.

"Had no choice," Micajah said. "I was awakened, saw his knife at the ready. He would stab her and then you'd be next."

Wiley nodded, smiling grimly as he stooped to pick up the knife Sadie had kicked.

"*You* could have killed *me,*" Micajah said, pulling his hand, reddened with his own blood, away from his side and holding the palm out for Little Harpe to see.

"Forgive me, brother," Wiley said, "but that isn't the first time I've shed your blood trying to defend you."

"Or in anger," Micajah added resentfully.

"Aye, that too."

"It's not deep," Big Harpe grumbled.

"You say he's Kegg?" Bett said. "Who is he to you?"

"Catoppas Indian," Wiley said without emotion. "Stalked me for over ten years. I killed his family."

Sadie wondered briefly if he'd killed the Indian's family during the war. That would have been much more than ten years ago. She knew she shouldn't ask.

"I crushed his right arm last time he came for me," Wiley continued, still without much emotion, "two years ago or more."

"Must have lost the hand," Micajah said, standing and looking over the corpse, "and took some time to heal." He kicked leaves and dirt toward the dark puddle spreading around the dead man.

Wiley took a deep breath, closed his eyes. "I thought he'd be done. He must have known he'd die, but his pride made him try again." He smiled crookedly.

Although shaken and horrified by the experience, Sadie was strangely pleased by the turn of events, for she'd had a vivid demonstration of the Harpes' willingness to protect their own.

"Break camp!" Micajah said. "I'll not sleep near the dead man's blood."

They packed up and moved forward along the trail another mile, relocating in a deep gully set into a heavily wooded hillside.

Sadie couldn't sleep for the rest of the night. Two images haunted her: The sight of the dead Indian, his blood spilling black in the cold moonlight, and the warmth of concern in Micajah's permanent scowl. Perhaps she should give up on competing with Bett for Wiley and go after the big man's favor. He was obviously the better defender. She'd be going up against Suesanna, but then the woman hated her anyway.

The next day on the trail, Sadie was miserable from lack of sleep. Micajah called numerous halts for brief periods throughout the day. Wiley complained about the delays. Each time he did, Suesanna glared at Sadie.

Eventually, Sadie realized that Big Harpe was allowing her time to rest. She was grateful.

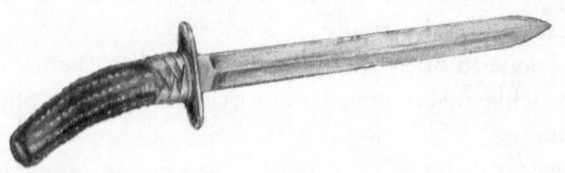

9
The Frontier

Sadie learned that the party followed trails that would take them over the mountains to the Holston River Valley of Tennessee. She tried to imagine what the other side of the mountains would look like. The dark forest she pictured was too strange to believe: Malevolent Indians painted with blood, peering out from behind most trees, and herds of wolves, bears, and cougars wandering the land, leaving only destruction and death in their wake.

The new moccasins Suesanna made for Sadie and Bett had thicker soles and were much more comfortable. Suesanna had worn deerskin clothing much like that of an Indian woman since the second day on the trail. Her moccasins went up to her knees.

Sadie's feet toughened quickly, and her body became leaner and stronger. Suesanna was unwilling to help Sadie learn the ways of the trail. The older sister taught her sister, however, and Bett shared the knowledge. Sadie learned how to forage for edible greens, tubers, mushrooms, berries, and insects, and in the water ways for fish and shellfish. Although the three women spent much of their time gathering food while the men pursued game, they'd had a difficult time keeping themselves fed ever since the dried pork ran out on the third day of their trek. Micajah needed twice as much food as any of the others, but put no more effort into securing it. Everyone seemed frustrated about that except Big Harpe. Nothing of the matter had been expressed since Wiley brought it up the first night of their journey.

Sadie followed Bett while foraging in the forest so they could talk. Unfortunately she gathered less that way because she and Bett went over much the same ground. If Suesanna saw her too close to Bett, she'd demand that Sadie search elsewhere.

During their conversations, she learned that Bett had known about her sister and the Harpes residing in the Tippens area for several months, and had visited and gotten to know Suesanna before running away to join them. Sadie also learned about Suesanna's name.

"My mother's name was Susan, but she always went by Sue," Bett said. "Suesanna's true name is Anna. Since she was Sue's daughter, the family always called her Sue's Anna."

Although Sadie had never thought she'd find anything delightful about the older sister, she smiled to hear the tale of her name.

"Why does she hate me so?" Sadie asked.

"Same reason she hates me," Bett said. "The men prefer us to her because we're younger, perhaps prettier."

"She doesn't mistreat you the way she does me," Sadie said, shaking her head.

"She can't. I'm family and she's bound to protect me. She isn't a bad person. Her suffering in life has given her an anger."

"There," Sadie said, pointing out some sweet tooth mushrooms growing at the foot of a white oak. She and her friend bent to pick the fleshy white fungi.

"Did you know about the Indian?" Sadie asked. "Kegg, was it?"

"Yes, that was the name," Bett said absently. "But, no, the brothers don't talk about the past much. I only know what little Suesanna has told me about them."

Sadie paused for a moment before asking her next question, concerned with how Bett might react. "Are they thieves?"

"They take what they want, what they need." Bett shrugged, yet obviously she found the question troubling. "Just as your father and mine took from us what they needed," she added hastily.

"Stealing isn't right," Sadie said, trying not to sound self-righteous.

Her friend turned and looked her in the eye. "A lot of things aren't *right*." Bett's tone was somewhat patronizing. "You and I haven't been treated right, even by our own families. Suesanna and my father weren't treated right by the Harpes during the war, but she's part of their family now, and with their help, she's done right by me."

Sadie nodded, more to show she understood what Bett had said than to indicate that she agreed with her.

"The brothers came to America as indentured servants and were sold to a cruel master. They ran away to live with the Indians before the war began. They weren't treated right during the war or after it ended. When the fight was over, folks held a grudge against them because they ran with the Indians, fighting for the Crown. They can't get honest work, so they do what they can. We're with *them* now. They've protected all three of us."

Remembering the night of the Indian's attack, Sadie nodded her head in vigorous agreement.

"Sadie!" Suesanna said harshly, "go look over there." She scowled and pointed into the distance to her right toward a stand of stout cottonwood trees far away from her sister, and Sadie moved to comply.

~ ~ ~

Wiley bedded both Bett and Sadie without seeming to have a preference. He did like having his hands on both of them while engaged in sex. He didn't bed Suesanna. She most often slept with Micajah, but some nights Bett was called to his bed as well, so Sadie had Wiley to herself.

"You too will go to Micajah's bed," Bett warned Sadie.

The prospect was frightening, as Sadie imagined the big man would crush her.

"Don't worry," Bett said. "For all his blustering manner, he's quite easy to handle and rather quick."

Sadie did her best to dismiss the idea. After all, Big Harpe was hardly willing to look at her.

In the first week of travel, they had met up with several other parties headed over the mountains. All went on foot or horseback since the trail wasn't consistently broad or smooth enough for wagons. Horses carried supplies or, in one case, an injured member of a party. Most of the groups included five or more men. The Harpes showed no interest in associating with groups of that size, and would call a halt in their own progress, allowing the parties to move ahead.

At the beginning of the second week, a smaller group of three men, headed for Knoxville, Tennessee, caught up with the Harpes and their women. They were clearly afraid of Micajah, but Wiley put the men at ease, engaging them in lively conversation. The oldest of the three, a man perhaps forty years old with flaxen hair, a strong nose and square jaw, introduced himself and his two sons with a heavy German accent. "I am Dieter Fischer, father of these fine young men, Dirk and Hans." He gestured toward the younger men, both of whom looked quite like him, one blonde, the other with a head of red hair. "We are on our way to settle in Knoxville, Tennessee, where we will open an office of dentistry. I am a tooth extractor," he said with great pride.

"Wir sind alle drei Zahnärzte," Dirk and Hans said in unison, smiling and nodding enthusiastically. Sadie could see that each of them had lost several teeth—more than most men were missing at their relatively young age—and she wondered if Dieter practiced on his sons.

Clearly Dieter didn't like his sons' interruption. He nodded and smiled tightly, displaying a full set of teeth. "My boys will aid me in my practice. One day, when they have learned English, they will overtake me and the practice will be theirs."

The young men nodded again, yet didn't speak.

"Are any within your party enduring toothache?" Dieter asked. "My services may be had for barter or coin."

Sadie, the sisters, and Micajah quickly shook their heads. Wiley didn't respond for a moment. He glanced at his brother. Big Harpe's nod was subtle. Then a grim expression crossed Wiley's face. "I had hoped it would go away," he said with obvious reluctance, "but the pain has become worse for a month now. I have a wee pistol you might find an attractive trade." He pulled his outer garment back to reveal the pistols tucked into his belt and pointed to the smallest of the four.

Dieter's eyes grew wide at the display, and his sons took a step back. Wiley gave them an innocent look. "One can never be too well armed in the wilderness," he said.

Dieter swallowed hard. After a moment he said, "Well…yes, that would be a *fine* exchange." He looked around, scanning the forest to either side of the trail. "The best we can do in the forest is to find a log for you to rest upon while I work. One that is inclined would do best."

"There will be blood," Micajah said ominously to Sadie and the sisters. The statement appeared to trouble Suesanna. "You will remain here," he continued, "while we search for such a log and the tooth extractor does his work."

Sadie thought Big Harpe's concern for the sensibilities of the women was unfounded. "I've seen much blood—" she began.

Suesanna grabbed her arm painfully. She had been exerting such discipline whenever Sadie showed the least inclination to question anything the Harpes said.

Sadie shook Suesanna off as the men moved forward up the trail. The Harpes and Fischers cast about for a proper log as they went. They disappeared beyond a bend in the trail and some time passed. Eventually Sadie heard Micajah's voice calling out, "There!" from some distance off the trail to the south. The indistinct murmur of the mens' voices moved farther in that direction until it was lost amidst the musical chatter of the forest birds.

Sadie didn't know how long the procedure might take, and decided to make use of the time. She spotted a small patch of wood sorrel off the trail on the right. She crouched down beside the patch and brushed the humus away from the plants with her hands. Using a blunted knife to loosen the loam beneath, she plucked the plants free, broke the stems, foliage, and flowers away from the tubers, and added the roots to the supply of food she carried. Glancing back, she saw the sisters pacing along the trail silently, apparently uninterested in occupying their time usefully.

Sadie had made a point of displaying to the men all the food she gathered, clearly an amount greater than what the other women collected. She watched to see what foods Micajah liked best, saved out extra portions of those items, and handed them over to him when no one was watching. He seemed most grateful, and on one of these occasions he revealed a slight smile, the first she'd seen from him. Thinking again that she was competing against the two sisters, Sadie was ashamed. She set the feeling aside, however.

Suesanna appeared uneasy as she paced, her eyes moving restlessly. Sadie remembered the woman was missing several of her front teeth. *She must have had bad experiences with tooth pain.*

Sadie went on with her work, and eventually a cry came from the direction the men had taken, followed by a deeper one. Neither utterance sounded like Wiley, but then having hands in one's mouth might change the voice dramatically.

Sadie crossed the trail to forage for more food.

"Don't go too far," Suesanna said. "You stay well away from the men and their business." The older sister watched her intently.

She's such a dour woman. Sadie wondered if Suesanna's temperament had always been so severe or if life with the Harpes had made her that way.

Sadie heard a trickling sound and saw a creek ahead. Knowing that black walnuts liked to grow near running water, she looked up and saw the distinctive odd-pinnate foliage of the tree mixed into the canopy overhead. She located the twigs holding the leaves, then her eyes traced them back to branches and followed those down to the trunk, rising from the earth not one hundred feet away from her. Indeed, the ground ahead was littered with the green and black hulls of the nuts. Squirrels and other forest creatures had harvested most of them. A few of the hulls were still whole and would contain nuts. She began to gather the bitter-smelling black ones since those were ripest.

Glancing up, she saw a bright redness sliding by in the creek. *Blood,* she decided, as Wiley cleaned up after his tooth extraction. As the red kept coming, she turned away from the sight, hoping he didn't suffer too severely.

Anticipating the return of the men, Sadie rejoined the women on the trail. All three had become restless before the Harpe brothers appeared on the path ahead, returning without the German family, carrying new gear.

"What happened to—" Sadie began.

Suesanna shoved her from behind, sending her stumbling. When Sadie had steadied herself, she glared at Suesanna and then looked at Bett. Her friend's mouth hung open as she looked at Wiley, whose outer garment was still open at the waist. The four pistols remained in Little Harpe's belt, including the one he'd said he'd barter for the tooth extraction. For a moment Bett's brow furled with concern and her mouth moved toward a grimace, but she pulled the expression back quickly and turned away from the Harpes.

"We bought some of their goods and sent them on their way," Wiley said. "I'm sure we'll see them again once we arrive in Knoxville." Blood dripped from his chin, yet he seemed to have no difficulty speaking after his tooth extraction.

Realization struck Sadie: Big and Little Harpe had harmed the Fischers! She knew she couldn't ask the brothers if that were true, however, and she truly didn't *want* to know. She imagined Big and Little Harpe robbing the German family and sending them running for their lives into the forest, hence the screams. Were the Fischers hiding out there somewhere nearby right now? She hoped so, but deep down she feared they had suffered much worse.

Still, Sadie looked at the brothers in horror. When she saw Wiley's eyes narrow and Micajah's jaw tighten, she knew they could see the terror in her gaze.

She quickly relaxed her features and said as brightly as she could, "I found some walnuts!"

Wiley smiled and Micajah's face relaxed. Suesanna nodded grimly. Bett's hand sought Sadie's in a death grip. Although painful, Sadie was glad for the warm touch as the party moved on up the trail.

10
Knoxville, Tennessee

As the Harpe party approached Knoxville at the end of their second week of travel in late July, Wiley went on ahead for reasons unknown to Sadie. The traffic headed along the trail grew steadily as they got closer to the town. Mixed with the other travelers were more women and children than Sadie had seen since leaving Tippens. A few men on horseback and an old fellow driving a wagon loaded down with supplies secured under oilcloth passed them by. Micajah had nothing to do with anyone they met, and most who saw him shied away.

Around noon on the last day of their trek, Wiley met them at a crossroads close to the settlement. Slanting gray and white columns of smoke from the town's many fires, no doubt mostly outdoor cook fires, appeared to support the overcast sky in the distance.

"I found a cabin on the French Broad River, away from the bulk of the settlement," Little Harpe said. "Indians and a flood drove the folks out. The Indians, we know. The floods…well, we'll need to be out by fall. Come with me."

His errand must have been to find us a home, Sadie decided.

The party turned south at the crossroads and traveled a few miles until they came to two cabins in a cleared plot of perhaps three acres. The French Broad River and a canebrake ran along one side of the roughly rectangular homestead. The place was in bad shape. Much of the topsoil in the field had been washed away. Most of an uprooted tree, detritus, and driftwood formed a deadfall up against the smaller of the two cabins as high as the roof and trailing away to either side. Cracks appeared between the logs at one end, but the chimney at the opposite end stood straight.

Less debris surrounded the larger cabin, and a way had been cleared to the door. The forces of the floodwaters had misshapen the building, having lifted the structure off its foundation of flat stones by a few inches on one side. The chimney was tilted slightly and would be unsafe to use.

"Chinking and chimney need repairs," Wiley said. "The shakes are sound. I opened the shutters so it'd dry out some. 'Tis crooked, yet solid."

He spoke with unwarranted confidence, Sadie thought. She was dumbfounded and saw that the sisters were none too pleased. "What if a flood comes before the fall?" she asked without thinking.

Suesanna pulled back to slap Sadie across the mouth. Bett grabbed her sister's wrist, looked her in the eye, and shook her head. The men watched the sisters without reaction. Also without reaction, Suesanna took her hand back and placed her palm atop her swollen belly. Sadie's question went unanswered.

"We can use the wee cabin as a kitchen," Wiley said.

Approaching the larger building, Sadie saw that its heavy door had suffered damage from an axe, but was still solid. Perhaps Indians had tried to break in. The inside of the cabin was moist and black with mold. The fireplace held sodden ashes. From the northern end of the structure to the southern end, the floor rose in elevation a few inches.

They set their bedding and possessions at the high southern end, where the wood was relatively dry, and set about to secure the structure for the coming night. Micajah installed a leather thong on the door latch, while Wiley made sure the swollen shutters would shut all the way. He used his knife to whittle the corner off one of the shutters to make it fit better. Suesanna dug clay from the field outside, mixed in fibrous detritus from the deadfall up against the cabin and began to fill the spaces between the logs where the chinking had fallen out. As Sadie and Bett moved to help her, the men conferred quietly.

"Micajah and I are going to town for supplies," Wiley said, and the two men walked out, leaving the door open behind them.

"What if Indians come?" Bett called after them with a look of worry. Sadie had wanted to ask the same question, but had held her tongue.

Micajah kept walking. Wiley stopped and turned. "We know most of those hereabouts," he said, then added ominously, "and they know us. Besides, no one has been here for some time."

Satisfied, Bett turned back to help her sister. Wiley ran to catch up with Micajah. Sadie watched the men for a moment as they made their way across the field, wondering if they intended to farm the worn-out patch. If not, why had they come here? Was the washed out homestead merely a place to sleep while they organized their next adventure? Again, she couldn't ask.

Sadie moved to the corner in which they had all stowed their possessions. The packs and extra supplies bought from the Fischers were stacked haphazardly, and would spill out onto the puncheon floor any moment. As Sadie reorganized the items, a leather satchel tumbled out of Micajah's large canvas pack and flew open, revealing a set of fine silver tools she suspected were dental instruments. She quickly closed the satchel and shoved the case back into Micajah's pack so Bett wouldn't see the contents, then turned away to help the sisters, vowing to forget all about the discovery.

11
Drunkenness

After the women patched the worst of the holes in the chinking, Sadie took a good look at herself and the sisters. Their hands were muddy from their work, but their clothing and skin were black in places with a mixture of sweat and dust from the trail.

"We should wash in the river," she suggested. Bett nodded her agreement, and she and Sadie gathered up all the clothing they could find, including garments belonging to the men. They walked outside, around the smaller cabin and its deadfall, and across the field to a split in the canebrake. Suesanna followed at a distance with a few more pieces of clothing.

The split in the canebrake was formed by a flat shelf of rock at the water's edge. The tall leafy stalks grew almost all the way around the rock, providing some privacy. In the weeds to one side sat an old dugout canoe, the sun-bleached silver wood so split from drying that the vessel would never float again.

Without soap, the women merely rinsed away as much filth as possible. While their bodies became fairly clean, the clothing remained hopelessly soiled. When finished with washing, the women sat semi-naked on the rock shelf, drying themselves in the sun. Sadie got a good look at Suesanna's swollen belly. The woman was six months or more along in her pregnancy.

They returned to the cabin at dusk to eat some of the dried fish and dried fruit that had belonged to the Fischers. Sadie tried not to think about where the food had come from. By her efforts to avoid the thoughts, they figured more prominently in her mind than they might have otherwise.

The men returned after dark while the women busied themselves mending their trail-worn moccasins. Loud and jovial, Wiley was heard for some time before he reached the cabin. A stranger's voice, hoarse and raspy, joined his in raucous conversation and laughter. "You say you got three women?" the new voice asked. "Why, that's enough for me to take one."

"You're a bampot drunk, you are," Wiley said, laughing. "The words fly like farts from your mouth."

Micajah's voice was absent from the conversation.

Sadie hoped the Harpes would not allow a stranger to take *any* of them. Could Wiley defend her if Micajah wasn't around to help?

Suesanna put down the moccasin she was mending and took up the chamberstick that held the one source of light within the cabin. Shielding the flame against the breeze, she stepped outside. Without the light, Sadie and Bett couldn't continue their work. They set aside their mending as well and joined Suesanna, standing in the night, peering into the darkness, trying to see the Harpes, and get a look at the newcomer. The men were quite close before they were seen. The stranger was leading a dark horse loaded down with the posts and rails of one or more beds. Sadie was relieved to see Micajah with them. Each man carried a sack and an earthenware jug.

The newcomer was a tall olive-skinned fellow with a prominent nose, shiny brown hair and beard, and an unnaturally protruding gut. Where had he come from? Had the men met him in town? By the way he acted, Sadie got the impression he'd known the Harpes for some time. Again, questions she should not ask.

The stranger tethered his horse to a limb of the dead tree resting on the small cabin, then started for the big cabin with the Harpes. He stumbled in one of the tangles of driftwood, but caught himself on Wiley's shoulder.

"Careful, Mose," Wiley said, giggling, "or you'll lose a limb. We've got enough dead limbs already!"

Mose hugged Wiley and laughed so hard that his voice echoed eerily back from the canebrake a hundred or more yards away. Wiley, still giggling, slapped Mose on the back several times and released him.

Micajah's lips formed a hard, thin line and his scowl deepened. Once he and the other men had entered the cabin and set down their jugs and sacks, he wasted no time on introductions. "Build the beds," he commanded.

The women kept out of the way as the men moved to unpack the bed parts from the horse and carry them into the cabin. Micajah took out of his sack two sailcloth mattress ticks, two lengths of rope, a straining wrench and an awl. Suesanna and Sadie lit two more candle lamps.

Wiley and Mose fitted the tennons of the rails into the mortises of the post. The first bed frame came together as Big Harpe threaded the rope through the holes in the rails and wove it in a pattern to support a mattress. He had tied a knot in the end of the rope before it passed through the first hole. He used the straining wrench and awl to tighten the rope and then put a knot in the other end to keep it from slipping through the last hole and coming loose.

He turned toward the women. "It'll be lumpy even with the empty sailcloth and all the bedding. You can find fill for the ticks tomorrow, perhaps cane leaves."

When the second bed was complete, Sadie and the sisters spread the empty sailcloth ticks and various blankets over the ropes. Mose flopped into the first bed finished and rolled, laughing and ogling the women.

"Out!" Micajah bellowed.

Mose leapt from the bed as if it were on fire. Sadie noted that despite his drunkenness, he knew to do as Micajah said.

Mose sidled up to Suesanna, who still fussed with the beds. He tried to steal a kiss. She shrugged him off.

"This one's the least pretty, but I'll take her," he said, his hoarse voice the breathless croak of a dead man. "She's got the biggest pussheads." He reached for Suesanna's breasts, and she dodged out of the way.

Big Harpe made a show of ignoring Mose. He sat with Wiley against the wall in the northwest corner of the cabin, and both men took drinks from one of the jugs.

Sadie and Bett returned to their mending, sitting together against the wall in the northeast corner.

As Mose drank from his own jug, Sadie saw a long scar on his throat, bobbing with each gulp. Damage to his throat might account for his coarse voice. He lowered his jug and caressed his great abdomen much the way Suesanna rubbed her own pregnant belly. His gut was much larger than Suesanna's, however, and looked about to burst any moment. His shirt, missing its lower buttons, failed to contain the bulge, and forty pounds of pale, hairy flesh and a distended belly-button hung pendulously over his crotch. Sadie wondered briefly if Mose was a woman in disguise, pregnant and perhaps near to giving birth.

No, he's too interested in women to be one himself.

Mose kept at Suesanna until she finally lost patience and kneed him in the groin. He dropped the jug, groaned, and fell to the floor. When his jug began to roll downhill, he ceased moaning. Watching it, he laughed. The rolling stopped when the vessel bumped up against Micajah's foot.

The big man righted the container before much of the contents spilled. Still laughing, Mose crawled toward the other men, retrieved his jug, crouched, and took another drink.

Suesanna, finished with her preparations, sat next to Bett.

Micajah clearly didn't like the way the drunkard was acting. Mose seemed oblivious to that as he sat next to Big Harpe.

"You try to snatch from Micajah's puss," Wiley said, "you're going to get hurt. She learned to defend herself when we lived with the Cherokee at Nickajack. Had three Indian bastards before she was done, but her quim hasn't suffered a stranger's prick since. You take care if you want to keep that thing of yours."

As Wiley spoke, a deep sadness gripped Suesanna's features. Sadie had never seen the woman's face so expressive except in anger. The melancholy lasted only a moment and then her features returned to their usual stoniness. The woman had feelings for one or all of those children, Sadie decided. She wondered what had happened to them.

Mose looked at Suesanna and made his face a caricature of fear. "She's not worth all that!" he said, laughing too loudly. "The other two, how much for one of them?"

"Not for sale." Micajah said flatly, his expression cold. He was clearly restraining himself.

"During the war, you boys were always willing to share," Mose said. "Nothing's changed."

So the Harpes did know Mose, Sadie decided, had known him for a long time.

He stood and moved toward Bett, stumbling in his drunkenness. Sadie was relieved to see he wasn't coming for her, but then he staggered, and when he got his feet firmly under himself again, he was turned toward her. She recoiled as he reached down to touch her hair. Sadie glanced at Bett. Her friend was minding her own business.

"You heard Micajah," Wiley said.

"A look is not a kiss," Mose slurred. He crouched beside Sadie and almost fell over.

Suesanna began to sing quietly:

"Why, cruel creature, why so bent
To vex a tender heart?
To gold and title you relent,
Love throws in vain his dart."

Mose became somewhat still, listening to Suesanna's song, a far-off look in his eye.

"Let glittering fools in court be great;

For pay, let armies move;
Beauty should have no other bait,
But gentle vows and love."

Apparently, Mose knew the song as he began quietly croaking out the tune along with her.

"If on those endless charms you lay
The value that's their due,
"Kings are themselves too poor to pay,
A thousand worlds too-flailing few:"

Although Sadie wanted to shove him away while he wasn't concentrating on her, she feared his reaction.

"But if a passion without vice,
Without disguise or art
Ah, Mira, if true love's your price
Behold it in my heart."

When Suesanna finished her song, she continued humming the tune.

Mose stopped, however, and turned his attention back to Sadie. He leaned toward her. She backed away from his oily face and pressed herself against the wall. His foul breath smelled of bad liquor and rotten, toothless gums.

"We have music," he said, nodding toward Suesanna. "Good etiquette requires that you cannot refuse a dance, and the gentlemen—" Mose stood and gestured elaborately toward the Harpes, "—must allow it."

The man was out of his mind with drink, Sadie realized. She glanced over at Micajah. His lip twitched angrily, but otherwise he remained still. Sadie knew his anger might move him any moment.

"May I have the honor of this dance?" Mose asked with his raspy voice. He extended a scabrous hand for her.

Sadie dropped her mending, crossed her arms, and remained silent. *Mose doesn't know what he's doing,* she thought. *I must say something, to save him a lot of pain.*

"She's not for sale," Wiley said, a warning in his voice.

Sadie glanced at Micajah again. His lip and the bridge of his nose quivered into a silent snarl, reminding her of the red wolves.

Mose seemed to notice her glance. "They won't stop me," he whispered. "We fought together, shared the spoils o' war, owe each other a debt." He reached for her skirts.

I must speak up, Sadie thought, *or he'll suffer terribly.*

Yet when Mose touched her, she found herself hating him, and decided he deserved whatever the brothers did to him.

Not long now, Sadie thought, *and they'll turn him out. Maybe they'll beat him before sending him to walk off his drunk on the long path back to town.* She liked the idea.

Mose had gotten his hand farther than she'd thought he would. Sadie was beginning to think he'd have his way with her.

Then, Micajah moved, and he was fast. He stood, hauled the man up by the hair, and dragged him flailing away from Sadie. Wiley got up and opened the door. Mose laughed. He clawed for something to stop his progress, got a grip on the door frame with both hands as Micajah tried to take him outside. Wiley pried Mose's hands loose and shoved him out the door.

Sadie and the sisters rose to their feet and followed the men outside.

"All right," Mose said, still laughing, "I give in."

"Too late," Wiley said.

The good humor clearly left Mose instantly with the sobering effect of sudden fear. "No!" he shouted.

Wiley smiled, but Micajah was all business. Still gripping Mose by the hair, he hauled the drunken fool to the hole from which Suesanna had dug the clay.

"W-we owe a debt to one another," Mose cried.

"Here's what I owe," Micajah said, as he lowered Mose toward the hole. Big Harpe drew a knife and cut the drunkard's throat.

Sadie screamed as Mose fell across the small pit. He struggled only weakly, his neck disgorging blood in pulses down into the earth.

"No," she cried, "no, no, no!"

Suesanna slapped her once across the face, and Sadie screamed again. The older sister slapped her a second and third time. The pain of the last blow took the volume from Sadie's voice. She cowered and sobbed.

Bett, standing nearby, had made no effort to stop Suesanna. The younger sister stared at the dying man, her expression void of understanding and emotion.

"You *would* have them defend you, would you not?" Suesanna shouted, hatred in her voice.

Yes, Sadie had wanted that. She'd begun bargaining for the Harpes' protection even back at the wattle and daub cabin in The Cut, but she'd hoped her father would be the one to suffer.

Wiley grabbed the dead man under the arms and hauled the corpse away, out of sight, behind the cabin.

Mose's death was Sadie's fault. She fell to the ground and wept.

Suesanna gave her a swift kick in the gut. Bett stumbled back as Sadie cried out in pain. Suesanna was drawing her foot back to deliver another blow when Micajah threw her to the ground. Suesanna looked away as the big man lifted Sadie. He smelled of blood and liquor. Sadie quaked with fear as he held her in his arms and carried her into the cabin to one of the beds. He lowered her to the rope-lumpy bedding and lay down beside her. The bed was a tight fit. He made no effort to quiet her, nor did he touch her.

Suesanna had returned to her mending. Bett sat next to her, and closed her eyes. Wiley came into the cabin some time later and returned to his drinking.

Eventually, exhaustion took away Sadie's fear. Her shaking ceased and she slept.

12
Fishing

When Sadie awoke the next morning, the cabin was quiet and all within slept. Slowly, so as not to disturb Micajah beside her, she sat up and looked around. Wiley wasn't in the cabin. She lay back down and tried to return to sleep, but memory of Mose's death filled her head with a repetitive and frightful muddle of sights, sounds, and words from the night before.

Wiley entered shortly thereafter, his leggings wet around his feet as if he'd been in the river. His hands and arms were tinted red with blood, though he'd obviously rinsed them. Had he been out burying the dead drunkard, then needed to clean up?

Sadie quickly shut her eyes when she felt Micajah stir and get up. She opened them just a crack to watch as Big Harpe joined his brother. They sat against the wall in the northwest corner, eating dried fish.

"Mose's gut was large because he had a great tumor, big as your head," Wiley told Micajah. "Had teeth in it, black hair, and something like toenails or maybe fingernails."

"A demon," Micajah said while chewing. He shrugged. "Good we killed it."

Perhaps Mose was pregnant after all, Sadie thought. She opened her eyes to get a better look at the Harpes' faces, to see if they spoke earnestly. Big Harpe caught her looking at him. Although she wanted to close her eyes again and pretend she wasn't watching, he wouldn't be fooled. He held her gaze for a while and she saw no threat in his expression. Indeed, for all of Micajah's ferocity, when he looked squarely at Sadie, she could see something beneath the scars and the scowl that wasn't frightening. To the contrary, she saw an ordinary man, wearing the body of a ferocious beast. No one, but perhaps Wiley, knew the extent of what he'd suffered during and after the war to make him that way. Sadie could still see the man inside, however. She knew something about suffering in silence.

Micajah turned away and talked with his brother so quietly she couldn't make out what they said.

Bett was right, Sadie thought. *We're with the Harpes now, and thankfully they protect us in a dangerous land.*

With all my crying, was I ungrateful last night?

Perhaps Mose was more dangerous than I could know. The Harpes knew him for many years. Micajah may have had good cause to kill him.

Her thoughts were interrupted as the sisters rose from bed. Suesanna slapped Sadie on the foot unnecessarily hard to rouse her.

The sisters, still dressed in their night clothes, broke out more of the Fischers' food supplies. Suesanna and the Harpes went about their business as if nothing momentous had occurred the night before. Bett was unusually quiet, her eyes frequently unfocussed and distant.

Sadie, still dressed in her clothes from the previous day, rose from bed to join the others. After what she had witnessed with Mose's death, she expected she wouldn't have much appetite, but surprised herself by eating a hearty breakfast of the fish, fruit, and dried biscuits.

Once everyone had had their fill, Micajah scooped up the rest of the fish and began to eat it.

Suesanna looked to Wiley, a pleading in her eyes.

"You know that's the last of the fish," Wiley said. "We have no meat, just the dried fruit, a few biscuits, and what the women have gathered."

"I'm hungry," Micajah growled.

"We're having trouble keeping up with that hunger," Wiley said quietly. "Have you looked for worm in your stool lately?"

Micajah dropped the last of the fish and grabbed Wiley by the collar, pulling him in close. Their faces mere inches apart, Big Harpe looked ready to eat Little Harpe. Wiley became stony-faced, except for his eyes, which darted about, seeking escape from Big Harpe's angry countenance.

"You've danced around this long enough," Micajah said, flecks of spittle and bits of fish flying with the words into Wiley's face.

Little Harpe finally fixed his gaze on Big Harpe's eyes. "You've gotten bigger," he said, and shrugged as if that might lessen the impact of his words.

"That's right," Micajah said, pushing Little Harpe away from his face and tossing him aside. "What have you to say about it?"

Wiley remained silent as he stood, straightened his clothing, and sat back down.

"You want I should carry most of the fight," Micajah said, "there's a price."

"Though you've always been big," Wiley said, "you carry a gut now, one that needs to be satisfied."

"Took me longer to grow up," Big Harpe said defiantly. He glanced at Suesanna and Bett, but his eyes sought Sadie's as if what she thought mattered to him. "I'm better in a fight now than when I was younger," he added.

She gave him a small, tight smile. He was in his late thirties, a time when many men grew larger. Sadie could understand that he might have concerns about getting older, about others seeing him as growing old. He'd want to keep up appearances for his women and even his brother.

"Aye, your size has always been a boon," Wiley said. "Never fear, brother. We'll find a way to better meet that hunger of yours. I have notions of what we would try. Let's go to town and see what we can see."

Micajah nodded. The brothers spoke in hushed tones for a moment, then stood and finished dressing.

"Suesanna, you look after the work while we're gone," Wiley said. "See if you can catch some fish. Fill the mattresses. Keep the others busy. My hope is we'll be back by nightfall."

The men grabbed their weapons and accoutrements and left the cabin. They were out of Sadie's view for a moment, then she saw them leading Mose's horse as they headed across the field toward town. When Wiley stepped over the dark spot where Mose had bled into the earth, Sadie noticed the hole had been hastily filled.

With the brothers' departure, she was apprehensive about being left in Suesanna's charge and going without the protection of the men way out at the edge of the Knoxville settlement. The Harpes might know the Indians in these parts, but Bett and Sadie did not. She could only hope that whatever respect or fear the Indians had for the brothers somehow extended to Suesanna as well.

Sadie picked up the dried fish Micajah had dropped on the floor, and put four strips back into the box in which they'd been stored. Making certain the sisters weren't watching, she slipped a fifth strip into a pocket of her skirt. She would give the food to Micajah later.

"Ready yourselves," Suesanna said. "We're going fishing." Once their toilets and dressing were completed, the older sister gave a great coil of rope to Sadie and a ball of horse hair fishing line to Bett. Suesanna led the way southeast toward the river, downstream of the canebrake, carrying a wooden box with a handle. As they walked along the eroding bank, she was looking for something in the river. Sadie was curious about what that might be, but not enough to endure the older woman's typically bad response to questions.

Bett still had the troubled, faraway look in her eyes that she'd had since the killing of Mose.

A half-mile downstream from the cabin, Suesanna poked around in the brush at a small feeder stream, finding another dugout canoe resting in the shallow water. She inspected the ground above on the river bank.

"Ask her what she's after," Sadie whispered to her friend.

"What are you looking for?" Bett asked flatly.

"Tracks," her sister said. "I want to know how often the canoe is used or if it's abandoned. If we have close neighbors, I want to know." Finishing her inspection, she said, "No one's been here for some time."

"Ask her if that's why we're here," Sadie said.

"We came here for that?" Bett asked.

"No," Suesanna said. She led them further downstream. "We're here to fish." They had not gone another fifty yards when she said, "There," and pointed downstream to a small, slow-moving whirlpool.

Bett seemed uninterested.

"The inside curve of the bend in the river," Suesanna said. "The water will be deep there. That's where we'll set our drift line."

She gave Bett one end of the rope. "Take that down just past the bend." Suesanna played out the rope as her sister moved downriver. "That's good. Now bring it back."

Suesanna opened the box she carried to reveal supplies for fishing. She demonstrated for Bett and Sadie how to connect fishing lines and cork floats to the rope at regular intervals close to Bett's end. All three women worked on the project for a time. Once they had connected twenty lines with floats to the rope, Suesanna tied a stone weight and hook to each one.

"Now we need bait," she said. "Small crawfish will do."

The women moved along the bank, turning over slimy rocks in the cool water and collecting the crustaceans in their skirts. Once Suesanna had set them on the hooks, their little legs still wriggling, she gathered the lines up against the rope carefully and held the bundle out to Sadie. "Hold it here and here." She removed her hands one at a time so Sadie could grip the bundle in the same way. "Carry it down the bank and stop just before the bend. Don't get the hooks caught in you!"

Sadie knew the woman's concern was for efficiency not safety.

"Bett, take up the rope halfway to Sadie," Suesanna said. "When I say so, both of you throw the rope out as far as you can." Suesanna tied her end to a small sapling up the bank. "Now, throw it."

Sadie did as instructed, as did Bett, and the rope, with its fishing lines now swinging free, sailed through the air and landed with multiple splashes in the sun-dappled water. The current dragged the combination downstream, right into the slow-moving whirlpool at the inside curve of the bend.

"Now to gather cane leaves for the mattresses, clean out the fireplace, finish the chinking," Suesanna said. She gave the younger women a dark look under her brow as if to warn them that she wouldn't tolerate any laziness.

Sadie was truly glad for the work as a distraction from her own thoughts, and as an excuse to look at anything other than Suesanna.

~ ~ ~

They returned to check on their drift line in the late afternoon as the sunlight, warm, golden and vivid, slanted down through the water illuminating clearly the rocks on the river bed.

Suesanna grabbed the rope and pulled, then gave a worried look. "Hold onto the rope," she said as she untied the end from the sapling. Bett and Sadie both held on, though the rope tried to get away from them.

"That's either many fishes," the older sister said, "or we've caught ourselves a drafted log." She began taking up the rope as they moved down the bank toward the bend.

Halfway to the bend, the women found that hauling the rope in further was impossible.

"Well, I swan," Suesanna said, a bead of sweat dripping down her forehead.

Sadie had not heard the older sister curse before. *She must be frustrated indeed.*

"Let's look and see," Suesanna said. She tied the rope to another sapling while Bett and Sadie continued toward the bend.

Sadie reached the whirlpool first and gasped at what she saw clearly through the ten-foot-deep water. Bett cried out and Suesanna came running.

Mose's corpse was tangled in the fishing lines. He appeared to stand on the bottom of the river, his left foot touching the riverbed, while his right leg was extended outward from his body at an angle, slightly bent at the knee. Although he faced away from the women, with his head tilted back and to one side, his features were visible.

"Damn! We'll never clear it," Suesanna said, showing not the slightest shock at the sight. She ran back toward the sapling. Halfway there, she stepped out into the water, grabbed the rope, and cut through the heavy cord with her knife.

As Sadie watched, Mose began a slow pirouette as if dancing an ominous and wicked jig, the rope and fishing lines spiraling about him. His head flung back, eyes and mouth open, he appeared to sing the silent song to which he danced. Recalled from the night before, Sadie heard Mose's croaked invitation in her head, "May I have the honor of this dance?"

When he had pivoted to face Sadie, she saw that his gut was laid open. Smooth river stones spilled out of the cavity, as fishes plucked at the great flaps of raw flesh undulating in the current.

Her stomach began its own sickening turn and she tried to vomit. She gagged several times, but hadn't had anything to eat since early in the day, and nothing came up. She swung around to hug Bett. Suesanna pushed Sadie away. The sisters stumbled off together, back toward the cabin.

Sadie walked alone, the image of the dead man still slowly dancing in her head. *One moment*, she thought, *he was fearless, alive, and laughing. The next...forever gone.*

Again, the breathless, croaking voice in her head. *May I have the honor of this dance?*

What little sympathy she had for Mose fled, however, as she thought of how he had reached under her skirts.

~ ~ ~

"No fish!" Micajah said. He tossed half a small butchered pig on the ground outside the cabin. Wiley dropped an armload of cooking equipment.

"We caught one too big to reel in," Suesanna said, standing in the doorway. "I didn't expect you'd dump the dead man in the river."

Sadie had never heard the woman make an attempt at humor until the present. The men remained stern. Suesanna stepped aside to allow them to enter the cabin.

"When have we *not?*" Wiley asked.

They put all their dead in rivers, Sadie thought numbly.

Suesanna shrugged. "We have more swine than we can eat." She gestured toward the partial carcass outside the door.

"Did Mose float?" Micajah asked urgently. "No," Suesanna said. "If he hasn't washed downstream, he's still in the deep, taking up the lines."

Micajah seemed satisfied and turned to other business. "The wee cabin is the kitchen. We got supplies." He gestured to the equipment Wiley had dropped. "Take the carcass, pots and pans. Cook the beast up."

Wiley hefted to his shoulder the half-pig, Suesanna grabbed the other end by the leg, and they hauled the dead thing away in the direction of the small cabin. Micajah followed, but walked past the cabin into the field. He seemed to be sizing the place up for some purpose. Perhaps he did indeed intend to put in some crops.

Sadie stacked the pots and pans, and put the pot hooks and a large iron trivet in the top-most kettle. She lifted the stack and followed Suesanna and Wiley.

Since the fireplace in the small cabin had a pot crane, those who built the homestead had no doubt intended the structure to be a kitchen, especially during the hot, humid summer months.

While Wiley busied himself butchering the carcass, Suesanna worked to start a fire. Once Sadie had set the equipment on the hearth, the older woman turned to her. "Get out," she said flatly.

Wiley never looked up from his work. For all his sweet words back in The Cut, he wasn't truly interested in Sadie.

Outside, she saw Micajah walking back across the field toward the cabins. Sadie walked toward him, and they met beside the open door to the large cabin. She pulled the dried fish from her skirt pocket and offered it to him. He gave the smallest hint of a smile as he took the food, put it in his mouth, and continued on toward the kitchen cabin.

Sadie turned to find Bett sitting on one of the beds watching her. "I know what you've been doing," she said.

"But I—" Sadie began.

Her friend cut her off. "I don't think any less of you." Bett hung her head, clearly distressed. "If I were smart, I'd make more effort to please."

Relieved her friend understood her need to gain favor, Sadie sat beside her. "Don't despair," she said.

"I'm afraid," Bett whispered.

The happenings of the last two days were so far outside Sadie's realm of experience, she didn't understand her own reactions. Her fear, anger, and sadness were mixed up, leaving her unfocussed and feeling distant from herself.

She caressed Bett's forearm.

"The sight of that man in the river," Bett said, "it haunts me."

Mose still danced in Sadie's head as well, the image cold and watery. *One moment alive and laughing,* she reminded herself, *the next, forever dead.* He would deteriorate with time. The fishes would take him apart and scatter his remains.

May I have the honor of this dance?

"I torment myself with fear and regret," Bett said. "I am to blame for you being here. I don't know what terrors tomorrow will bring."

"Don't think about it," Sadie said. "If we are alive, it's only for the

moment. You saw what happened to Mose. One moment he was alive, the next, he was gone. He was laughing almost to the end."

Bett frowned, and Sadie found herself trying to decide what her own words meant. "That's life, isn't it, one moment follows another, each with its own trials, until the end?"

Bett's frown darkened further.

Sadie could see that her friend saw only the anguish in what she said. She shook her head. "Thinking about the past, I have regret, and looking to the future, I feel dread, but those are torments of fancy." She shrugged. "If I have none of it, and live only *now*, come what may, I'll at least be safe from the wretchedness of my own making. I could laugh until the end, just like Mose."

Bett seemed to think about that, then she turned a somber face to Sadie and hugged her. Although Sadie found that her own words seemed reasonable, she didn't know if she could live that way. *I must try*, she told herself.

To start with, she was glad to be alive. She also felt safe and well-protected with the men nearby. Doing her best to banish all other thoughts, she concentrated on the feeling of gratitude and the well-being that came with feeling safe. Sadie found that way of thinking exciting. For the moment, she was able to set aside her feelings of responsibility for recent events. Somehow, she knew life wasn't that simple, but for the present, all was as it should be.

Tonight Sadie was safe and happy, glad for the Harpes' protection, and willing to benefit from anything provided through their efforts. Tonight she would eat well and sleep soundly, untroubled by her own conscience.

13
Jealousy

For the second night, Micajah placed Sadie in his bed, and Suesanna slept with Wiley and Bett. The older woman had given Sadie the evil eye before retiring.

Again, Sadie slept through the night unmolested. When she awoke and opened her eyes, Micajah was looking at her. He lay beside her in the bed for some time calmly gazing at her face. She wasn't frightened until the question occurred to her and she couldn't keep from asking, "Why?"

She ducked her head in fear of his reaction. He gently placed a hand on her shoulder, and she relaxed. The big man was silent a moment, then he whispered. "Suesanna is broken. She will do anything we ask, but the light is gone from her eyes. The girl she was died long ago. Bett has only fear and she too will die inside. You don't turn away when I look at you. Wiley doesn't care, but I want…" He shook his head and looked away.

Sadie caught a glimpse of something she found endearing: The big man was embarrassed. She could see that he cared for her beyond mere physical attraction. Micajah had a human weakness after all—a weakness for Sadie—and somehow that made him attractive to *her*. But how could that be? He was second only to Quinton in ugliness. Of course, she'd had feelings for him as well.

Feelings for him?

Is that what she had for Micajah? She realized she had somehow mixed up having feelings for someone with attraction. Although she shook her head at the thoughts, her wonder wouldn't go away.

Micajah got up and left the cabin. Sadie sat and looked around. Wiley must have gone out before Big Harpe. The sisters remained in their bed, eyes shut. Sadie lay back down. The newly stuffed mattress was a delightful cloud to rest upon. Despite her decision not to dwell on the past and future, she thought of Micajah's words and what they might mean in time to come.

He had referred to a light being gone from Suesanna's eyes, and Sadie had the impression he still saw such illumination in her own. She also believed he would fight to protect that light. Feeling untroubled, Sadie closed her eyes and tried to return to sleep.

Moments later, she felt something hard and sharp against her throat. "Be still or I'll cut you," Suesanna whispered. She lay atop Sadie, pinning her. The older woman's rotten breath escaped with each word. Choking on the foul odor, Sadie panicked. She wanted to lash out against Suesanna, to pound the sides of her pregnant belly, to beat her sullen face. With the older woman's legs on Sadie's arms, she had no leverage. She opened her mouth to cry for Bett, but the older sister pressed the knife harder against her throat.

"You will be quiet."

Sadie nodded slightly. Had Suesanna heard what Micajah had said? Even if she did, they were the big man's words, not Sadie's.

"Two nights you have been with my husband," Suesanna spat.

She merely wants to punish me, and then will let me go, Sadie told herself. She didn't truly believe that.

"You will not take my man!" Suesanna seemed to shout, although still whispering her words.

"I haven't tried to win him away from you," Sadie lied desperately. She knew she was about to die. "I didn't ask to be in his bed."

The Harpes would return to the cabin to find her bloody corpse. Wiley wouldn't care. Micajah would mourn her for perhaps a fortnight. To protect Suesanna, they'd gut Sadie, load her with stones and sink her in the river to join Mose.

May I have the honor of this dance?

"Please," Sadie said, "I will say *no* to him."

"Wouldn't do any good," Suesanna said, then pressed her mouth into a hard line. "I will fare better if you're gone." She bore down with the blade on Sadie's throat.

Feeling the sting of sharp steel as the blade cut through her skin, the fight rose up in Sadie. "Cut my throat," she coughed out, "and see what he does to you!"

Suesanna's eyes became wide and darted about, seeming to search the dim interior of the cabin for an answer, while no doubt searching her own mind.

The pressure of the knife decreased.

"Suesanna!" Bett said. She stood at the foot of the bed.

The older woman didn't respond. She was quiet for a moment as Bett, her eyes also wide, moved to the side of the bed to better see what was happening.

Suesanna pulled the blade away. She put her rotten mouth next to Sadie's right ear. "A good accident should do the work for me. Look for it another time."

Bett drew her sister off Sadie, and took the knife away. The sisters lay back down on the other bed. All was quiet in the cabin except for the pounding of Sadie's heart and the sound of blood rushing through the vessels in her neck. She wiped away the trickle of blood that flowed from a small cut on her throat.

At present, the worry she'd hoped to banish returned with a vengeance and she could think of nothing but the future. One day, soon perhaps, she'd have to respond to another attempt on her life from the older woman. A dread of each passing moment gripped Sadie.

If I tell Micajah what Suesanna has done, will he protect me from her like he did from Mose? Would she lie if he asks her about it? Yes, she would, and Bett would not give her away.

She won't risk his wrath openly. I'll have to remain on guard and become ever closer to Micajah.

Sadie did fear the future. For her own survival, she must make herself ready. However, she refused to regret the past any longer.

~ ~ ~

Wiley and Micajah entered the cabin, carrying hunks of roasted pork. They were deep in conversation, despite stuffing their mouths with greasy chunks of meat. They sat in their usual mealtime spot, leaning against the wall in the northwest corner.

The sisters got up and left the cabin. Sadie remained in bed, listening.

"But we'd have to go to Chota to make an agreement with the Red and White chiefs," Micajah said. "They won't—"

"No, it's simpler than that," Wiley said in an exasperated tone. "We don't have to work with any of them. If we got the Cherokee to help, they'd want a share of the take. Folks hereabouts fear the Indians, so we don't even have to make threats. Fear of Indian attack will do the persuading for us. We tell folks we can provide protection because the Indians are our brothers. We tell them that anyone who pays us will not be attacked."

"Then those who don't pay have to be attacked," Micajah said. "If we don't have the help of the Red and White chiefs, how are we going to get them to attack?"

"*We* do it. *Alone. You* and *me.*" Wiley paused to allow that to sink in. "We attack at night, when no one sees it's just us. We burn their barns. If they still don't pay, we do worse."

"What if a real Indian attack comes against one who pays?"

"We say it was another tribe, one we don't know."

Micajah, his eyes seemingly focused on some possible future beyond the walls of the cabin, nodded his head slowly. "I think it's a good plan."

Sadie got dressed and left the cabin. She walked to the hole Wiley had dug in a stand of willows by the river. Squatting to relieve herself, watching the pale green leaves flicker in the breeze against the blue sky, she thought about what she'd heard. She understood only that Wiley and Micajah thought they'd found a new opportunity that would pay, one that might require more fighting. The violence came with the wilderness, Sadie had decided, an unavoidable aspect of frontier settlement life, and she felt lucky she was with men who were good fighters. She was certain the two brutes were equal to the task, whatever the campaign entailed.

She thought back to the night the wolves had treed her. The animals were dangerous, they were opportunistic, casting about for whatever they could take to survive, but they were her wolves that night. She'd slept well, knowing her father couldn't get to her without going through them first.

Micajah and Wiley were like the wolves. The fighting, the violence, the struggle for survival would be worth the effort if the adventure paid in coin.

Her involvement was limited to more domestic concerns. They protected her without once expecting her to commit violence. Safe and happy, she'd stay at the cabins, away from the fighting. Sadie didn't even have to know about it.

With a little money, they would eat well and prosper. They could fix up the cabins of the washed-out farm, or perhaps buy a better piece of land and build a new home, become respectable members of the Knoxville settlement. Bett might emerge from her fearful state. Suesanna would become happy, setting aside her hatred. Sadie could imagine getting along with the woman.

Thinking about Suesanna, Sadie reminded herself to be vigilant. She looked around, but the woman was nowhere to be seen. Sadie relaxed and finished her toilet, then headed for the kitchen cabin to find something to eat. Entering, she smiled. The smile sat uneasily on her face. She kept the expression all the same, for if she could use her imagination to torment herself, she could use that same creative vision to persuade herself that she was happy.

14
The Young City

The months of August and September were a pleasant time for Sadie. As she had imagined and hoped, the Harpes' enterprise paid off and they had money to spend. Everyone within the household was well-fed. They made trips into town to buy cloth to make new clothes, a table and chairs so they'd have a place to sit in the kitchen cabin while enjoying their much fuller meals, feather pillows on which to lay their heads in bed at night, and many other small things to add comfort to life.

The Harpes acquired shovels, axes, wedges and pry bars, and with the help of the women, they set posts and split rails to build two enclosures in the washed out field, one for pigs and one for sheep. They also set posts for a picket line for horses. Shortly after the pens and picket line were complete, the Harpe brothers rounded up livestock for them. Sadie assumed that some of the Harpes' clients bartered the beasts for the brothers' service. The horses were the only animals fed. The sheep and pigs were held just until the brothers got around to slaughtering them, which most often occurred only when their hungry bleating became too much of a nuisance. When the Harpes went to town, their business included selling meat they had butchered. Occasionally someone came by the place to bargain for one of the horses.

Micajah didn't take Suesanna back to his bed. Sadie slept with him every night, and she knew that he'd require sex from her eventually. She could only imagine Suesanna's growing hatred, for the older woman ceased to exhibit the signs. Indeed, she seemed somewhat happy at times—as Sadie had imagined might happen. One morning Suesanna had saved an extra corn fritter from breakfast to give Sadie. With the food, the woman also gave her a smile and a nod that conveyed resigned acceptance.

Sadie's father had made such genial overtures too. Inevitably, he followed them with more pain. She wasn't about to let her guard down for a fritter and a smile.

~ ~ ~

On her first visit to town with the Harpes and the sisters, Sadie noted that the citizens of the Knoxville settlement were much like the people in Tippens, but for their clothing, which was often ill-fitted, lacking in color, and frequently fashioned of unevenly spun wool in coarse knits and weaves. The men were more heavily armed than those of Tippens, and several of them wore buckskins. Sadie saw five Indians, four males and one female, and two black men. Compared to Tippens, there were fewer women and children in proportion to men in Knoxville.

The town had nine muddy streets, four running north to south, five running east to west. Sadie counted about forty-five houses, mostly of log construction, although a couple were simple frame houses and one was built of limestone. Under the bright blue sky, surrounded by the cool green of the endless forest, the town was somber grays and browns. Sadie wondered if the drab hues said anything about the virtue of human endeavor.

Along with the delightful smells of freshly hewn wood, cooking, and baking, the town also smelled strongly of smoke, particularly the piss odor of burning elm. Sadie presumed the people of Knoxville were frugal frontier folks who couldn't afford to set aside any resource, such as the elm, merely because the wood smelled bad when burning. She identified two smoke houses by their salty, savory odor, and a makeshift tannery by the smell of old urine coming from a collection of barrels surrounding an enclosure of wooden baths. Beyond the baths were racks of stretched hides. Without the pleasant breeze blowing the odors northward, Sadie knew the place would have smelled much worse. Beside the tannery squatted the long log structure of the slaughterhouse where the brothers sold their butchered meat. The air around the building was alive with flies.

The closer they got to the center of town, the more the sound of human voices overlapped; quiet conversational tones, clear and insistent instructions from men and women working together, laughter, arguments, and singing. Above the voices rose the sounds of a blacksmith's hammer, sawing and chopping, horses and wagons, and barking dogs.

Gay Street, in the center of town, was a long, deeply rutted series of mud puddles. A puncheon walkway ran on either side of the road in front of the houses and businesses. Still, to cross intersections meant walking through thick, brown mud while avoiding the ubiquitous piles of manure and the harrying flies that bred in them.

The Harpe party received pleasant, if curt, greetings from the towns-folk. Several men bowed slightly to greet the Harpe women. Some men shook the brothers' hands warmly, exchanging trite pleasantries, while others did so exhibiting a touch of unease. The women of the town stared, but Sadie found that if she looked one who was staring in the eye, she'd receive a polite smile. No one made more than a cursory effort to engage in conversation with any of the Harpe party. That suited Sadie, for she had nothing to say to anyone.

The Harpes and their women walked about town with their heads held high and did business at the mercantile. For most of the day, they steered clear of the rum joints, makeshift gambling parlors, and whore houses. Even so, Sadie got an eyeful of the rowdies in town, as they stumbled about drunk and made nuisances of themselves, urinating in public, cursing, and harassing most everyone but the prostitutes.

Wiley must have seen her concern. "Most of those rough fellows work on the river," he said. "They won't bother us."

Indeed, Sadie noticed that the rowdies, as drunk as they were, carefully kept their distance.

The Harpes appeared to know quite a few people in town. Except for simple greetings and an occasional "good day," Micajah said little.

Wiley hailed a short, plump, bearded man on the street. "Hey, Baudin," he said. "If you're not careful, I'm coming to town soon to get drunk with you!"

The man nodded and laughed. "Let's meet up at Hughes' and play some cards," he said. Sadie remembered passing Hughes' Tavern on the way to town. The two men spoke briefly, and then the Harpe party moved on. That was the most Wiley had said all day.

Sadie presumed that the majority of the talking the Harpes did, getting to know folks and setting up their enterprise, they'd done in private. She imagined the threats they delivered would not be well received in public.

At a distance, Sadie saw a man who looked like her father, tall, black hair and beard, dressed all in darkness. He had the same strutting stride as Reverend Rice. She quickly ducked behind Bett to keep from being seen by the man.

He's looking for me!

Bett looked at her curiously. "Are you not feeling well?"

Sadie risked a look over her friend's shoulder. The man was gone. Perhaps he'd entered a place of business. "I thought I saw my father."

Bett grasped Sadie's hand and gave a reassuring squeeze. The gesture was warm, but a worried look played about her friend's features.

When calm returned, Sadie realized she hadn't seen much of the man's face, and that many men had dark hair and clothing. Most likely, he had been a stranger with some resemblance.

Even so, she imagined him trying to wrest her free of the Harpes and take her home. *They would kill him.* Sadie liked the thought of that.

Toward the end of the day, they bought pastries made with honey from a woman selling on the corner of Hill and State Streets. Suesanna pulled from the sack she carried an old, gray piece of calico, folded the cloth around the pastries, and placed the bundle in her sack.

The Harpe party stopped for a meal at Hughes' Tavern outside of town. The food was forgettable, not so the experience. The place was crowded with all manner of rough and raucous men. Laughter among the patrons did not sound like the product of good humor, having instead a derisive, mean-spirited edge. The few women in evidence were prostitutes, their halfhearted participation in the drinking and eating a mere pretense to get close to the men. Two fights broke out in the tavern while the Harpe party ate, one ending in a near-fatal knifing. The loser was carried out of the place. Although obscured much of the time by people walking the sawdust strewn floor, Sadie was certain a man in one corner of the establishment had sexual intercourse with his whore even as he drank and spoke to his companions.

Sadie would have been afraid of the place if she hadn't been with the Harpes. She saw no one within the establishment she thought could stand up to the brothers or pose them any real threat. Indeed, the tavern's patrons appeared to make efforts to avoid looking at the Harpes. The brothers didn't react as if they felt slighted. On the contrary, they were the lords of the tavern. Their table, an island of calm within a maelstrom of activity, was centrally located, but the other patrons carefully gave them plenty of room. Big and Little Harpe kept to themselves, happily watching the debauched goings-on while they ate. Although they didn't communicate with anyone, they seemed right at home among the coarse revelers. Sadie thrilled to feel immune to the dangers and above the iniquities of the place.

While walking home in the waning light, they ate their honey pastries. Sadie had never eaten anything so sweet and delicious before. By the time they reached home, lightning bugs were flashing in the misty air above the washed-out field and crickets sang in the shadows.

She had a warm feeling as she lay down for the night, but the warmth fled when Micajah turned to her and drew her into an embrace. Her mind filled with the worst imaginings as he groped her with his giant hands and nuzzled her. Sadie's bones would be shattered beneath his weight! He'd suffocate her. With his powerful thrusts, he'd split her in two and perhaps not even notice he'd done so until the next morning. To protect his brother and the sisters, he would gut Sadie, load her abdomen with stones, and drop her into the river to join Mose.

May I have the honor of this dance? She heard the man's croaking laughter in her head.

But, no—she found Micajah surprisingly gentle. Unseen in the darkness, he wasn't so frightening. When he was ready to enter her, he placed her on top. His manhood being smaller than Wiley's, she had difficulty maintaining a rhythm without it falling out. As Bett had said, he was fast. When he was done, she wanted more, but didn't know how to ask him to continue. He rolled over and went to sleep. Sadie lay awake for some time, worried about Suesanna's reaction.

~ ~ ~

Sadie's relationship with Suesanna did not seem to change. Showing no increased hostility, the woman was cold, sensible, and no-nonsense in her communication. Still, Sadie maintained her wariness.

She took a new pride from her status with Micajah. When he wanted sex, she willingly gave herself to him, and was surprised to find much pleasure in the act.

~ ~ ~

In September, the weather delivered more frequent rains. Nothing more was discussed about finding a new place to live, however. Sadie trusted the men to deal with the matter in due time.

During the Harpe party's visit to town at the beginning of September, their reception was colder, and only became worse with each subsequent visit. On a Sunday at the end of the month, folks on the streets and in places of business gave the Harpes and their women a wide berth. Sadie noticed that even those in their Sunday best would endure walking through the muddy wagon wheel ruts in the middle of Gay Street rather than continue on a course that would bring them into contact with the Harpes. She saw small groups watching the brothers and whispering to one another. While no one seemed willing to show the Harpes any disrespect, they gazed at Sadie, Bett, and Suesanna with open hostility.

Sadie wondered if they somehow knew of the arrangement the brothers had of sharing their women. She wouldn't be surprised.

Micajah and Wiley either turned a blind eye to the affronts or they truly didn't notice, but if Sadie's mistreatment in town was the only thing to dislike in her new life, she could live with it. She certainly didn't feel any more isolated than she had in Tippens, where folks did their best to turn away from the sight of her bruises.

The people of Knoxville can talk all they want, Sadie thought. *It won't do them any good to treat us poorly. They might instead come to harm if they displease the Harpes, for we are a strong family.*

Sadie had a sense of power over life for the first time, borrowed from a fearless and bold man perhaps, but one that she would readily claim as her own.

~ ~ ~

In early October, the last time Sadie went to town with the Harpes, a burly fellow, not quite as large as Micajah, confronted the brothers at the corner of Gay and Main Streets. He strode up and planted himself on the puncheon walk directly in the brothers' path. They stopped ten feet away and glared at the man. The fellow had dark hair and eyes like those of Sadie's father. She hated him instantly.

Perhaps he was the man she'd seen at a distance and mistaken for her father on her first visit to town two months ago.

"I hear tell you two act alone," he yelled, "that you're rogues and thieves."

His shouting reminded Sadie of her father bellowing his sermons on a Sunday. Apparently, he wanted everyone nearby to hear what he said.

"If I were you, Grimes," Wiley said calmly and quietly, "I'd put away my tongue, turn around, and walk off."

Suesanna remained still. Bett hid behind her.

"I ain't afraid, and I ain't payin'." Grimes's face turned red as he yelled at the top of his lungs. His fists balled. He appeared willing to take on the Harpes then and there.

Sadie got a thrill from her head to her toes. She found her excitement somewhat frightening and shameful, for the man didn't truly deserve to suffer. Still, he reminded her so much of her father.

"Other folks see me stand up to you," Grimes cried, "maybe they'll stand with me."

Micajah looked under his brow at the man, his lip twitching like that of a growling wolf. He said nothing, though, and Grimes didn't look intimidated.

"You have the terms of our contract," Wiley said reasonably, without the slightest sign that he felt insulted. Sadie was impressed with his ability to control himself. "It's up to you whether you choose to accept our offer."

People had gathered to watch the altercation from a distance. Micajah glanced around at them, as did Wiley. Suesanna and Bett kept their eyes on Grimes. Although Sadie used to think of her friend as brave, Bett was clearly afraid. Perhaps Micajah was right about her when he suggested she would die inside like Suesanna.

"Everyone in town knows you two are no good," Grimes shouted, gesturing toward the onlookers, "but they're afraid of you. We all know the meat you sell is from stolen livestock and that you're horse thieves. Word is, you ran with the Indians during the war, took a bounty from the Crown for scalps, burned people out of their homes."

Sanctimonious dolt, Sadie thought. *Folks barter for all sorts of things. Grimes doesn't know where the Harpes get their animals.* He would judge the brothers harshly, as Sadie's father would have done. *No doubt he too breaks a few laws to provide for himself and his family.*

The onlookers were growing in number and discussing what Grimes and the Harpes said.

"There are always rumors," Wiley said. "The truth has a way of getting lost crossing the mountains."

Micajah struggled to restrain himself, his eyes squinted to hard slits. Wiley put a calming hand on his brother's shoulder.

Grimes gestured widely. "We all know there haven't been any Indian troubles of late, but barns have burned."

"Horses have been stolen," Wiley said. "Mose Doss went missing. Express Rider was robbed. Just because you don't see them commit the deeds doesn't mean the Indians aren't up to mischief."

"Doss was a drunk, no doubt fell in the river and there he remains. Express Rider, that was in April, well south of here, long before you fellers arrived. I'm not gonna stand here and argue with you. You come near my property, or that of my family and friends, I'll kill you both."

Micajah lunged, and then pulled himself up short. Even so, Grimes stumbled back, his eyes wide, one hand out for balance, the other moving toward the knife at his belt.

Micajah reached for his knife, but didn't pull the blade from his belt. Wiley quickly stepped between the two big men, suddenly looking rather small, though Sadie knew he could defend himself.

"We don't want any trouble, Grimes," Wiley said. "Our offer is a friendly one, truly a benefit to the community we've joined." He looked around, raised his hands to show Grimes and the onlookers that he held no weapon. Micajah released the haft of his knife and raised his hands as well.

Sadie was disappointed when Grimes stepped back and took his hand away from his knife. Again, she found her reaction shameful.

"You've heard what I have to say about your offer," he said, "and you'd better heed my warning."

Wiley nodded. Micajah merely stared hard at the man. Finally, Little Harpe took his brother by the arm and led him away. Sadie and the sisters followed closely. As he walked, Micajah glanced back numerous times to keep a wary eye on Grimes.

Once the man was out of sight. Little Harpe looked Big Harpe in the eye. Something, an understanding of what must happen next perhaps, passed between them and they both nodded.

Sadie would get her wish. Big and Little Harpe would pay Grimes a visit to redress their grievance. Too bad she wouldn't be present to see the man, who looked and acted like her father, put in his place.

15
Challenge

A week later, well into October, a quiet evening was interrupted.

Suesanna had made popcorn in the dutch oven. Sadie, Wiley, and the sisters sat at the table in the kitchen cabin amidst the fatty, toasty aroma of the cooking, gambling for kernels of the treat while playing loo. The door and the single window shutter stood open to help dissipate the heat.

Micajah didn't like card games and had stepped out. From time to time, he did that alone, and Sadie didn't know what he did out there. He was never gone long enough to go to town or meet up with anyone, and he didn't bring back any game. She imagined him wandering around in the forest, chasing deer, arguing with the mocking birds, asking the cardinals for forgiveness.

A voice Sadie recognized as belonging to Grimes emerged from the dusk outside.

"Harpes," he said, "step outside. We have business."

Suesanna and Wiley each doused a candle flame, and the interior of the cabin was plunged into shadow. "Get away from the door," Little Harpe whispered. "Don't stand up."

Sadie could see Wiley dimly as her eyes adjusted to the darkness.

Grimes has saved the brothers some trouble, she thought, *coming all this way for his punishment!*

Suesanna grabbed up the rifle Micajah had left behind and began loading it.

Wiley peered out the door, trying to find an angle from which he might see the man.

"I brought my cousins, Tom and Odell Metcaf," Grimes said with little emotion. "We shared the barn you burned. Their sister is married to Hughes. You don't want him against you."

So they did burn his barn.

"Does he mean the man who owns Hughes' Tavern?" Suesanna asked.

Wiley nodded, still angling for a view. "He's strong among the men of the river trade. River Rowdies, he calls his men. Truly they're pirates set up through his groggery to control the market."

Sadie had never considered the idea that there were more powerful outlaws than the Harpes in Knoxville. With dread, she imagined the River Rowdies running the Harpe family out of the area. They'd have to hit the trail, wandering hungry and exposed to the dangers of the wilderness again, with only the hope of finding opportunity somewhere, perhaps further west in ever more dangerous territory.

"I see him," Wiley said quietly. "He and his men have rifles."

No, Sadie thought, *we can't stand against three with Micajah gone!*

"You'll have to pay for the barn one way or another," Grimes said.

"Tell him we're not here," Wiley whispered to Suesanna.

She nodded. "The brothers are off hunting, Mr. Grimes. Don't expect them back for some time."

"Then you won't mind if we come in and wait for them?" The sound of footsteps approaching the cabin came from without.

Wiley picked two pistols up off the cabinet by the door, and stood in the doorway. "Stop where you are," he said.

"What kind of coward needs a woman to speak for him," Grimes said. He and the Metcafs stood perhaps fifty feet away from the cabin door.

Despite the insult, Wiley appeared unperturbed.

Night was falling fast, and the three men spread out away from one another, becoming worse targets in the grayness with each passing moment.

"Your troubles with the Indians belong to you, Grimes," Wiley said. "You could have sold them to us, but now it's done."

"Where's the big one?" Grimes said. "Why don't you send him out?"

"He's out there in the night," Wiley said, "keeping watch."

Tom and Odell looked around, their silhouettes shifting uneasily from foot to foot as they turned. One of them said something to Grimes that Sadie couldn't hear clearly.

"Calm yourselves," Grimes said. He remained motionless, a great block of darkness within the waning light.

"You out there, Micajah?" Wiley called.

"Right behind them," came Micajah's voice from out of the shadows.

The Metcafs crouched. One spun around, as if trying to locate the source of the voice. The other took off running.

"Stay where you are, Odell," Grimes said to the one remaining.

"This is your fight," Odell said. "I'm going back to Hughes." He took off after his brother.

"Nigh on stupid to come alone to such a fight," Wiley said.

Grimes raised his rifle, and fired, but Wiley had dodged back inside out of the way, and the shot popped loudly into the log beside Sadie's head. She gasped and dodged away too late to avoid the splinters thrown into her face. Her blood pulsed faster in her veins.

Another gunshot sounded as Grimes charged toward the doorway with his knife drawn. His blocky silhouette bucked as he ran and he uttered a sudden deep moan, as if the breath was knocked from him. He stumbled and veered off out of view. Wiley stepped outside to fire a pistol. Micajah's voice came out of the darkness again.

"Let him go," he said. "No sense wasting shot on him. He won't get far."

Wiley and Sadie followed Grimes. She could see he'd been shot in the back. He seemed to wander aimlessly in the washed-out field.

Sadie had never experienced anything so exciting in her life. She couldn't understand the Indian attack at the time the violence occurred. The fight with these men she understood. Grimes had come to harm her family, and Micajah defended them. Grimes would fall any minute. Then, sadly, the drama would end.

He suddenly changed course and stumbled past the animal pens, headed toward the river. The sheep bleated their hunger as he blundered by.

"Don't let him get to the water," Micajah shouted from across the field.

Wiley raised a pistol, aimed and fired, but his shot went wide. Grimes was fifty yards away, moving fast. Wiley lifted his other pistol, fired, and missed again. He dropped the weapons and chased the wounded man, Sadie following him through the growing darkness. Before Wiley could catch the long-legged fellow, Grimes reached the split in the canebrake and passed through. A splash followed, and Sadie knew he'd crossed the flat shelf of rock and leapt into the river.

With his wound, he'll drown and sink to the bottom, she decided. Since Mose would have someone to dance with, perhaps his invitations to Sadie would cease.

She took a couple of deep, satisfied breaths as she watched Micajah run across the washed-out field toward the split in the canebrake. Wiley went through the split onto the rock shelf and returned moments later cursing.

"Prick jumped in," he said to Big Harpe.

Micajah slugged Wiley in the face and down he went. Big Harpe stood over Little Harpe and kicked him in the ribs. Wiley cried out and tried to roll away from his brother. Suesanna started across the field from the cabin in response.

Sadie stood not knowing what to do.

Wiley scrambled to his knees, and Micajah punched him in the face again. Little Harpe didn't go down. He turned and ran, and Micajah went after him. Wiley hauled himself up several branches high in a willow near the water's edge, beside the rock shelf. Micajah stopped at the base of the tree and cursed Little Harpe while catching his breath.

Big Harpe had gone insane, Sadie thought, but still Suesanna headed toward him. Sadie moved cautiously to join her. She didn't get as close as the older woman did, however.

"You don't want to hurt Wiley," Suesanna said.

"Aye, woman, I do," Micajah said. "He let another one get away."

Sadie could only assume that the other was the boy Micajah had spoken of weeks ago, the one that Wiley failed to kill.

"You said he wouldn't get far!" Wiley cried, his voice wet and choked. Despite the darkness Sadie saw blood, black in the dim light, dripping from his nose and mouth. She smelled its metallic odor on the slight breeze.

"Aye," Micajah said, regret in his tone, "I did, but he was a big man."

"He'll drown if he isn't dead already," Wiley tried.

"He had fat on him. He'll float," Micajah countered.

"So he'll wash up somewhere south of here and folks will blame the Indians," Wiley said, a note of hope in his voice. "That will only do us good."

"His cousins will tell a different tale," Micajah said. He sat in the dirt and hung his head. "If I hadn't've shot him in the back, we could say we were defending ourselves."

"Tom and Odell—you saw them—they're so scared, they won't say anything." Keeping an eye on Big Harpe, Wiley started out of the tree. When he dropped to the ground, Sadie heard a splash. She looked to see water standing at the base of the tree.

With the recent rains, the river was nearly even with the top of the rock shelf, reminding Sadie of the potential problem of flooding. The present was not the time to point that out to the brothers.

Sadie had never seen Micajah in despair. The sight of him, sitting in the field in the descending darkness with his head down, took her courage away, and she saw within her mind another militia coming for them.

But then Wiley stood beside her. His nose was broken and he was a bloody mess. His eyes were clear and unafraid, though, and Sadie found herself moving to embrace him. He took her in his arms.

"We'll cover up the blood and keep watch for a while," Little Harpe said. "When Grimes doesn't show up, there won't be anything to prove, no matter what the Metcafs say."

"I hope you're right," Micajah said. "I'm tired of roaming, and we had a good life started here."

Sadie heard Micajah saying something beneath his words, that he was getting too old to stay on the trail and would like to settle down and make a home.

"Come with me," Suesanna said, reaching for him. Micajah took her hand and slowly stood.

Resentfully watching the older sister lead him back toward the cabins, Sadie tried and failed to imagine herself comforting the big man. She knew she wouldn't know what to do with him in such a melancholy state, and so she let go of her jealousy.

"You know I'm right, big brother," Wiley said.

With the look in Wiley's eyes, Sadie couldn't help but believe him. Luck would favor her and her new family—she *knew* it.

Those bold enough to take what they want, she thought, *most often have their way. Micajah can have what he wants. We can all have what we want.*

They walked back to the big cabin to find Bett in bed, the covers pulled up over her head.

Sadie looked at her doubtfully. She sat on the bed next to her friend. *Bett is now the sort of coward I was.*

Sadie felt possessed of a power over life. Having lived in terror of her father, she found the new feeling deliciously intoxicating.

Bett lifted the quilt draped over her head so that only Sadie could see her. "We must get away from the Harpes," she whispered, the sober look in her eyes startling.

Sadie knew instantly that the power she felt was mere drunkenness, that what she borrowed from the Harpes was a blustering swagger meant only to intimidate others. At present, she was the one who was piss proud. What did that matter if the posturing worked, though, as it had for her father? Wasn't she entitled to a little drunkenness after all she'd been through?

Without responding to Bett, Sadie turned away and sought the eyes of the men.

16
Starting Over

The Harpes were missing, and Sadie was uneasy not knowing what had happened to them. They had left on a Monday morning on horseback, headed for town to sell butchered mutton. Tuesday morning, Bett asked her sister if the absence of the brothers was unusual. Suesanna shrugged.

When the older sister went out to do her morning toilet, Bett set down the pot she'd been scrubbing and turned to Sadie who was cleaning plates and cups. "We should take this chance to leave. We could be so far away by the time they find out we're gone, they won't bother looking for us."

"Not much will keep the Harpes from coming after us," Sadie said. She didn't want to leave, but somehow didn't want to admit that to her friend.

"Distance," Bett said. "If we put enough distance between them and us. If we become part of another community. We could go to Nashville."

"You know they have skills for tracking man and game alike. They won't give up their possessions easily. We would not survive such a trek alone."

"You *like* how we live here, don't you?" Bett said. "I've seen the change in you."

"Of course not," Sadie said, grimacing for lack of a more convincing facial expression. *Why does the question cause me shame? No, I won't think about it.* She *was the one defending the crimes of the Harpes not long ago.*

"No, truly, I'm frightened of the savage fighting," Sadie said more persuasively, "but cruelty has always been part of my life and yours. What's different now is that I'm not the one being harmed. I like that much better."

Bett had nothing to say to that and didn't speak to Sadie again until Wednesday, when Suesanna had set them to work rendering fat and leaching lye from ashes to make soap. They were halfway through with the pro-

96

cess before Suesanna left them to their work unsupervised. With the older sister gone, Bett spoke again to Sadie about leaving.

"One day soon," Bett said, "one of the men will turn on you. He will beat you much as your father might have done. We should leave before that happens."

"Why does it have to be *we?*" Sadie asked, careful not to allow her exasperation to emerge with her voice. "You could leave without me."

"Yes, you'd like that, *wouldn't* you, having Micajah all to yourself?" Without knowing the truth behind her words, Bett sounded petty and small. "Remember, Suesanna will still be here. You could never stand against *her.*"

"I won't have to," Sadie said flatly.

"You think the brothers will protect you from my sister?" Bett sounded incredulous.

"I think she's afraid of what they'd do to her if she tried to harm me."

"Oh, she *means* you harm and *will* find a way." Bett gave Sadie a penetrating look. "That's yet another cause for you to leave."

"So now it's just *me* leaving?" Sadie stopped stirring the simmering white soap mixture and looked her friend in the eye.

Bett lowered her gaze with a look of shame. She was silent as she helped Sadie pour the soap into a wooden box to cool and harden. "I brought you into this," Bett said when they had finished. "I'll never forgive myself if I don't get you out safely."

Sadie gave Bett an even look. "I have never been so safe. You should go if you need to."

Bett's features were grave. "I—I can't, not without you."

"You're a good friend, even when you're trying to anger me into taking action, but you needn't worry."

"Oh, yes, I should." Bett gave her a long, sober look.

Despite the unhappiness in Bett's eyes, Sadie's heart warmed to find she had not lost her friend.

~ ~ ~

Wednesday evening, a deep baritone voice hailed the cabin, "We're looking for the Harpe brothers."

Suesanna opened the window shutter a crack and looked out, then opened it further. Sadie saw ten or more men standing about a hundred yards from the big cabin in the gathering dusk. She barely made out Tom and Odell Metcaf, Grimes's cousins, among the group. Suesanna walked out to talk with the men. She spoke with them for a moment, and returned to the cabin.

The group's spokesman said, "Search the other cabin and surroundings." Most of the other men dispersed in all directions, while he and another man entered the large cabin with pistols drawn. The spokesman was a tall, blonde-haired man with a square face and a lazy left eye. The other man was short, stocky and completely bald.

"This is the sheriff of Knoxville," Suesanna said, indicating the tall blonde man.

He showed no interest in introductions. They checked under the beds, but that was the extent of their search within the cabin, for anyone could see the brothers weren't present. Still, they lingered, scrutinizing the women. The short, bald one wasn't much of a threat. The sheriff was clearly a man of grit. Sadie felt a chill as his lazy eye lingered on her after his other eye had moved on to inspecting Bett.

"You see the Harpe brothers," he said slowly and quietly, "and you don't let me know about it, you'll be charged as accomplices to their crimes."

"What crimes are those?" Suesanna asked evenly. She was clearly unafraid, while Bett kept her head bowed and her eyes averted from the men.

The sheriff didn't answer. He left the cabin, gathered his men, and headed back toward town.

Once they had gone, a silence filled the cabin. Sadie remained quiet for fear that one of the men had remained and still listened. Finally Suesanna broke the spell, speaking to her sister.

"Don't fret," she said, and Bett merely shook her head.

"Do you think Grimes was found?" Sadie asked.

Suesanna shushed her, and the women passed what remained of the evening in relative silence.

~ ~ ~

Sadie slept fitfully Wednesday night. Worry that her new life unraveled kept her awake. When she dozed off toward dawn, she dreamed the Harpes were hanged in the Knoxville town square. Side by side, they swung and twisted in unison at the ends of their ropes, dancing a faster, more frenzied version of the wicked jig Mose performed in the river. She awoke in a sweat and cried out.

Someone was knocking on the door.

"Open up, Suesanna," came Wiley's voice.

Sadie's heart skipped several beats as she wondered if she were still dreaming.

Suesanna opened the door.

When Sadie saw Wiley unharmed and seemingly untroubled, she experienced a deep relief. She realized she was holding her breath, let it go, and inhaled deeply. The muscles in her neck and back were sore from tossing and turning, but now she began to relax.

Out of breath and with dried blood on his hands and shirt, he stood in the doorway and glanced back toward the retreating night. "They'll be coming for us," he said, "if they haven't been here already."

"They have," Suesanna said. "The Knoxville sheriff and some men, yesterday at sunset. Where's Micajah?"

"Coming up behind me."

Excited, Sadie got up and moved toward the door to see the big man's return. She was concerned about the danger the brothers brought with them, but had confidence they were up to defending against whatever came. Bett got out of bed. Her mouth was set in a grim line.

"What happened?" Suesanna asked.

Micajah appeared in the doorway. "Seems Tom and Odell Metcaf fished their cousin out of the river," he said, panting for breath. He too had blood on his hands and clothing.

Wiley looked somewhat sheepishly at his brother. As he stepped aside to allow Big Harpe to enter, Sadie saw that Little Harpe sported a fresh purple bruise on his stubbly left cheek.

"Clappin' crap-devil lived long enough to condemn us," Micajah said. "Weren't for Baudin tipping us off in town, the law would've had us straight away. We got out of Knoxville. They had a posse formed quick, though, and give us chase up toward the Cumberlands."

"Caught us when we stopped to rest the horses," Wiley said, his expression grim. Then his lips and eyes took on a crooked, self-satisfied smile. "As they were hauling us back to Knoxville, we leapt from our mounts into the thicket, and they couldn't keep up."

Suesanna looked at Micajah and grinned. Sadie had never seen such an expression on the woman's face. Suesanna's face was transformed, and Sadie knew that the older woman truly had an affection and admiration for the big man. Again, Sadie knew the resentment of jealousy.

Wiley had seen the smile too. "*I'm* the one who leapt first and led the way," he said, angling to catch Suesanna's eye. She apparently liked the play for her attention and gave the smaller man a smile as well.

"I knew the Metcafs would meet as they do every night at Hughes' Tavern," Wiley continued. "I ran the whole way back along the trail, big brother hardly keeping up. We got to the tavern late because we took a longer route to avoid being seen, but Tom and Odell were still there, after business hours, playing cards with Hughes himself. They couldn't believe we'd come back for them when their posse-friends had all gone home to their soft beds." The cackling with his words was frenzied and frightening.

Sadie saw a petulant child in Wiley for the first time. She realized that, although rash, Micajah was all that kept Little Harpe reined in. No wonder their lives had become such a misadventure.

"We'd've been here sooner if Wiley hadn't been on his fool's errand," Micajah said. "I should've left him to it and come home."

"If you had," Wiley scoffed, "the sheriff might've got hold of you again. Suesanna says they were here last evening."

The older woman nodded her head for Micajah. "Tom and Odell and some others with him. The Metcafs must have gone on to Hughes' from here."

"Still," Big Harpe said, "leaving no witnesses out on the trail in the middle of nowhere is one thing…" He started moving about the cabin, organizing equipment and throwing articles of clothing into a pack. "…but tearing up Hughes' to get at those men?" He paused and glared at his brother. "When word gets out what we did tonight, it'll only harden folks against us."

They killed the Metcafs, Sadie told herself. *They deserved it, just as Grimes did!*

Little Harpe turned on Big Harpe. "You tell me right now that revenge against Tom and Odell didn't feel good." He turned back to Suesanna, smiling crookedly again. "Seems my brother has become more particular than he used to be."

Micajah grabbed Wiley by the collar and jerked him in close. "You want another one of those?" he asked, pointing at Little Harpe's bruised cheek and swollen nose.

Wiley didn't answer, became stony-faced.

Micajah threw him away. The small man bounced off the log wall, and kept his feet. Wiley stood with his gaze downcast, his features trembling with frustration. To Sadie he looked like a boy made to stand in the corner for punishment.

"Better to be particular than to have the whole country against us," Big Harpe grumbled, as he continued to gather belongings. "But you've done it now! We're at war again."

"You helped me last night!" Wiley shouted.

"Only to get you out of Hughes' alive," Micajah bellowed back twice as loud. "I could not dissuade you from going after them!"

Silence filled the cabin for a moment, and all within remained still. Sadie realized she held her breath again, and let it go.

Wiley grabbed up his firearms and accoutrements, and stormed out of the cabin. "Where are you going?" Suesanna called to him.

"Rains are coming," he said. "We have to be gone from here anyway."

"Let him go," Micajah said. "I know which way he's going."

"Have we a new home?" Sadie asked hopefully.

For once, Suesanna did not try to silence her. Clearly the woman was interested in the answer to the question as she looked at Big Harpe expectantly.

Micajah looked around at the women. Bett would not meet his gaze. "No," he said sadly.

Suesanna's shoulders sagged and she looked away.

"Pack light," Micajah said to all of them, "but you'd better take what you want since we won't come back. We're hitting the trail again."

Sadie's world instantly flew apart. All that had transpired in the last couple of months—the struggle to survive, the deaths—was for nothing. They would leave the comforts of a home behind to start over. Sadie had to wonder how anything might turn out differently a second time, and if she could survive the ordeal again.

Tears sprang from her eyes as she sat on the floor, leaning against the wall. Exhaustion combined with lack of sleep put Sadie in a fog. Suesanna demanded that she get up and help them pack and leave. Sadie wouldn't respond, and the older woman made as if to strike her.

Micajah stepped between them. "Leave her be," he commanded.

A flurry of activity went on around Sadie as she remained on the floor. Finally, Micajah lifted and carried her outside to the picket line. As he placed her on the only animal remaining to the Harpes, a sturdy old gray horse, the big man whispered, "There will be more struggle for a time, but I'll find us a new home where we will not have to fight so hard." In her delirious state, Sadie wasn't certain if she had dreamed his words. The idea of having a home was just what she wanted to hear from him.

Her legs were indelicately spread to either side of the horse and she lay forward, hugging the animal's neck. Beneath and behind her, across the back and rump of the beast, were loaded various packs of their possessions. A blanket was draped over her and tucked in around the packs to give her stability. The horse began to move, and Sadie heard dimly the footsteps of the others.

After a time, she lost awareness of her surroundings, and her head filled with odd dreams; her father giving a sermon about the evils of honey to a church attended only by wild animals, Bett pleasuring herself with her stepfather's cane, and Wiley blubbering like a baby as he apologized to Micajah for killing Tom and Odell.

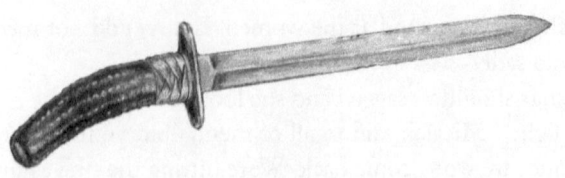

17
No Excuse

Sadie awoke still draped over the horse's back. Looking dejected, Wiley walked along beside her. The party must have caught up with him at some point while she slept.

Sadie sat up and looked around. Micajah led the way. The sisters followed behind the gray horse. Although Suesanna was so large in the belly she looked ready to burst forth with child any moment, she easily kept up. She looked at Sadie with glaring resentment.

The dense forest through which they passed presented fall color: yellows, oranges, and a bit of red foliage mixed with the green. Birds sang on all sides. A flying squirrel glided from one tree to another, while the earthbound variety, clinging to branch and trunk, chattered their disapproval.

Sadie didn't know where they were, where they were going, or what was the time of day. Knowing better than to ask if the brothers had a plan, she considered Bett's advice about getting away from the Harpes for the first time.

No, she decided a moment later, *I'm surrounded by deadly wilderness again. I need my wolves for protection.* As with so many situations involving her survival, Sadie arrived at the decision by calculation. The feeling that accompanied her resolve, one of affection for Micajah, was troublesome. She would never be truly proud of her relationship with him. Indeed, Sadie experienced a deep shame at the thought that she belonged to such a coarse, brutal man, but that didn't blunt her desire to be close to him, for him to gaze upon her with longing, to feel his touch, and even to make love to him. Was *he* the shapeless man she'd dreamed of falling in love with when she was still a child, merely three months ago? Certainly not! The conflict between her shame and desire left her with a profound mistrust of herself and a feeling that the ground beneath her feet would remain unstable wherever she stood in the future.

As the trail rose and then became level again, a fellow traveler came into view ahead, a man moving slowly on a dun-colored horse that was burdened with numerous saddle bags.

A dread rose up in Sadie. She opened her mouth to cry out for the man to put heels to his mount and flee, but he turned at that moment and shouted a greeting. With the friendly gesture, the spell of her urge was broken and she thought of the consequences of alerting the fellow. The Harpes wouldn't tolerate a warning. Whatever the Harpes intended for the stranger, the man's poor nag was so burdened with packs of supplies, he didn't stand a chance of escape anyway.

He stopped his mount and waited for the Harpe party to catch up with him. In his middle years, he had long, straight brown hair, a beard, and friendly green eyes. "A pleasant autumn day to you folks."

"Hello to you," Wiley said brightly.

The stranger took in the Harpe party, looking somewhat startled when he got a good look at Micajah. "My name is Peyton."

Wiley came up on his mount's left side and Big Harpe moved around to the other side.

Sore from riding, and suspecting she'd want to be on her feet and ready for whatever happened, Sadie dismounted.

"I'm a peddler with plenty to barter or sell." Still facing Wiley, he glanced somewhat warily over his shoulder at Micajah. "Few comestibles. Plenty of small wares, however. Pots and pans, utensils and the like. I'm certain the women would find something among my stock of sewing needs."

"Yes," Wiley said, "we'd like to see what you have."

Peyton dropped the reins, dismounted, lifted a couple of saddle bags off the cantle of his saddle, and settled to the trail to untie the bags. Micajah remained on the nag's right side. As he took up the horse's reins, Peyton glanced over at him again.

"She'll stay put," he said.

As Sadie realized Big Harpe held the reins in case the animal spooked, she knew what was coming. Instead of shouting a warning, she turned away to avoid seeing what Wiley would do with the knife he'd drawn from his belt. Sadie heard the slice, a gagging, burbling gasp, and her skirt was splashed with warm wetness. Without turning back, she ran off the trail, Bett following closely and screaming. They crouched together in brambles beneath a mock orange tree, thorns plucking at them painfully. Sadie, hugging Bett around the waist from behind, saw the peddler's bright red blood gleaming on her own skirt. She listened to the activity back on the trail, Bett's fitful breathing, and the blood pounding in her own neck. Bett began to sob, but Sadie found herself strangely numb. Still she hugged Bett tighter, and made a discovery: her friend was pregnant.

"How long?" Sadie asked, touching Bett's swollen belly.

Bett made an effort to contain her sobs and control her voice. "Since early August."

"Why didn't you tell me?"

Bett didn't answer for a time. Sadie saw through the underbrush beyond her right shoulder, the head and shoulders of Micajah moving backwards as he dragged a heavy load into the forest.

"Because I didn't want anything to prevent you from leaving," Bett said.

Sadie was surprised to find Bett willing to steal away with a child belonging to the brothers, and couldn't keep her astonishment from showing. "Your child *is* a Harpe, isn't it?"

"Yes," Bett said, vexation in her voice. "though, I'm *not* my sister."

"Wouldn't they have more reason to find you, to take back their child?"

"Suesanna has given birth to five infants, and they're not with us," Bett said. "She won't say why, but I can't think how children could live with these men."

Sadie wondered if Suesanna's children were left somewhere or if they had all died. Out of five, at least one might have lived beyond its most vulnerable early years. Then came the thought that the Harpes might have killed them. As she began to picture in her mind such horrible and pitiless acts, she quickly pushed the idea away.

Bett shook her head. "I would leave with my bastard so he could live. I would choose to live, though I'd suffer the stain on my character."

"I understand," Sadie said.

Bett turned to face her and embraced Sadie.

Micajah, walking upright in the distance, headed back toward the trail. "All clear," he called out. "The danger is past."

"I don't want to go with them," Bett moaned against Sadie's neck. "The Harpes *are* the danger."

Sadie pushed her friend away enough to look her in the eye. "We must," she said. "We cannot stay out here on our own."

Bett swallowed hard, wiped her nose and mouth. She looked away, apparently lost in thought for a moment. Finally she turned back to Sadie. They stood, untangled themselves from the bramble, and walked slowly back toward the trail.

Wiley and Suesanna rifled through the peddler's saddlebags.

Micajah stood on the trail, waiting for Bett and Sadie. "The peddler had a pistol in his pack," he said. "Wiley was only defending us."

Wiley looked up from his task to scoff at Big Harpe's words. "They're smarter than that, brother."

Micajah gave Wiley a hard look, then turned away to go through the clothing that had been removed from the dead man.

"Micajah is trying to save our feelings," Sadie whispered to Bett. "There is *some* goodness in him."

Bett stared at Sadie, long and hard, her mouth open in an expression of surprise, an unformed question in her eyes.

Sadie looked away and watched as Wiley handed Micajah one of the emptied saddlebags. Big Harpe hung the bags back on the saddle of the dead man's horse and then stowed gear in them.

"I know," Sadie said, "I speak foolishness, but I can't think that all is lost."

Bett's expression turned to one of understanding and she embraced Sadie again.

No excuse existed for the killing, such as defense of life, property or honor. The peddler had died merely because the Harpes wanted his horse and some of his other possessions. Sadie knew, perhaps had always known, that the German tooth extractor and his sons had suffered a similar fate. Big and Little Harpe had no regard for human life.

Still, she believed that Micajah knew what was in his own best interests. He might be ruthless on the trail, but he knew better than to kill indiscriminately when part of a community. His displeasure with Wiley's bloodlust at Hughes' was evidence of that. Once they'd found a new place to settle, just as he'd said, they wouldn't have to fight so hard.

How to say all that to Bett eluded Sadie. She decided that her friend would follow if she led, however. Sadie released Bett and walked toward the brothers.

Suesanna stood up from rifling one of the saddlebags. She'd used her bulging abdomen as something of a shelf to help her thin arms hold more. She was burdened with numerous spools of thread, packages of pins and needles, a couple pairs of scissors, and a cleaver. An unmistakable look of shame crossed her features as she glanced at Sadie and headed back toward the gray horse to stow her booty.

When Wiley finally stepped back from ransacking the peddler's goods, the trail was littered with combs, a hairbrush, cast iron pans, balls of hemp, knitting needles, a couple drop spindles and various "notions" useless to the Harpe party.

"Let's go," Micajah said, leading the dun nag as he went. Wiley, Sue-sanna, and the gray horse followed dutifully.

Sadie started after them, but paused and looked back. Bett stood off the trail where Sadie had left her, slowly shaking her head, her brow knitted in concern and cheeks still wet with tears. No one else had noticed her hanging back. Sadie held out her hand in a beckoning gesture toward Bett and nodded encouragement. Bett swallowed hard and looked at her feet as if she had to will them to carry her forward. Finally she moved, caught up with Sadie, and the party continued up the trail.

18
The Endless Trail

The Harpe party spent the remainder of October traveling the Wilderness Road up into Kentucky. Headed nowhere in particular, at least no place of which Sadie and Bett were made aware, the party kept moving without any apparent intention of settling down. Sadie suspected they walked back the way they had come several times, and by early November that was clearly true.

She wanted to ask Micajah about how and when they would find a place to settle down, however, he'd become more irritable and less approachable with each passing day. Sadie began to think she had indeed imagined his promise to find them a new home. She knew she must find a way to talk to him.

The Harpes avoided those parties on the trail with five or more men, pausing to allow such groups to pass on up the road. Since the Harpe party had little, and food was scarce, they fell in with the smaller groups with the intention of robbing them of their supplies. Before doing so, Wiley was friendly, striking up conversations with the intended victims and thereby gathering news from along the trail.

They heard of a posse out of Knoxville after two brothers named Harpe, also known as Big Harpe and Little Harpe. The scoundrels, so folks said, were the worst sort of murderers and thieves. They were blamed for four murders in Knoxville, one of which was the body of a man found tangled in a drift line in the French Broad River. Word was the body had been hidden in the water by a method the Harpes were rumored to have employed in North Carolina and Virginia in the past, which involved gutting the victim and loading into the abdominal cavity enough stones to keep the corpse submerged. In the case of the body sunk in the French Broad, the method had failed or that victim might never have been found. The brothers assumed the other three murders were Grimes and his cousins, the Metcafs.

The posse turned back, having lost their quarry somewhere in the Cumberland Mountains, but not before putting out word among the communities growing up along the Wilderness Road that the dangerous and desperate men were abroad. Several murders along the Wilderness Road were also attributed to the Harpes. Some were victims of Big and Little Harpe. Obviously, several others were not.

Once Wiley had gleaned what news he could from the intended victims, the violence began. Big and Little Harpe left no witnesses behind. The forest to either side of their trail was littered with the rotting corpses of those they murdered, and several of the streams along the way held fish fattened on human flesh. Micajah dropped all pretense after his failure to provide an excuse for killing the peddler. He merely warned Sadie and Bett to hang back or hasten up the trail out of sight, preferably out of earshot as well, until their business was done.

Although Bett didn't say so aloud, she clearly desired nothing more than to get away from the Harpes. Sadie felt certain her friend wouldn't leave without her, however.

With each killing, Bett's eyes sought Sadie's. Over time, the younger woman learned to not look back.

One evening after they had finished eating fish taken from a young black man whom Wiley had killed on the banks of the Green River, the brothers consulted one another quietly, then Micajah turned to the women. "Other posses may come for us," he said. "If we get separated, head for Cave Inn Rock on the Ohio River. We have friends there. They'll take care of you if we aren't there yet."

Bett asked Suesanna about Cave Inn Rock, and Sadie overheard the older sister's answer.

"It's a cave on the Ohio," Suesanna said, "where river pirates live and prey upon the river traffic. They aren't our friends, but they're not enemies."

As night descended, Micajah took Sadie by the hand and led her to their bedrolls. She assumed he wanted sex. Once they were tucked into their blankets, though, nothing happened.

The others remained by the campfire.

Micajah did not try to sleep. He seemed to simply want to hold Sadie. He appeared troubled.

She decided that the present would be a good time to ask her questions. She screwed up her courage and cleared her throat. The big man looked at her.

"Where will we go?" she asked, her voice cracking in fear.

"West," he said curtly.

Sadie swallowed and tried again.

"When will we find—"

"In the spring," he said, cutting her off. "There's nothing for us in winter."

Gruffly, he disengaged from their embrace, and turned away from her.

He was right, Sadie realized. People did little in the wintertime but stay warm, make repairs, prepare for spring planting. Opportunities would be few and far between.

She gathered the blankets more tightly about her.

If we can make it through the winter, she told herself, *we'll be all right.*

19
Wilderness within the Wilderness

More frequent rains and colder weather warned of the onset of winter. Fortunately, two large sheets of oilcloth had been acquired from two of the Harpes' victims. The murdered men, named Batts and Pacca, were merchants from Maryland who had come to Kentucky with the hope of opening a small store in Harrodsburg. The travelers met on the road between Crab Orchard and Stanford. Batts and Pacca were leading a black packhorse loaded with supplies. Wiley proposed that he and his companions might travel with the Marylanders as long as they headed in the same direction, to which the merchants agreed.

Soon, they were in a torrential downpour. The Marylanders pulled two broad sheets of oilcloth from their supplies, and the parties crouched, each under its own weatherproof covering, within a thick grove of trees. Moments later, Wiley complained that the single sheet of oilcloth was too small to protect all five of them, and he asked if he might join the Marylanders.

"Yes," they said in unison, both of them eager to help their fellow travelers. The word was the last one either of them ever spoke. Big and Little Harpe tossed the dead men into a deep ravine.

Much of the Marylanders' belongings were useless to the Harpes. They took the sheets of oilcloth, a folding knife, some dried fruit, vegetables and meat, but the bulk of their supplies were left on the ground near where the men died. The packhorse, a slow-moving beast, was tethered to a tree beside the road for the next traveler to discover.

When the Harpe party camped at night, usually in lean-tos of various construction, the oilcloth was used to help keep the makeshift dwellings drier. When the seemingly ceaseless rain fell in the daytime, the party split into two parts to walk along the trail, each group wrapped in an oilcloth to help keep out the wetness. Their feet remained wet for days on end. Sadie found the damp and cold nearly unbearable.

She had sympathy for Suesanna and Bett, who carried the extra weight of pregnancy. Her friend had not yet felt much discomfort. The older sister experienced swollen legs, a sore back, and occasional dizzy spells. Sadie was comforted to think that Suesanna would likely commit no violence in her present state.

At dawn on a particularly miserable, cold morning in mid-December, the Harpe party stood under the oilcloths in the rain outside of the Farris Inn, a place where they had been twice within the last month. The establishment was one of several taverns and inns spaced twenty to thirty miles apart, that being the approximate distance folks were willing to travel within a day along the Wilderness Road. The Farris Inn stood at the edge of an area referred to as The Wilderness, to distinguish the region as an especially wild and dangerous territory within the ordinary wilderness of Kentucky. Less than fifteen miles of the Wilderness Road passed through the area, but it took travelers a full day to traverse a steep and densely wooded landscape. Criminals and Indians found the region a perfect place to ambush travelers headed northwest toward Stanford, Danville, Boonesborough, and beyond. The brothers haunted The Wilderness because folks were expected to go missing there, making the job of hiding corpses less critical, and decreasing the likelihood that the blame for the murders would fall on Big and Little Harpe.

Lone travelers frequently came to the Farris Inn to join up with other parties traveling through The Wilderness to gain safety in numbers. At present, the Harpe party waited outside the establishment with the hope that a small party might come along and ask them to become traveling companions. Two weeks earlier, such a party had joined up with the Harpes for the added protection, never realizing that they would be traveling in the company of the very danger they meant to avoid.

Although miserable in the rain, the Harpe brothers and their women could not go into the establishment without the price of a meal, and they currently had no money. As they stood and lounged outside for a couple of hours, the weather cleared a bit, while the sky remained overcast. A large group of travelers assembled outside the Farris Inn, too large and with too many men to suit the Harpes' dark purpose. Micajah and Wiley merely watched them gather and head up into The Wilderness. Some within the big party looked at the bedraggled, dirty brothers and their women suspiciously, but strangers waiting outside the inn to join other groups wasn't an unusual sight.

A slim young man with a clean-shaven face, wearing an elegant felt hat on his head, rode up on a fine horse. He was alone, and his few belongings were neatly tied to his saddle behind him. As he dismounted, he seemed to consider the Harpes, and appeared to find their filthy appearance somewhat unsettling. Still, Wiley smiled at him. Micajah looked away casually so as not to frighten the man.

Not wanting to get to know the Harpes' future victims and beyond desiring to warn the innocent, Sadie looked away as well.

Within moments she heard a new voice and turned to see the young fellow addressing Wiley.

"Greetings," he said, his accent unusual, perhaps northern, Sadie thought. "My name is Lankford."

"We are the Logans," Wiley said.

"Will you be traveling through The Wilderness, perchance?" Lankford asked.

"Yes," Wiley said, "but we're hungry and must hunt first, for we haven't eaten in some time and are without the price of a meal at the inn. It might be some time before we're ready."

Wiley, Sadie knew, was practiced at not seeming too eager.

Lankford seemed to think for a moment. He got a better look at Micajah, took a deep breath, and nearly shied away. He looked down the road toward The Wilderness. "I've heard there are dangers aplenty along that road."

"Aye," Wiley said. He raised his eyebrows and nodded while tilting his head, presenting a look of pure seriousness. Sadie found the expression subtle, yet utterly convincing. If she didn't already know The Wilderness, Wiley's simple agreement would have frightened her.

Lankford looked down the road again, paused for a moment, then turned back. "If you will travel with me," he said, "I would gladly pay to have you all fed."

"That's most generous," Wiley said.

Micajah nodded without looking at Lankford. The Harpe Party followed the young man into the inn.

～ ～ ～

After the delicious meal the young man provided on a day when they were all truly hungry, Sadie had difficulty accepting his demise at the hands of the Harpes. At least the death had been fast and therefore relatively painless—a quick slice to the neck, and the life drained from his eyes even as he fell. Since he'd been so generous, Big and Little Harpe might have let him go on his way, but when he'd paid for the large meal at the Farris Inn, he'd allowed the brothers to see the purse of silver he carried.

For the rest of the day, Sadie wore in her hair a delicate ivory comb Micajah found among Lankford's possessions. The only feminine item among the young man's effects, the pretty thing was perhaps meant as a gift for a woman he loved. That night, as Sadie removed the comb before going to sleep, she tried not to imagine the sweetheart who might grieve for the loss of Lankford. The woman was as shapeless in her mind as the man Sadie dreamed of one day loving. As she lay down in the lean-to, using Micajah's shoulder for a pillow, Sadie allowed the two shapeless ones to meet in her imagination. They instantly fell in love, and she imagined them going off together. Although a pitiful payment on the debt owed for her part in the Harpes' crime against the man, sacrificing her dream love to comfort Lankford's possible sweetheart felt right and proper. Still, she had given up her dream and now felt alone and in despair.

Such foolishness, Sadie thought, but she cried herself to sleep as the big man stroked her hair.

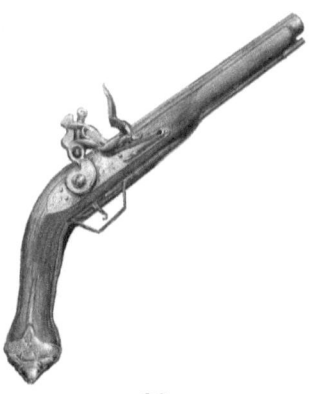

20
Christmas Day

Sadie awakened to the sound of men shouting. Opening her eyes, she saw at least ten strangers, each with a rifle trained on her or another member of the Harpe party. Dully, Big and Little Harpe and the sisters emerged with Sadie from their lean-to into a stinging drizzle.

Their horses had served in the night as a windbreak. They'd been hobbled and tied between trees on the windward side of the lean-to. The strangers had unhobbled them, and one of the men held them to one side. The shifting wind and the clicking of freezing rain had masked the sound of the ambush.

Sadie wondered if they were being robbed. *Will they kill us and take everything we have?* Somehow, that seemed a fitting end after all they'd done.

A gloss of ice coated the foliage and twigs of the surrounding trees. Plumes of vapor rose from the many mouths and noses surrounding them. All the strangers' eyes held fear and hatred, except for those of one man.

His eyes were calm, his attitude businesslike. With his long gray hair and great barrel chest, dressed as he was in buckskins with tassel fringe on the arms and waist, he looked like an aging Indian fighter or longhunter. He stepped forward and demanded, "Show your hands." Sadie, the Harpes, and the sisters brought forth their hands. "Now, raise them over your heads," he said.

The Harpes moved slowly, but they complied, as did all three women.

The surrounding strangers moved in closer with their rifles. The barrel-chested man searched Big and Little Harpe and removed their weapons—a knife from Wiley, the stone tomahawk from Micajah.

Sadie noticed another man who had a calm, businesslike attitude about him. He was maybe twenty to twenty-five years old, had sandy hair and a red beard. He hung back a bit from the rest. While the other men swung their rifles around somewhat carelessly, aiming at the Harpes and the women, he kept his steadily pointed in the general direction of the Harpes, yet aimed at the ground. When she looked at him, he held her gaze for only a moment, then looked away.

"You are the Harpes," the barrel-chested man said, "are you not?"

The brothers didn't answer, and a moment later the man said, "Tie their hands, Oaks. String them together, and let's be about our business. If we don't hurry, we'll miss *all* the festivities."

The Harpes and the sisters said nothing, and although Sadie had many questions, she was too frightened to assemble her words into anything understandable. She mumbled out a "why" and a "where." Her words hung in the air with nothing to support them but frozen vapor, and no response forthcoming.

The man referred to as Oaks, almost as large as Micajah, with bulging gray eyes and great fleshy lips, stepped forward with heavy cord and tied together the wrists of each of the Harpe party, starting with the brothers.

The frozen rain was irritating as it struck Sadie's bare arms and face. Once the women were similarly bound, Oaks passed a length of rope through the loop of cord knotted around each set of wrists so the entire Harpe party were strung together like beads on a necklace. Blankets from among the Harpes' possessions were draped over the women to provide some protection from the rain. The barrel-chested man took up one end of rope and Oaks took up the other.

A thin fellow with a tricorne hat went through their belongings under the lean-to. Sadie, the brothers, and the sisters all watched him resentfully.

"Early," the barrel-chested man said, "help Ball gather up their belongings."

The calm red-bearded fellow Sadie had noticed earlier leaned his rifle against a tree and set about helping the fellow with the tricorne hat roll the Harpes' camp into bedrolls, then roll those into the two oilcloths taken off the top of the lean-to. The longer the task took, the more grumbling emerged from the other men. Before the job was finished, the barrel-chested man spoke again. "You boys'll catch up. We're headed back."

As Ball and Early continued their work, the bulk of the captors turned without another word and walked away from the rising sun.

The slack was taken up on the rope that bound Sadie's wrists and she followed the others, walking between Bett and Suesanna. Despite the fear and anger in their abductors' eyes, they were relatively clean and well-dressed. They were not wolves like the Harpes, and that realization gave her a vague hope.

Once the group of strangers had recovered their horses in a nearby clearing and mounted up, they led the Harpe party for three hours along trails and then a broad road leading to Stanford.

Since Sadie, the Harpes, and the sisters were the only ones not on horseback, they struggled to keep up. Obviously their captors were in a hurry to return to festivities of some sort. The men spoke in hushed tones despite the barrel-chested man's frequent commands for silence.

The rain let up after a couple of hours. Sadie remained warm enough under her blanket, but her lungs became raw from breathing deeply of the frozen air in her physical exertion.

Ball and Early caught up with the procession about halfway to Stanford, riding up while leading the Harpes' stolen horses. Sadie saw all their possessions packed on the beasts.

"Mr. Balinger, sir," Early said, addressing the barrel-chested man, "the women are stumbling in their effort to keep up."

"I see that," replied the man identified as Balinger.

"Don't you think we could slow down a bit?" Early said.

A moan or two rose from the rest of the company of strangers.

"We're all in a hurry to enjoy ourselves with our families," Balinger said. "The women will survive, I'll see to that."

As they approached the town, children and adults alike emerged from their log homes to watch them go by. Several of the onlookers followed at a respectful distance as the procession made its way, crunching through the frozen mud of the road toward the center of town.

Sadie assumed that she and her party had been captured to face trial for their crimes. Exactly what charges might be brought against them, she couldn't say for certain, but her imagination had many possibilities from which to choose. As she tried out several in turn, not the least of which were murder, robbery, and horse theft, and then thought about what the onlookers must think, she hung her head in shame.

The crowd grew larger the closer they got to the center of town. Little was said loud enough for Sadie to understand until they reached a large log building within a crude town square.

"Open up, Kennedy," Balinger said.

A plump fellow in his middle years, with a beaver cap, heavy coat, and mittens emerged from the western end of the building. He held a pistol in one hand, a set of keys in the other. "I fear it's not very warm yet, Mr. Balinger."

Balinger smiled. "Got to be warmer than standing out in the cold," he said. He and Oaks, both still holding opposite ends of the rope, dismounted and tethered their horses to a rail beside the building. Balinger pulled a pistol from his belt. He pointed the weapon at the Harpes, and with Oaks leading the way, he ushered them and their women into the log structure.

The first room inside ran the length of the building, but half the width. A fire roared in the fireplace in the eastern wall. The air within had yet to take up the warmth. Beside the fireplace was a desk, two chairs, and a tall cabinet. The interior wall of the room held two heavy, iron-reinforced doors with small windows in them. Sadie knew the building was the town jail and that she and her companions were being locked up. Her shame deepened and she struggled to catch her breath.

Early entered and stood by the door, watching. Occasionally his eyes met Sadie's. Something about his gaze was pleasant and not the least bit threatening. The rest of the posse clustered outside the door to the building, their rifles at the ready. They spoke with those of the community who came up to see what was going on. Sadie saw that the Harpes were aware of the armed men outside as well.

The man with the keys, Kennedy, had followed them back inside. He trained his pistol on the Harpes.

"I take your lack of protestation to mean you know you've committed crimes enough to be here," Balinger said to Micajah.

Big Harpe turned away, sucked on his stained teeth, and spat on the floor. Next to the well-groomed Balinger, Sadie thought Micajah looked like a mangy bear. Again, she experienced chagrin at the thought of belonging to Big Harpe. Then, hating that sense of shame, she swung to a defiant pride, looked past the trail grime and the dishevelment of the big man, and saw the noble savage who had defended her life more than once.

Oaks opened one of the heavy reinforced doors, the one farthest from the fireplace.

"All right," Balinger said, "both you men, in you go." He pointed the pistol in his left hand toward the door.

Big and Little Harpe looked at each other for a moment, as if deciding whether to take an alternate course of action. Sadie feared she'd see the brothers shot then and there. Balinger trained his pistol more carefully on Micajah's heart while Kennedy approached with his pistol pointed at Wiley's. After a moment, Big and Little Harpe nodded to one another and moved toward the door. Before they passed into the room beyond, which Sadie presumed was a cell, Oaks allowed his end of the rope to slip out of the knotted loops of cord around the brothers' wrists. Kennedy shut the door and turned a key in its lock.

Balinger turned to Suesanna. "The Wilderness is no place to celebrate Christmas," he said.

She turned away, but Bett caught the man's attention with a question in her eye.

"Didn't you know?" Balinger asked.

Bett shook her head. Sadie glanced at Early, who remained by the door. He nodded at her.

"Yes, ma'ams," Balinger said, "this is Christmas Day."

Bett smiled. Seeing the expression, Sadie couldn't help grinning. Much as the Harpes and the sisters had shown no emotion throughout the trip to town, she too had allowed no expression of feeling since awakening. Her face felt strange stretched into a grin, and she wondered how much time had passed since she'd smiled.

Balinger looked at the two friends in astonishment for a moment. Then he smiled too. "I suppose the wilderness isn't entirely Godless this time of year." He chuckled and gestured toward the door closer to the fireplace. "If you will," he said.

Suesanna led the way, and Bett and Sadie followed. Inside were two crude beds, a basin, and a chamber pot. The cell had two small windows up near the ceiling and one in the door.

"We'll bring another cot in and blankets," Kennedy said. He turned away, shut the door, and locked it.

Balinger looked into the room through the small window in the door. "If you behave yourselves and don't give Mr. Kennedy and Mr. Early too hard a time, I'll have some of my wife's delicious Christmas turkey and stuffing delivered to help you celebrate the season." Then he was gone.

Sadie sat on the floor to allow the two pregnant women to use the beds. They both collapsed on the cots, moaning, then faced the wall.

Sadie was already warmer than she'd been in more than a week. She smiled at the thought of a hot meal. Terror lay in store for her in future. She decided she wouldn't think about it. For the moment she had something to look forward to, and she hardly deserved that.

21
Jailed
Stanford, Kentucky
1800

The dawn of the new century occurred without ceremony in the jail. Celebration would have seemed out of place, Sadie thought, considering what lay in store for the Harpe party in the new year.

Before a pretrial hearing on January 2, Kennedy trussed up the Harpe brothers with cord bindings that limited the movement of their legs and held their arms tied behind their backs. The women were not bound. Kennedy and Early escorted their prisoners slowly across the square to the log courthouse in the cold yet sunny early morning to face three prominent members of the community. Kennedy referred to the trio of town fathers as squires. The courthouse was jam-packed with others from the community curious about the Harpes and the proceedings.

Sadie kept her head down throughout the hearing, concentrating on a fingernail on her left hand that was spilt down to the quick and quite painful.

Asked to state their names, the sisters and the Harpes gave their true first names, but they all said their last name was Walker. Sadie told the squires she was Sadie Rice. When asked if they would plead guilty or not guilty, the Harpes and Suesanna quickly said, "Not guilty." Bett looked at her sister. Suesanna elbowed her, and Bett said, "Not guilty." Sadie followed with her own "not guilty" plea.

Balinger testified that a man named Dickens, whom he had hired to drive cattle to Crab Orchard, had come upon Lankford's dead body in The Wilderness. Dickens had hauled the deceased to the next dwelling he encountered, which turned out to be the Farris Inn, where witnesses, including the proprietor and his daughter, said they had seen the young fellow with the Harpes and their women. Farris and his daughter testified that they heard Lankford and Wiley Harpe discuss traveling together through The Wilderness and that they had all left the inn together.

Philip Ball, who Sadie recognized as the man wearing the tricorne hat on the day they were arrested, gave testimony. He said he was a close acquaintance of Lankford's, and that he found numerous of his friend's possessions among the belongings of the Harpes, including his friend's handsome horse.

The Harpes and Suesanna sat still throughout the hearing with dull, stuporous expressions on their faces, their eyes focused on nothing in particular. In her own unease, Sadie could not leave her split nail alone, at times worrying the small wound mercilessly until blood flowed. Bett sat chewing her lip and teasing out the threads from the hem of her left blouse sleeve. How, Sadie wondered, could the Harpes, even Suesanna, find no interest in the proceedings? She could well imagine they had been arrested on other occasions. Had they been through similar experiences so many times they had become immune to concern, or was their demeanor an act?

The three squires, jowly, gray-haired old men, seated together behind a great oak bench at the head of the room, consulted with one another, then the one in the middle spoke.

"The prisoners are remanded to the jail to be tried for the murder of Tom Lankford before the judge of the district court of Danville in the April term."

To cease thinking of the implications of the squire's words, Sadie bore down on her split nail. She was barely aware of anything but her aching finger as Kennedy and Early rounded up the prisoners and walked them back across the square to the jail.

~ ~ ~

Early in her incarceration, despite fears of the future, which Sadie could not completely shut out, she experienced the blessed relief of time to relax with little to do. No new terrors were possible in the jail, at least not until April.

Meals were prepared and brought to her and her cellmates. The food was good and came with a regularity much preferable to what she experienced on the trail. At first, she'd gorge herself at each meal, then regret it when she became nauseated and vomited up the food.

Early, who introduced himself as Mr. Daniel Early, brought books for the women to read: a copy of the *Bible* and one of *Travels into Several Remote Nations of the World, in Four Parts. By Lemuel Gulliver, First a Surgeon, and then a Captain of Several Ships* by Jonathan Swift. To touch the *Bible* gave Sadie the feeling her father watched her, and she avoided it. Strangely, Suesanna was most drawn to the *Bible*, and spent hours reading the book.

Sadie delighted to feel free of her cell with the adventures of Gulliver's travels. She and Bett took turns reading the stories to each other. Sadie lost track of how many times they read the book after the seventh time. Although Suesanna called the stories foolishness, she seemed to listen attentively every time the words were read.

Whenever both Kennedy and Early were out of the jailhouse at the same time, a rare and brief event when it occurred, Sadie heard a splitting, crackling noise coming from the direction of the Harpes' cell.

She struggled with her strong desire to remain close to the Harpes, particularly to Micajah, because she found the yearning simultaneously unreasonable and undeniable. Knowing they were in the next cell, she couldn't help but feel comforted. She relished the moments when she overheard them speak to their jailers or when they quarreled with one another loud enough for her to understand their angry shouts.

Sadie's period of relaxation ended on January 29, when Balinger and another man, a tall rawboned fellow with a bulbous red nose and wild white hair, arrived to question the Harpes and their women. Big and Little Harpe no doubt denied everything. When Balinger and the white-haired man, introduced as Hiram Petrie, were finished with the Harpes, they met with the women in their cell.

Sadie and the sisters gained much more information than did their interrogators. The corpses of the Marylanders, Batts and Pacca, had been found in a ravine just off the road near Crab Orchard. A folding knife, with Pacca's name carved into the handle, had been found among the Harpe brothers' possessions. Although the Marylanders were partially devoured by wolves, cut marks on their neck bones indicated that their throats were cut. When asked, Sadie and the sisters denied knowledge of the dead men.

"Your companions in the next cell say they found the knife on the road," Petrie said. "Can any of you confirm that account."

Sadie thought she should support what the brothers had said, and opened her mouth to speak, but Suesanna jabbed her with an elbow. Petrie glared at the older woman as Sadie covered her mouth and pretended to cough.

The interview continued with questions about the deaths of the four Tennesseans, Mose Doss, Grimes, and the two Metcaf brothers. The women denied knowledge of these murders as well, and their interrogators left.

~ ~ ~

Far from a blessing, having little to do became a curse as Sadie began to worry. She knew that eventually the body of the peddler, Peyton, would be found. The Harpes had taken his horse and saddle bags. She recalled that the man's initials appeared on the underside of one of the bags, carved into the leather.

She thought of the comb that had belonged to Lankford. If the law found out she'd worn the beautiful ivory item, they would surely condemn her at trial and put her to death. Sadie tried to come up with a reasonable explanation. She thought perhaps the best thing to say was that she'd found the comb on the road, but the story was too close to the one the Harpes told about the folding knife. Thinking of several other unlikely stories and rejecting them, she fell into despair. Even if she came up with something believable, she knew she couldn't tell the tale in a believable fashion. After all, her father had never believed her lies. The law in Danville would see through her, much as her father had. Sadie decided that her life would end soon and became despondent. She tried to sleep away time, because, while she slept, she was free of worry. After a week of fretting over the matter, however, she became less emotional and more reasoning in her approach to thinking about the problem and soon decided there was no way anyone could know she'd worn the comb.

She asked Bett if she thought they would all hang for the murders the Harpes committed.

"They wouldn't do that to three young mothers," Bett said.

"How did you know?" Sadie asked. She had not truly admitted the reality of her pregnancy to herself until the moment Bett acknowledged it.

"We live so closely, we're like sisters," Bett said, smiling. "You have been sick to your stomach often, and there has been no fresh blood from any of us since we've been here, well over a month."

Sadie couldn't return the smile; her thoughts were far away, considering a dark future. Her child would be a bastard unless she could persuade Wiley to marry her. Micajah was already married to Suesanna, so he wasn't available. Bett had expressed a desire to leave the Harpes behind, so Sadie presumed her friend wasn't in competition for Wiley.

If the brothers were convicted and put to death, Sadie would have to somehow persuade Wiley to marry her before his execution, which didn't seem likely while they were separated by a log wall and the law. Making matters worse, his interest in her had waned over time. If they all survived the trial without conviction, however, she would have more of a chance to prevail upon him.

Micajah's desire for Sadie had grown more powerful. If they all survived the trial without conviction, and Suesanna were to die, the big man would become available. An accident could remove Suesanna as an obstacle at any moment. Micajah had lost interest in the woman anyway, and she was a danger. Although she had shown no signs recently that she still intended Sadie harm, there was little reason to believe otherwise.

To kill Suesanna would be self-defense, Sadie told herself. *Could I do it? If I asked Micajah to do it for me, would he kill her? Either way, could I live with it?* She didn't think so.

Although her preference was for Micajah, she decided that she'd have to settle for going after Wiley.

Since she was not able to communicate with the men, all her speculation and plans were moot until the litigation of the charges against them produced an outcome. With little to do, Sadie spent many hours over the course of several days going over the possibilities, powerless to alter her situation and stewing in frustration.

～ ～ ～

Suesanna went into labor shortly after noon on February 8. A midwife was called to the jail. She prescribed tea with sugar for Suesanna to treat nausea and vomiting. The two younger women were each given a cup to enjoy as well. Sadie had rarely had sugar before and savored the first few sips. As the struggle of Suesanna's labor intensified, the pain was clear to see, and Sadie found she could taste the sweetness of her drink no longer. She'd thought she would enjoy seeing the woman in distress, but Suesanna's suffering was difficult for Sadie to bear without feeling sympathetic pains.

Thankfully, by three o'clock in the afternoon the worst was over, and the older sister had given birth to a healthy baby boy.

In the next few weeks, Sadie threw herself into helping out with the infant to give her mind something to do other than worry. Bett helped less since her own pregnancy gave her much discomfort. She didn't sleep well at night and suffered back pain.

One evening in mid-March, both Kennedy and Early left the jail to respond to a fight at a local tavern. Sadie expected to hear the same sort of noises from the cell next door that occurred when both jailers were out. The sounds had been louder each time. Those she currently heard, a crackling, rending noise that ended in a series of loud pops like rifle fire, were earsplitting. The Harpes' muffled voices mixed with other commotion for a time, and then the jail became quiet again.

Sadie stood to look out through the window in the door, but Suesanna got there first. She struggled to find an angle from which she might see in the direction of the brothers' cell.

"Micajah," she called, "Wiley, are you there?"

"What's happened?" Bett asked.

Suesanna waved her question away and continued calling out to the Harpes. Fear rose up in Sadie when still there was no response from the men. Suesanna gave up, sat on the edge of her cot, and hung her head. Sadie moved to the window and looked out at the empty jail office.

"What's happened?" Bett asked again.

"They've busted out," Suesanna said.

"No!" Sadie spun around.

"Yes," Suesanna said, "and left us behind. I know it."

"They wouldn't do that." Sadie heard the panic in her voice. "They wouldn't leave us here."

Bett glanced at her with a look of surprise.

Suesanna's expression became contemptuous. "They cannot help us. Surely you would not begrudge them their freedom."

"They'll be at the cave on the Ohio River," Sadie said. "What did they call it?"

The pain on her friend's face was easy to read—Sadie's desire to be with the Harpes wounded Bett.

"Cave Inn Rock," Suesanna said flatly.

Bett hugged her great round belly and looked away.

Sadie's frustration deepened, her stew thickening.

~ ~ ~

Several days after the discovery of the Harpes' escape, Kennedy spoke to the women through the window in the door to their cell. "Mr. Balinger rounded up a posse and even now pursues your men," he said, then paused for reaction.

Sadie and the sisters had no comment so he continued. "Mr. Early has spoken on your behalf before the squires. He asked them to take pity on you as women burdened with children abandoned by their fathers or, in the case of Miss Rice, one too young to be held responsible for the horrible deeds of the men. They do not believe you had a hand in Tom Lankford's death, and would save the expense of sending you to Danville for trial. They would consider releasing you, but want assurances you will not rejoin the Harpes and aid them in further crimes."

Sadie had difficulty trusting her ears. The man seemed to be saying she might get out of jail without a trial.

"We've been talking about that very thing," Suesanna said. "As the men have abandoned us to answer for *their* crimes, our feelings toward them have changed. We have all three agreed that we have no desire to see the scoundrels again."

Bett nodded her head vigorously. Sadie merely stood, eagerly waiting to hear more. When her friend elbowed her, Sadie shook her puzzlement loose and nodded.

Kennedy stood eyeing the three for a moment, then said. "I'll carry your words to the squires."

"Before you go, Mr. Kennedy, sir?" Suesanna said.

"Yes, Ma'am?"

"May I ask, just how did Wiley and Micajah get away?"

Bett and Sadie stood closer to the door to get a better view of the man as he answered.

"I have an agreement with the court not to discuss it," he said, then walked away.

Sadie didn't know what to think. Escape couldn't have been easy for Big and Little Harpe—the logs of the jailhouse walls were at least ten inches thick—and after all Sadie and the sisters had been through, attaining their freedom didn't seem likely, despite the ease with which Kennedy talked about the possibility. Still, she found herself with a small hope for the future, which hinged on finding and persuading one of the Harpe men to marry her. If Wiley would not have her, Sadie would have to come up with some way to get rid of Suesanna. Whatever she had to do, she would learn to live with the deed. Although she told herself she was motivated by the need to provide her child with a father, she knew she was more driven by her troubling desire to be with Micajah Harpe.

22
Freedom

The squires who presided over the hearing had set Sadie and the sisters free. The women spent a week preparing to leave. They allowed the impression that they would go back to Knoxville, never to see the Harpe brothers again. In private the two sisters had long, whispered arguments about what to do.

Suesanna had every intention of going on to Cave Inn Rock.

Bett wanted to go to Nashville, Tennessee, and make a fresh start. She begged Suesanna to go with her. The older woman refused.

Sadie stayed out of the discussion as long as she could. When she realized that Bett made plans for her, though, Sadie finally spoke up. "I must have a father for my child. Bett, if you don't want Wiley for the father of yours, I'll go with Suesanna to find him and ask him to become my husband."

Bett looked at Sadie with surprise. Suesanna scoffed, yet appeared satisfied that Sadie sought Wiley instead of Micajah.

"You will die," Bett said simply.

"Perhaps," Sadie said, "but I would not suffer the abuses of others for bearing a bastard. My child would suffer even more without a father."

Bett turned away, and again didn't speak to her for more than a day.

~ ~ ~

Mr. Kennedy asked Sadie to step out of her cell for a conversation. She was concerned that he'd overheard her planning with the sisters and knew they weren't returning to Knoxville. The sisters seemed curious about the conversation as she exited the cell.

"Please, Miss Rice," Kennedy said, gesturing toward the other cell. Curiosity about the condition of the chamber after the Harpes' escape drove her forward, and she entered. Mr. Early stood inside the windowless chamber. The beds were pushed against the walls. The northwest corner of the cell, the corner of the building itself, looked to have been repaired. One of the logs close to the floor in the northern wall had a long diagonal split that ran from the top of the timber to its bottom for about ten feet. The log had been repaired, the split pulled back together with heavy bolts. Sadie could only assume the builders of the jail had simply chosen for their construction a highly flawed log that, in drying over time, had split nearly in two. Big and Little Harpe must have somehow worked at the split until the log broke into two parts. Then they pushed one piece out of their way and crawled to freedom.

Two chairs sat facing one another on the floor. Kennedy stepped out of the cell, and Early gestured toward the chairs. "Please have a seat."

Sadie took the one facing the door, and he sat in the other. She became uneasy as he glanced at her, looked at his hands, then back at her again. He took a deep breath, lowered his gaze back to his hands, and began in a timorous voice, "I hope we have treated you well while you've been here."

Sadie had never heard a statement that seemed so out of place for the circumstances. She glanced at Kennedy who had reappeared silently in the door to the cell behind Early. He had a smirk on his face. Unable to think of how best to respond to Early's statement, she merely nodded.

"I would like you to consider staying in Stanford," Early said. "The town is growing. We have a fine Presbyterian Church. We…" he paused uncomfortably. "The fishing is good hereabouts." He produced a tight smile and shook his head.

Sadie didn't know what to think. Kennedy rolled his eyes. No doubt Early was unaware the man stood behind him.

Early wrung his hands, widened his eyes and rubbed his forehead. Then in a rush, he said, "My aunt Euvie, a widow, is willing to take you in, if you will help with the children." He sat back gulping breath and trying not to look at Sadie.

Kennedy cleared his throat as if about to speak.

Early spun around. "This is none of your business!" he said, his voice shrill.

"You had me go get her—"

"Yes, and now your job is done."

Kennedy shook his head, backed off out of view.

Sadie knew in that moment that Daniel Early had amorous feelings for her. She remained silent, thinking for some time before she spoke. Looking back over his reactions to her in the past, she could see that there had been some small evidence of his tenderness all along.

She didn't know how to respond, because she had no feelings for him.

"What is it that you see in me, Mr. Early?"

He frowned, looked at his hands again. "Miss Rice, I'm a good judge of character."

So he thinks, Sadie thought.

"You aren't a willing participant in the terrible crimes of the escaped men," he continued. "You don't protest your innocence or see fit to explain yourself, and I won't ask you to do so, but I don't believe you are with these people by choice."

Half-truth.

"On the day we met, your face, your eyes, told me the truth. While the others kept their eyes downcast, as the defiant outlaw is wont to do, you looked us—those of the posse—full in the face and your shame was plain to see. You've made no complaint while here."

"Nor have the Walker sisters," Sadie said.

"No, but they don't look me or anyone else here in the eye." He took a deep breath and sighed. "I've been in Kentucky since Mr. Boone established the settlement at Boonesborough. I was raised from an infant there. My earliest memories are of the fighting we had with the Indians and the British. There was much suffering and many widowed women, my mother among them. Being a practical woman, she remarried. He was a man—I won't say his name—who she believed would provide for us. And he did provide. He was a brutal man, though, an outlaw, as it turned out. She stuck with him to keep me fed. As I got older, I argued with her about leaving him. By then she'd decided she had nothing else in the world and must stay. I left to find my way in the world, with the hope that I might become established well enough that she'd come live with me. Shortly after I left, he killed her while in a drunken rage."

"I am *not* your mother," Sadie scoffed.

Early blushed. "Nor do I think of you that way. But I do find attractive that practical quality that aids the will to survive. I grew up around many women of such determination and grit, hardy women who did what they had to. They have a look about them. I see the same in your eyes. This wilderness takes its toll on all of us. Whatever you've done, I know it has been for the sake of your own survival. You needn't explain it to me."

"You are a handsome man," Sadie said dismissively. "I'm certain there are plenty of young women in Stanford who yearn for your attentions."

Early smiled sadly, looked at the puncheon floor. "Perhaps," he said, then looked a bit embarrassed as he added, "I find most of them have rather frivolous concerns."

Sadie realized that he had indeed judged her character fairly well. Despite having made choices in a practical manner, however, her feelings had developed quite independently. She tried to imagine settling down in Stanford with Early and having a safe life, but knew she'd miss Micajah terribly. Although the desire to be with him was shameful, she thought of herself as belonging to Big Harpe, and knew that she'd become reconciled to the situation.

"Aunt Euvie is also willing to take in the Walker sisters, at least until Miss Bett Walker has given birth and is ready for travel. She is so advanced in her pregnancy, I fear travel is not a good idea. You might stay at least that amount of time. Please extend the invitation to your companions."

Sadie knew the sisters could not hear the conversation. She didn't want Bett, in particular, to know of Early's invitation, for she might well want to stay, and Suesanna might stay with her. Sadie needed Suesanna to help her find the Harpes and to survive on the trail while looking for them. "Thank you for wanting us to stay," she said. "The Walker sisters are in a hurry to travel back to Tennessee, and I must help them. Perhaps in the future...."

The last four words, delivered without conviction, hung in the air awkwardly for a moment. Sadie barely noticed the wounded look on Early's face as she struggled with her betrayal of Bett. The treachery left a coldness in the pit of her stomach. Sadie decided she would live with it. She could only hope Early never said anything about his invitation to the sisters.

A moment later, Early nodded his head in a knowing manner. He struggled to produce a smile for her as she slowly got up.

"We are rounding up clothing and provisions for your trip, Miss Rice," he said. "They should be ready for you when you're released in three days. In the meantime, please let me know if there is some way I can help."

"Thank you, Mr. Early," Sadie said, and she returned to her cell.

"What did he ask you?" Suesanna said.

Sadie was certain the sisters didn't know she had been speaking with Mr. Early. "Mr. Kennedy is still suspicious about our intentions," she said. "I think he believed that since I am the youngest, he might trick me into admitting we will rejoin the Harpe brothers. Perhaps he and Balinger hoped I'd say where they are. Kennedy was clever, but I told him nothing new. He seemed satisfied and told me that supplies have been assembled for our trip back to Tennessee."

Suesanna and Bett readily accepted her explanation, and were more interested in hearing about what she'd seen of the Harpes' breakout. When Sadie had told them about the split log, Suesanna commented, "Micajah is very strong, and Wiley is, well…he's wily."

~ ~ ~

Sadie awoke in the night. She discovered Bett, crouched on the floor beside her. Suesanna was snoring in her bed in the far corner of the cell.

"Wiley will not make you his wife," Bett said.

"I must try."

"If you follow Suesanna with no one to look out for you, she'll kill you in your sleep. She hates you."

"She knows I go to be with Wiley, not her husband."

"She knows too that Micajah will not care that you are legally bound to his brother. He will have you whenever he chooses."

Sadie hoped that was true. In fact, she counted on it. "I must try," she said.

Bett became quiet for a long time. Sadie couldn't see her friend's face in the darkness, but could imagine Bett's frustration. She was trying to help, yet perhaps only to salve her conscience. After all, she'd said she felt responsible for Sadie becoming involved with the Harpes, and admitted that she could not live with herself if Sadie came to harm while with them.

Finally, Bett returned to her own bed, and Sadie went back to sleep.

~ ~ ~

On April 1, the day of their release from the Stanford jail, while Suesanna gathered up her few belongings, Bett spoke quietly to Sadie. "I will go with you to find Wiley and help you persuade him to marry you, if, once he has done so, you will come away with me and be done with the Harpes."

What was one more deception on top of the lies Sadie had already told? She nodded her approval of Bett's plan, although she had no intention of leaving the Harpes, particularly Micajah, unless something horrible happened to them. In the event that something horrible *did* happen to Big and Little Harpe, an eventuality not the least bit out of the way, Sadie would not want to remain alone in the wilderness. Bett was an ally, however misguided she might be.

~ ~ ~

Before they left the jailhouse for the last time, Sadie helped Suesanna situate her baby in the infant sling the woman had fashioned from an old blouse. Daniel Early met Sadie and the sisters in front of the building where he had assembled what they would need for their journey. He had organized the charitable giving of the townsfolk of Stanford, and proudly offered up clothing for the infant, clothing and shoes for the three women, packs of provisions, and an old mare. Among the supplies were two sheathed knives, a hatchet, an old pistol, a shot pouch with twenty balls, a small powder flask, and a spare flint. The firearm would be no good for hunting, but useful in fending off attack. He also returned to them the two sheets of oilcloth confiscated upon their arrest. They had been cleaned and folded neatly.

Although glad for the charity, Sadie also felt stung by the generosity of the people of Stanford; she and the sisters were not worthy of such largesse after lying about their estrangement with the Harpes.

Early accompanied them out to the edge of town on the road that led to Crab Orchard. Before parting company with them, he pulled Sadie aside. "If you change your mind and decide you'd like to return to Stanford, please write to me at the courthouse. I would be most pleased."

"Thank you," Sadie said. "I will remember your invitation and your kindness whether I come back to Stanford or not."

Early smiled as Sadie turned away with the others and began to walk.

She'd thought freedom would uplift her spirits, but fear of what lay ahead dampened her mood.

Within a short time, Bett could not go on at the pace Suesanna demanded. Watching her friend, Sadie imagined a time when her own pregnancy would be as advanced, and wondered if she'd suffer the same. All women responded differently. Sadie had suffered little more than morning sickness. She could only hope that when she was near to giving birth they would finally be in the new home Micajah had promised.

Bett was placed on the mare with the infant and the party continued. A few miles down the road, they found a well-worn trail headed south and followed it for about ten miles until they came to the Green River. A thin path ran along the river bank and they followed that one northwest. Suesanna inspected each feeder stream they crossed, looking under the overhanging brush where the flows entered the greater body of water. Sadie wondered what the woman was doing. Still, she kept her curiosity to herself. They passed a tilled field, and came upon a stream where Suesanna's odd ritual ended differently; she found a dugout canoe resting in the shallow water, hidden among tree roots and tied in place.

"How did you know it would be here?" Bett asked.

"I didn't, but a dugout is too heavy to carry far and must be kept wet or it'll crack. If I lived here," she said, gesturing toward the tilled field they'd passed, "this is where I'd hide mine. I would *not* leave paddles with it." She pointed to the two paddles resting within the charred interior of the boat. "Luck is with us."

They loaded their supplies into the dugout, then turned the mare loose. The three women got into the canoe and began the long trip to the Ohio River and Cave Inn Rock.

23
The Rivers

Without Suesanna, Sadie and Bett would never have survived the river journey. Sadie lost track of the days after the first two weeks and the sleepless nights following the difficult birth of Bett's baby girl. The night of the birth in mid-April, Sadie knew that at any moment criminals or Indians would assail them from out of the forest, for Bett's painful cries were surely heard for miles around. Even so, the night passed without a violent incident and they resumed their water voyage the next day.

They paused in their journey to fish, forage, rest, and relieve themselves. Their sleep was frequently interrupted by crying infants. Of the three women, Suesanna was the most talented at quieting the children and most frequently took on the task. Still, Sadie was kept awake: with each outburst, she feared for their lives. She assumed that dangerous men were everywhere, prowling the countryside, waiting for a sign of weakness as a signal to attack. What clearer sign of weakness, Sadie thought, than a wailing infant?

Suesanna had fashioned an infant sling for Bett, much like the one she wore. The difference was that the older sister's sling also carried the pistol. She kept the weapon close at hand since she was the only one among the three women with experience using firearms. She also kept one of the knives and Sadie kept the other.

With no rifle, and Suesanna unwilling to stop long enough for trapping, they went without meat. Despite that, with foraging efforts organized by the older sister, they ate well.

The weather warmed as they progressed. Spring had come, bringing with the season changes along the river. The dugout passed silently under brilliant green curtains of young foliage that hung from limbs dipping down over the water. Wildflowers and blossoming trees added color along the shores. The chicks of water fowl struggled to keep up with their mothers in the shallows. Swallows danced in the air above the sparkling surface of the river, feeding on early insects of the season.

At times, Sadie found her surroundings so beautiful, her passage so soothing, that she might have thought she moved through a dream, except for the need to keep a lookout for other travelers on the river. If any were spotted, the women put into shore, hid their dugout and themselves in the underbrush, and waited until the strangers had passed by. Similarly, if one or both of the infants began to cry, they hid until the fussing ended.

Sadie enjoyed sharing the duty of holding and cuddling the infants. As cute as they were, with smooth skin, soft hair, and sparkling blue eyes, she had difficulty seeing the Harpe brothers in them. Neither infant had been given a name. Sadie had known periods when disease was rampant in Tippens and new mothers delayed giving newborns names to help forestall attachment to a child that might be lost. Although she understood the point of view, she was disturbed to think the sisters expected they might easily lose their children. In honor of the sister Sadie had lost, she thought of Bett's girl as Virginia. Suesanna's boy, Sadie thought of as Quinton, after her teacher. She said nothing to the mothers about the names.

They reached the Ohio River without incident and headed downstream on the broader waterway. The second day on the Ohio, they slept at the base of a bluff a hundred yards from the water.

In the night, Sadie awoke to a commotion. She sat up to see a man in a broad brim hat looming over Suesanna. His knife was poised to thrust into her chest, but she held his wrist. In one fluid movement, she twisted out from under him and brought her own knife up to slash at his belly. Sadie recognized the man as Wiley.

The silhouette of another man, also wearing a hat, appeared behind him. "They are our *wives!*" the figure bellowed, and Sadie knew he was Micajah.

Little Harpe danced out of the way of Suesanna's knife. Both infants were crying. Bett stood with Big Harpe. Sadie assumed he'd snuck up on her friend with knife at the ready, before discovering she was Bett.

Wiley tried to back away from Suesanna. She made one last slash at him, connecting with his hip. He yelled.

"Just desserts," she cried.

Wiley moved toward her and swung again, and missed. Micajah came up behind his brother, grabbed the wrist of the hand holding the knife, and twisted. The weapon fell, Wiley sat down hard, and Micajah held him down. Little Harpe looked bewildered. The fight was gone from him. While he sat and nursed his wounded hip, Bett offered him a strip of cloth for a bandage. He ignored her.

Big and Little Harpe didn't usually wear hats. That and the cloth garments they wore had prevented Sadie from recognizing them quickly.

"He must have swallowed a wild hare," Micajah said, "because he's been mad for some days."

Sadie had never been so glad to see anyone in all her life. She wanted to hug the big man, but knew she couldn't. He was breathing hard, which caused her some concern, and he sounded weary as he continued. "For his larks at Cave Inn Rock, we were driven out. He's had a blood lust since."

Sadie spread blankets for Wiley, and he lay down. Bett offered the strip of cloth again. Sadie took it and sat to bandage Little Harpe's wounded hip.

"There's been a posse after us out of Fort Massac for almost a week now," Micajah said. "They're soldiers, some of them. They kept us running, and we haven't had much rest. For now, we've lost them. We should get to the other side of the river."

Sadie had never heard him speak so much at once. He was indeed fatigued for his mouth to run on so.

"Tomorrow," Suesanna said. "You need rest."

Done with her bandaging, Sadie watched with chagrin as Suesanna led Micajah to the bed she'd prepared for herself and lay down with him. He allowed her guidance without a single glance at Sadie. He hadn't even acknowledged her presence.

Suesanna had been an invaluable guide along the rivers, and she was a good mother to her beautiful baby boy. She also had a claim on Sadie's man that had to be broken. Suesanna would not keep Micajah. Hatred welled up in Sadie's heart.

She lay down to return to sleep, but couldn't. Instead she examined her resolve, picturing possible future events in which she might effect the older woman's death, and assessing whether she'd be capable of following through with the needed action. Yes, she decided, she could do whatever was necessary. She would bide her time and find the right moment to end Suesanna's life. Micajah would belong to Sadie again. She'd see to that.

24
Crossing the River

They sat together in their camp at dawn, eating the last of their recent catch of fish.

Sadie tried not to look at Suesanna. Micajah still appeared exhausted. As the sun burned through the early haze and warm light slanted down on them through the trees, Sadie saw that Wiley was heavily bruised about the head and face. Several of the bruises had turned green and yellow with time, while others were a fresh purple and blue. Where his hair parted haphazardly on the right side, she could see the bruising extended across much of his scalp. A feral look in his eyes, one wilder than he'd possessed in the past, prevented her from asking him about the injuries.

Big and Little Harpe were dressed in cloth garments and each wore a hat. Micajah wore a nankeen coat and breeches, grey leggins, dark blue woolen stockings, and leather shoes with hard soles. Wiley dressed similarly except that his coat was a gray surtout and his leggins brown. Sadie found the dress so out of character, she knew they must intend their new appearance to help them remain hidden from those searching for outlaws in buckskins.

When Micajah leaned forward and his coat opened, Sadie saw that he had replaced the stone tomahawk taken from him by Balinger with a new one. Although made of fresh flint, wood, and binding, it was stained from use and handling already.

Bett motioned with her head toward Wiley while looking at Sadie. Clearly, she was in a hurry for Sadie to snag the man for her husband so they could leave the Harpes. Sadie shook her head curtly, and Bett gave her an exasperated look.

The Harpe party loaded the dugout and headed across the river while the morning was still young. Suesanna and the Harpes swam alongside the canoe while Sadie and Bett rode within, each holding an infant.

Sadie mused about holding Suesanna's head under until she drowned. Of course, such action against the woman would have to wait.

The paddles lay unused among the supplies as the swimmers propelled the craft. The Harpes had also placed in the vessel their hats, shoes, coats, four rifles, and seven pistols. Sadie could only assume all were stolen from various victims of the brothers.

"Keep your eyes on the bank we've left behind," Micajah said to Sadie and Bett. "Look up and down river. You see anyone, you let me know."

All was quiet for a time, but for the splashing and trickling of water. Then Micajah spoke again, his voice muffled against the side of the canoe. "We'll set up camp on the other side and rest."

"We're low on food," Suesanna said. "Some meat would be good."

"Can't hunt until we're well away from Fort Massac," Micajah said. "Don't want to alert anyone with gunshot."

"Why not?" Wiley said in a distant, dreamy sort of way. "They still won't know where to find us. We're everywhere, after all, killing everyone."

"What does he mean?" Suesanna said.

"The countryside is up in arms against us," Micajah said. "On the way to Cave Inn Rock, we did some killing. Wiley, he did some things…." He shook his head.

"What'd you do?" Suesanna asked.

"Killed a boy for his sack of flour," Wiley said, giggling. "Sunk him in the creek."

Sadie didn't want to believe him, but Micajah offered no denial.

"Killed a calf," Wiley continued. "Made a meal of veal and biscuits."

"We were running, and hungry," Big Harpe explained. "Balinger came for us with another posse, fifty or more men. Saw them at a distance a couple times."

Sadie watched a fish jump in the distance and plop back into the water. The cool breeze and the warm sun on her skin increased her awareness that she was alive and rooted to the present. The story the Harpes told of the past didn't seem real.

"Suesanna, big brother and I can cast spells and be two places at once," Wiley said.

"What is he going on about?" the older sister asked. She didn't seem to trust Little Harpe to answer.

"What we heard after we'd been at the cave for a time," Micajah said. "Some of our earlier business was discovered. Many other killings, no matter where, we get the blame. We're everywhere. Folks have begun to think we have evil magic, that we're cannibals. Kentucky governor put out a bounty. More posses."

Because Micajah spoke so seldom, hearing his voice had always been a singular experience for Sadie. Hearing him speak at length, she found herself drawn to his voice, although she didn't like what he said.

"If he hadn't killed that boy..." he said, and paused, shaking his head. "Lad must've floated up."

"You *want* me to kill boys." Wiley said. "Wanted me to in the past. Not anymore. Rules change and big brother has to have his pound of flesh."

"You did this to him," Suesanna said.

Although her tone made the words more a statement than a question, Micajah answered her. "Aye," he said with no sign of regret. "I beat him then, and again after his prank at the cave. His blood lust got worse each time. He's been addled since the last beating."

A dreadful expression grew on Bett's face. She shook her head vigorously. Suesanna and the Harpes, busy guiding the dugout, didn't notice. Sadie believed her friend was trying to discourage her from seeking Wiley's hand in marriage.

"He couldn't sit a horse properly," Wiley said. "Thought to teach him a lesson, that's all." Again, he giggled.

Micajah didn't wait for the inevitable question from Suesanna. "He took one of the river pirates' prisoners to the top of the bluff above the cave, a hundred feet up or more. He tied the man to a horse and put a sack over the animal's head. He smacked the horse's rump, and sent man and beast over the edge to die on the rocks before the cave mouth. A tarnal sight of blood and bones. So used to all manner of wickedness, it takes a lot to shake the river pirates, but with that, the pirates had seen enough of us."

The look on Bett's face darkened further as she listened to Wiley giggle like a little boy. Her mouth gaped and her eyes squinted painfully. She took Sadie's hand. "You mustn't, please," she whispered. "Better your child were a bastard than that."

Again, Suesanna and the Harpes were unaware of Bett's response, the sounds of their swimming providing cover for her words.

Sadie didn't want to respond, but thankfully she didn't have to—the canoe bumped gently into rocks. The brothers dragged the canoe into the shallows. They had arrived at their destination, and Sadie could busy herself helping to set up their next camp.

25
Confluence

The Harpe party moved east, and set up camp against a steep, thirty-foot-tall rocky prominence in the forest near the confluence of the Cumberland and Ohio Rivers. They built their lean-to into a V-shaped space cut out of the stone formation where the roots of trees growing among the rocks provided solid anchors for the structure. Oilcloth was tied onto the roof of the lean-to to keep out the rain.

Sadie wanted to find a chance to talk to Wiley about marriage, but there wasn't time before the men prepared to leave again. The Harpes planned to travel over forty miles upstream on the Ohio River and slip into the settlement of Shawneetown at night, to steal another canoe and whatever supplies they could find.

While the brothers were gone, Suesanna taught Sadie and Bett how to locate fish hiding among the roots and overhanging brush of undercut sections of the river bank. Sadie learned to feel along under the water, explore holes, wiggling her fingers. When the fish, mostly catfish, saw the digits moving like worms, they bit down on them. With her fingers in the mouth of a fish, Sadie could grip its jaw, wrestle the creature out of its hole, and throw it onto the bank.

Suesanna organized the building of a fishing weir. Using the hatchet provided by the good people of Stanford, the women cut approximately one hundred wooden stakes to drive into the gravel riverbed in a row, each about six inches apart, forming a line that angled out from near the shore to about forty feet into the river. At the end of the line closest to shore, the row of stakes curved into a circle that wrapped back on itself. Fish following the inside edge of the line of stakes would enter the circle at the end and not find their way out. The women hung vegetation on the stakes that stuck up above the surface of the water to help keep the structure from being recognized by anyone passing by on the river.

At first, the women ate most of the fish they caught. As time passed, however, they needed a way to store excess. The fish were kept alive in a large depression formed within the bedrock at the river's edge. Suesanna removed the oilcloths from their lean-to, folded them into two makeshift buckets, and all three women took turns using them to haul water from the river to keep the depression filled. Although their little fish pond wasn't quite water tight, its walls were high enough to keep the fish from jumping out. Occasionally, one would die and they'd toss it out, but as time passed their supply of fish grew.

When not fishing, the women foraged for food in the forest. They ate well and stored what would keep for their upcoming travels. Both infants, being breastfed, were well nourished.

The men had left behind three pistols. Sadie couldn't imagine using one, even if a posse or other dangerous men attacked.

To reduce the risk of being discovered, Suesanna built smokeless fires to warm and to cook. She dug two holes a few inches apart, each a little over a foot deep. Reaching down to the bottom of one of the holes, she punched a tunnel between that one and the hole next to it. Then she loaded combustible material into one hole and left the other empty to draw air. When lit, the fire burned so hotly, little or no smoke appeared in the air above.

With all their activity along the river's edge, they spent as little time as possible in the open to minimize the chance that others might spot them.

~ ~ ~

The Harpe brothers returned a week later with another dugout canoe, unnecessary equipment for fishing, additional clothing for themselves and the women, a twenty-pound sack of salt, one of a similar weight filled with corn meal, and strips of smoked venison.

The first evening after the return of the men, Sadie overheard Suesanna asking Micajah how Wiley acted on the trip to Shawneetown.

"A bit dafty, is all," he said. "I told him he couldn't kill anyone. He sulked, but held back, and nobody died. He's hungry for it, I can tell. We got what we needed and left with no one the wiser."

"Killing?" Suesanna asked.

"Aye."

Sadie didn't tell Bett about the conversation. Wiley had become more frightening, yet he kept mostly to himself. Although he slept with Bett and Sadie, there was no sexual activity. He wasn't disagreeable, merely odd.

~ ~ ~

Suesanna set about salting and drying their store of fish. She found flat rocks exposed to the sun on a bluff half a mile from the river. Some were loose enough that the brothers were able to pry them away for the women to use in pressing the fish. Suesanna, Sadie, and Bett gutted, skinned, split, and salted the fish which were then pressed between the slabs of flat rock during the daylight hours. At night, all of it was taken to the camp.

Suesanna directed the building of a fish flake in a sunny spot on top of the stone prominence at their camp in the forest. Once most of the moisture had been squeezed from the fish by the pressing, they were hung on the flake to dry. Both the men and women took turns in pairs guarding the fish at each stage of the process, by day on the bluff, day and night in the camp. They kept smokeless fires going at the bluff and in their camp to discourage predators. A black bear made a couple visits to the camp. The creature was unfortunate to have done so each time while Micajah stood watch. The second visit, the big man tried to add bear flesh to the Harpe party's diet, but he only succeeded in wounding the beast with a shot from his rifle. The animal did not return.

~ ~ ~

The first time Sadie took a turn guarding the fish on the bluff with Suesanna, a dawn to noon shift, the older woman brought her infant with her, and they took turns attending to the infant's needs. Suesanna seemed to like standing at the edge of the precipice, holding her child and looking out at the bright ribbon of water in the distance. During the shift, Sadie got close to the edge only while she held the infant. Otherwise, she kept away from the precipice for fear the older woman might throw her off the sixty foot drop.

Many months had passed since Suesanna had threatened Sadie. Perhaps the older woman had set aside her anger, since Sadie had been such a help with the infant boy. Suesanna's attitude was difficult to assess because she so seldom spoke or made eye contact.

Sadie had not set aside her hatred, and thought about pushing the woman off the cliff, but wouldn't as long as Suesanna held the child.

The second time the two shared the duty, several days later for a noon to sunset shift, the older woman left her infant with Bett. Suesanna climbed to the top of the bluff with Sadie and they stood watch with little conversation as the afternoon progressed. The longer she watched Suesanna standing at the precipice, the more Sadie came to believe she might get away with giving her a deadly shove. If she did that, she'd willingly take on the responsibility of the infant boy.

The sun was setting, and they'd soon have to gather up the fish to take back to their camp. Sadie stood and stretched, yawning. Suesanna ignored her completely. She'd hear if Sadie approached, but that wouldn't matter if she had little time to react. If Sadie ran at the woman, she would rebound off her. Suesanna would go over the edge while Sadie would remain on the cliff.

Sadie took a step toward Suesanna, and, trying not to think, several more in rapid succession. Then she did think; she pictured the woman in a bloody heap of torn flesh and broken bones at the base of the cliff, and decided too late that she couldn't go through with it. Sadie cried out as she tried to stop her forward momentum. To her horror, Suesanna turned at the last moment, grabbed her by the hands, and swung her out over the drop. As Sadie fell, Suesanna turned her hips, threw her legs out behind her, and went down onto her chest, still holding on. The breath was knocked from the older woman. She remained on the rock, however, her grip firm. Sadie dangled as Suesanna held her hands and looked her in the eye.

"No," Sadie gasped.

"Yes," Suesanna hissed.

"I'm sorry."

"I know you are, *now*."

Sadie's palms were slipping through Suesanna's hands. "Please!"

The older woman's grimace might have come from the pain of holding on, her swollen breasts crushed against the rock, or from hatred. "I see myself in you," she said. "I too had to learn how to live, to…continue."

"Yes, I'm like you," Sadie agreed out of desperation.

"Surely you don't think that's a good thing."

Sadie didn't know how to respond.

"I wasn't going to hurt you," Suesanna said, adjusting her grip. "If it wasn't you, he'd find another. He always comes back to me, yet I had to do something."

"Help me!" Sadie felt tears sliding down her cheeks.

The older woman struggled to get to her knees, and lever herself up by her elbows.

Sadie clambered with her feet for purchase on the rocks, got a toe into a crevice.

Suesanna began to rise and pull Sadie back up. When they were both upright, but Sadie still leaned out over the edge, Suesanna stopped.

"The worst I can do to you is to let you live with what you've done. I know this because I've had to do the same."

Sadie didn't think about what the older woman said, she merely nodded.

Suesanna pulled her to safety and they fell together.

Sadie was terrified to think she'd intended to kill one who did not truly mean her harm. The woman had indeed threatened her, perhaps partly out of jealousy. Still, Sadie understood Suesanna's need to defend her place within the family. The older woman had made decisions, much like those Sadie herself had made, driven by a need to survive.

Sadie hugged her, for she realized they were indeed much alike.

After a moment's hesitation, Suesanna returned the hug and stroked Sadie's hair.

When they rejoined the others, neither Sadie nor Suesanna said anything about what had happened.

~ ~ ~

While guarding the drying fish in the camp with Wiley, Sadie sought a way to talk to him about marriage. She settled next to him as he sat feeding the smokeless fire hole. The others had left the camp, attending to other duties.

Sadie remained quiet for some time, uneasy about speaking suddenly. He seemed hardly aware of her, and she didn't want to startle him. Quietly, she said in a warm tone, "I'm going to be a mother."

"I'm sorry," he said, glancing up at her. His sad gaze lingered a moment.

Did he think so little of life? Sadie supposed that he did. Why else would he kill so frequently, so willingly? Even so, he struggled to survive. He was a loyal defender of his brother and his women.

"Could be a good thing," she said. "Might be your son or daughter."

"More's the pity."

Sadie had quickly come to an impasse in the conversation she'd hoped to have. He was in a bad mood. She'd have to try again some other time.

As she turned away, he must have seen her downcast look. "You will make a fine mother," he said, as if feeling the need to say something good.

A moment of silence passed, and Sadie thought he was done, but he continued wistfully. "I might have liked being a father. My bairn were all lost. Comes a time, big brother finds them vexing, and they have to go. There was one I would claim was my own because he so favored me. I might have taught him a few things."

Sadie didn't want to know what he meant by having "lost" all his. Indeed, she was inclined to end the conversation with him. Since he was talking and feeling sentimental, however, she thought she might as well try again.

"We could be married. Then my child would be yours, no matter the truth."

Wiley smiled. "You've been a good hen, hardly any trouble at all."

Sadie felt foolish, and became certain he was making fun of her.

"Aye, I could take you for my wife," he said with a chuckle.

Yes, he thought her funny. Sadie lowered her gaze and bowed her head, but he reached out with a finger to her chin and raised her head so she'd look at him. Would he laugh in her face?

No, he had a tender look about him. "I will marry you, lass," he said, "if you truly want me."

Momentarily speechless, Sadie looked at him. She struggled to smile through sudden shame. She didn't love him. Indeed, she had serious doubts about marrying him. Little Harpe was the brother who caused all the problems. He didn't kill when he should, and did so when he shouldn't. No doubt only Micajah's loyalty to his brother as family prevented him from killing Wiley for his blunders. That very loyalty would serve Sadie well when she was married to Wiley—the fact that she would be Little Harpe's wife would draw her that much closer to the big man. Still, the shame held her tongue. A moment longer and he'd turn away from her—she knew it. Desperation had driven her into his arms before and, as she found her voice, the same wretchedness did so again.

"Yes, I *do* want you," she said.

"Are you certain?" he asked, perhaps disappointed with her long delay in answering.

"Yes! I-I was lost in thoughts of the pride I'd have once we're wed."

"Then, when we can find a preacher, we'll get to it straight away."

Although they were engaged in guarding the fish, Sadie allowed her betrothed to carry her to their bed. When they coupled, Bett was not a part of it. The only other time Wiley had bedded her alone was on the day they met. Sadie hid her fear and did her best to please him. Luckily, no bear or other predator appeared to challenge their possession of the drying fish while they were preoccupied.

The next day, Bett was delighted with Sadie's news and clearly hoped to find a preacher for the couple right away. Since Big Harpe planned for the party to travel southeast up the Cumberland River, through Kentucky to Tennessee, and didn't want to be seen in any borough in Kentucky, Sadie feared she'd have a long wait.

Before they were all arrested and thrown into the jail at Stanford, Sadie had asked Micajah where they would go to find a place to settle down. He'd answered with a single word, West. Since Nashville was on the Cumberland River, and that was west of where they had been when Sadie asked the question, she wondered if that was where they were headed. She would have to find an appropriate time to ask him, but, once again, he had become unapproachable, his thoughts seemingly far away with concerns he did not share with anyone.

~ ~ ~

Within two weeks, the Harpe party was ready to travel again, with a supply of food that would last perhaps a month if they were frugal. In late May, they set out, moving upstream on the Cumberland River to reach Tennessee.

26
Against the Current

Their passage up the Cumberland was plodding because they kept the two canoes in the slowest moving parts of the river. All the adults rowed or poled. Each vessel carried a swaddled infant within its bow. Suesanna rode with Micajah while Bett and Sadie rode with Wiley. Supplies were stored in the stern of each canoe to add more weight there than at the bow, thus the task of keeping the vessels steered into the current was made easier. When the water was too rough, the current too strong, or the river too shallow, they attached lines to the canoes and hauled them upstream while walking. On occasion, for short distances, they were required to lift the canoes and carry them.

Sadie's back ached much of the time. Her shoulders were sore at the end of each day. She felt the movement of the child growing within her, and was constantly hungry. She was irritable and at night endured half-remembered, bad dreams. Knowing that complaints would fall on deaf ears, she kept her troubles to herself, and was thankful that her pregnancy experience thus far was less painful than what Bett had suffered.

Wiley's bruises faded away and he regained his wits with time. Smiling and hailing travelers on the river or along the bank, he tried to entice others to join with the Harpe party. However, a few choice words from Micajah, muttered just loud enough for Little Harpe to hear, and Wiley relented each time, making excuses if necessary, and bidding the folks a safe journey. He eventually gave up trying to talk to people and merely smiled and waved at them. Sadie joined him in the effort, figuring if people saw canoes full of friendly folks, they were less likely to think they were looking at men with bounties on their heads. Apparently Micajah saw no harm in that.

When they pulled in to shore to camp for the night, Sadie was so exhausted, she usually ate and then went straight to sleep. On occasion, she heard Micajah and Suesanna arguing with Wiley over whether he'd stay in the camp at night.

"I'm not letting you wander around looking for trouble," Big Harpe said more than once.

They couldn't watch him all night, however. When awakened by a bawling infant in the dark morning hours, Sadie noted Wiley's absence on four occasions. One morning, after he'd taken off in the night, he returned with blood on his clothing.

"Where did the blood on your blouse come from?" Micajah asked.

"Had a dream I was eating a joint of rare beef," Wiley said. "Been a long time since we had anything like that. I bit my tongue chewing in my sleep and woke up bleeding."

Micajah looked at Little Harpe suspiciously, but asked no more about it.

Sadie remembered that leading up to the night in question, he'd become increasingly restless and ill-tempered, and for a time afterward he was calm and good-humored. She didn't know what to make of his moods, yet suspected he'd killed one or more people in the wee hours. The frightening idea came to her that somehow killing provided him with needed tranquility.

Three weeks into their travels on the Cumberland River, they arrived just downstream of Clarksville, Tennessee. They dragged their canoes into a small feeder stream, and Micajah told them what he intended. "We'll set up camp along the river, out of the way, and steal into town to get what we can in the dead of night."

"Need to find a preacher so I can marry the young lass," Wiley said.

Sadie found herself suddenly much more interested in the conversation. Bett leaned in to better hear what was said.

Micajah looked at Sadie, and she nodded. His gaze lingered until she became uncomfortable. "Not here," he said, finally.

"Why not?" Wiley asked. "What did we stop here for?"

"Because we're almost out of food." Big Harpe sounded impatient. "You know Clarksville is part of the land grant to veterans. It's full of folks who know how to fight, so we won't want to rouse them to anger."

Wiley shrugged.

"You listen to me, little brother. It's too dangerous. We don't know what folks here know about what went on in Kentucky. We're close to the state border, so word might have reached. You'll have to wait until Nashville."

"They won't know us here," Wiley said. "Surely a stranger pokes his head in that town from time to time. Don't you want to go into town for a drink?"

"No!" Micajah said. "Do you understand?"

Wiley shrugged again, looking sullen.

Micajah got in his face, asked louder, "Do you understand?"

"Aye!" Wiley growled irritably.

Bett turned away, shook her head. Sadie wanted to get the wedding done while he was perhaps more than willing, but found herself strangely relieved that she would not yet become Wiley Harpe's wife.

Several columns of smoke rising into the sky in the distance to the southeast told Sadie they were close to the settlement. She knew Wiley had become restless again, and suspected he wanted to go to town for more than a drink. With so many lives within his easy reach, she feared the worst.

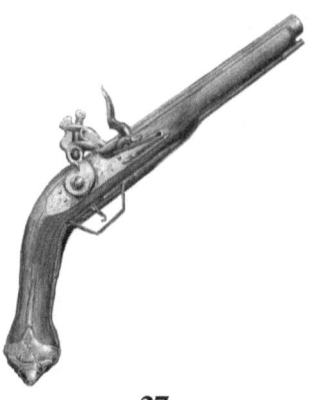

27
What's Known

Despite Sadie's trepidation, Wiley behaved himself while they were in the Clarksville area. Within a few short days they were resupplied and moving east on foot in the early morning of June 5, following a trail that led to Nashville.

Although Sadie had yet to discuss the subject with Micajah, she had a feeling they were on their way to the new city to settle down. Massaging her back as she walked, she dreamed of having a bed with a straw mattress to rest upon. If the big man could keep his little brother reined in, she decided, they might have a chance for a good life. The walk in the warm summer air was pleasant enough, despite her aching back and frequent crying fits from Suesanna's baby boy. He'd been fussy for several days now.

"Keep your bairn quiet," Micajah said.

Suesanna stepped away from him and hugged her child tighter. "He's teething."

"I don't care if crows are pecking out his eyes," Micajah said. "Keep him quiet."

Suesanna dropped back to walk at the rear of the party. The distance didn't muffle the sound much, but no more was said for a while. Still, Micajah looked irritable every time the baby started up.

"We need to find out what folks know about us," Wiley said. "How do we know if we're even in danger?"

"Well," Micajah said dismissively, "it wouldn't be smart to ask somebody if they know there's a bounty on us."

"No," Wiley said with uncharacteristic patience, "we'd pretend to be looking for news of the Harpes. If it came to it, we could say we were hunting them for the bounty."

"With three women and two bairns in tow?"

"So we leave them back a ways. All we've got to do is run on ahead a bit." He turned and addressed the women. "If you three start to catch up, just hang back some. Keep an eye out, and if you see us talking to some folks, step off the trail and hide before they see you."

Micajah seemed to consider the plan. "It'd be good to know what's known. A'right, then."

~ ~ ~

Micajah had given Suesanna two pistols. The women walked on their own, not knowing how far ahead the men were. Sadie worried that the Harpes had continued on at a fast pace and unknowingly left their women behind in the wilderness. She was encouraged, however, to see that Suesanna seemed unconcerned.

Several hours passed before they heard conversation on the trail ahead. Sadie recognized Wiley's voice. The three women stepped off the trail as they'd been instructed. Suesanna set her swaddled baby boy within an embrace of tree roots. Once their movements had ceased, Sadie could make out the words of the conversation, starting with Wiley's voice.

"...heard tell of wild men named Harpe, brothers they say, causing trouble in Kentucky?"

"Yes, sir," came the voice of a stranger, "terrible men. Murdered folks in The Wilderness and along the Green River. We just heard of a family down the Cumberland a ways killed a week ago. Folks say they were thrown in the river with stones in their bellies like some of the Harpes' victims in Kentucky and last year in the East, so we fear the murderers have come back to Tennessee. Me and my brother were talking about maybe going after them. We could make good use of that three-hundred dollar bounty."

"Now, that's drafted strange, it is," Wiley said. "You two look something like what's described of these men, the Harpes."

"No," Sadie heard Micajah say. "No, they don't!"

"Mister," came a similar but deeper stranger's voice, "we're the Brassls, Robert and Jim."

"I don't believe you!" Wiley shouted. "I'll turn you in for the reward, I will."

"Stop it!" Big Harpe shouted.

"Stand back," one of the Brassls said.

Sadie heard the sounds of a scuffle.

"Tarnation, Wiley," Micajah cried. "You're a fool!"

She and Suesanna ran from their hiding places toward the men. Rounding a tight bend in the trail, Sadie saw Micajah holding on to one of the Brassls, while Wiley tried to wrestle a rifle away from the other one.

"We're Big and Little Harpe, you bawbag twallies!" Wiley cried.

At that, Micajah threw the man he held down onto the road. He pulled his tomahawk from his belt and stove in the fellow's head. The skull cracked open like a sun-dried gourd, and the contents flew in spatters.

Seeing his brother's death, the other Brassl screamed, let go of the rifle, and ran off the trail, moving west. Wiley gave chase. He tripped and fell, picked himself up and continued. His quarry was getting away.

Suesanna ran off the trail after the man, paused, raised a pistol and fired it. The shot struck the man in the right shoulder, sending out a spray of bright red in the dappled sunlight. She raised her other pistol, but Wiley was too close to her target.

Not knowing whether to run, scream, or find some way to help, Sadie merely stood watching.

"God damn it!" Micajah bellowed.

Wiley and the Brassl fellow disappeared into the forest.

Suesanna approached Big Harpe.

"I didn't want to do that," he said, looking at the dead man, "Wiley left me no choice."

She helped him haul the dead Brassl off the trail and hide the body behind a fallen log. Returning to the bloody spot where the man's head had been split open, Micajah and Suesanna began to clean up the red mess. Sadie helped the older woman gather up the leaves, sticks, and pebbles with blood on them, while Micajah used his knife to cut away the soil stained red. They hid what they had gathered up with the body, then scattered other detritus over the spot where the man had died.

By the time they finished, Wiley was coming back through the trees. Although his head hung low, Sadie could see the fear in his eyes. Clearly, he expected punishment.

Why then had he committed such a cruel, foolish act? Had he thought his actions might stir Micajah's own blood lust enough that Big Harpe would rise to join him in an ecstasy of killing?

Yes, she supposed that he did. Sadie could see that Micajah enjoyed killing. The war years and running with savage Indians had perhaps given him a taste—no, an appetite for it. He had a practical side, though, that Little Harpe lacked. Micajah only killed with purpose; he killed to defend himself, his family, and property or for the taking of property from others while leaving no witnesses. As cruel as the latter may be, Sadie had come to respect his decision to take such action for the sake of his family's survival in the dangerous environment of the frontier wilderness.

She would punish Wiley herself if she were able, but if she expected the man to stand before a minister with her, she couldn't show any sign of her horror at his betrayal.

"You can't beat him again," Suesanna said to Big Harpe. "It'll kill him this time, if you do."

Apparently unwilling to look at Little Harpe, Micajah looked at her, his face grim and stony. He stared at her for a time, then nodded. "You're right, I'd kill him."

Wiley stopped a hundred feet away from Big Harpe.

"You didn't even get to enjoy it," Micajah said, without looking at his brother, "did you?"

Wiley didn't answer.

"They'll know we're moving east," Big Harpe said, "so we'll have to take the first trail headed north or south."

Suesanna's infant had begun to cry again. She hurried to pick him up and quiet him.

Sadie's heart sank as she wondered how Micajah's decision might affect their plans to head for Nashville.

28
New Knowledge

The Harpe party headed north, moving rapidly, easily putting ten miles between themselves and the spot where the Brassls were attacked. As the sun began to set, they ate and rested by a creek twenty yards off the trail. Wiley wanted to press on, but Micajah hadn't made a decision. The women, Bett and Suesanna, having carried infants on their backs, and Sadie, starting her seventh month of pregnancy, were exhausted.

"Load the pistol you fired, woman," Micajah said.

Suesanna turned to him. "I have done."

"You rest," he said, looking at both sisters and Sadie, "while we look for a good spot to camp."

The men headed back to the trail and moved north again. The women sat and soaked their sore feet in the cool waters of the creek. A half-hour passed before Sadie heard anything more from the direction of the trail. When finally she did hear something, she got up in anticipation of greeting the returning men.

"That's the sound of horses," Suesanna said, getting up.

Bett pulled her feet out of the water and began putting on her shoes.

Suesanna and Sadie, barefoot, moved toward the trail, keeping low among the underbrush, and peeked out from behind trees. Twenty or more armed men on horseback came toward them from the south on the trail, which ran straight in both directions for quite some distance. Sadie saw among them the Brassl who'd gotten away. His right shirt sleeve had been torn away and a bloody bandage was wrapped around his right shoulder.

The riders had drawn close to her hiding place by the time Sadie pulled her head back. She looked up the trail in the other direction, worried about the brothers running into the new posse upon their return.

Just as she turned her head, Big and Little Harpe stepped out onto the trail, caught seemingly unawares, about a hundred yards away.

The man at the head of the posse called a halt.

Micajah made as if to step away quickly, and Wiley grabbed his arm. Big Harpe glanced at his brother, who said something Sadie couldn't hear.

Although she couldn't see the men of the posse from her position behind the trees, she heard clearly those in the lead and the fretful murmurs of those behind them.

Micajah had turned back toward the posse. He and Wiley planted their feet firmly and donned their fiercest expressions.

"Be still," said the man who was obviously the leader of the posse.

She heard the shuffle and clunking of hooves on the trail, the rustling of gear, the snort and whinnying of horses further down the line, but no other voices for a moment.

Then, "If we don't make a threatening move, perhaps they'll just go on," came a timorous voice from near the front of the posse.

She recognized Brassl's voice as he spoke. "Are you *cowards?*" he asked, sounding incredulous.

"Be quiet, Brassl," the leader said. "They are deadly men, and we've lost the advantage."

Sadie knew the Harpes could not hear the conversation among the posse. They stood confidently in the middle of the trail, still glaring.

"I've heard they've killed more than anyone knows," came a young voice from further back along the line. "Some never turn up because the Harpes eat them."

"Aye," another posse member said, "and they cast spells to travel great distances in a trice. That's how they kill so many across the frontier each day."

For the first time Sadie knew something of what the world had been like for those outside the Harpe party over the last few months. People on the frontier were more than merely frightened of these men. She knew Big and Little Harpe were blamed for more than their share of murders. They had created such havoc and gotten away with the violence for so long, folks had begun to think they were more powerful than ordinary men. Obviously, rumor had invested the Harpes with supernatural powers.

"Barker," Brassl said, "bloody order your men to move on them."

"I can't," the leader said. "They're afraid, and they'll panic. The Harpes won't. We might get them in the end, but at what price?"

"You're the one who's afraid," Brassl said, then he shouted, "They killed my brother!"

"Shut up, Robert," the leader said. "They'll hear you."

Sadie was certain the Harpes *did* hear Robert Brassl. Still, the outlaws stood their ground, their terrible expressions held firm and illuminated in the last orange rays of the sun.

"I don't care what the tarnal dogs hear!"

"Cooper, Amsing, train your pistols on Brassl," the leader said. "Take his rifle. Don't let him move."

"Yes, sir," two voices said nearly in unison.

"Turn your horses, men," the leader said. "We'll fight another day."

"You are a coward," Brassl said, "no better than those who killed my brother!"

Listening to the shuffle and clomp of hooves, the creaking and clinking of the horses' tack, Sadie wanted to poke her head out and get a look at the retreating posse. She remained hidden, however. As the sounds began to diminish, Brassl addressed the Harpes, shouting, "You'll die horribly, you will! You'll die for what you've done. You'll die a death for each of them, again and again for eternity!"

Sadie had not heard such vehemence from one of the Harpes' victims, but then none had lived long enough to express anger. Brassl seemed to speak for the many who could never speak again. Startled by the ferocity of the voice, feeling the hatred expressed, Sadie was left stunned. She truly did not know what to do with her new knowledge.

Finally, she glanced back along the trail, just as the posse was disappearing around a bend. Brassl's shouts became incoherent and faded into the distance.

Suesanna tugged on Sadie's sleeve and gestured back the way they'd come. "Our men are coming," she said. "We should prepare to leave quickly. Those men—their fear will not last. Brassl will shame them into action."

Sadie saw the Harpes walking toward them, and she followed Suesanna mechanically, her thoughts far away.

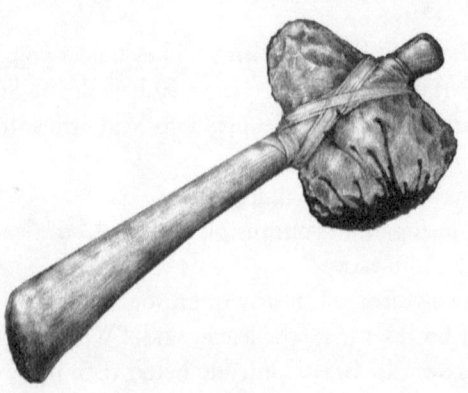

29
Carved Out of the Wilderness

The Harpe party left the larger trail where they had met the posse, and took a smaller one. They walked on into the night, then slept in a spot where creepers were swallowing the trees. The network of vines blocked the wind and formed crude hammocks that were fairly comfortable. Sadie awakened with small black and orange beetles crawling around inside her clothing. The others experienced the same, and once they were all up and around, they spent some time helping each other get rid of the insects.

They continued on the small trail for a few hours, then turned northeast onto a broader one. While crossing a wide, shallow valley that had signs of having burned in the not-too-distant past, Micajah announced, "We're back in Kentucky."

"Could be that Barker fellow can't bring his men over the line," Suesanna said. "He sounded like a constable."

Big Harpe nodded. "John Tooly lives near. We'll stop at his place. He'll give us a rest."

"They've been here before?" Sadie asked Suesanna.

"They ran in this wilderness shortly after the war," the woman said. "Few but Indians lived here then, and the Harpes could have their way."

Sadie could well imagine the campaign of blood the Harpes had waged before the white man's law had come to these parts.

~ ~ ~

The Tooly place was a cabin and maybe ten acres carved out of the wilderness. At the outer perimeter, Sadie could see the trees had been killed by girdling.

As a small child, she'd gone with her father to community gatherings to help farmers clear land. She'd never seen such hard work as she did while wandering among the working men, serving them water from bucket and ladle. The plots at the Tooly place looked to have been cleared much the same way. Once the trees were girdled and had died, they were burned away, but their stumps remained among the young crops of corn and wheat.

The Harp party hailed the homestead as soon as they emerged from the forest. Several small children ran for the cabin. A tall, muscular fellow with a red and black coat emerged from the building carrying a rifle.

"John," Micajah called, "it's the Harpes."

The man hesitated, looked around. Finally, he leaned his rifle against the log wall behind him and said, "Come ahead, then." Sadie noted that he kept a hand on a pistol tucked into his belt.

As the Harpe party approached the cabin, a rawboned woman with thinning black hair and poorly fitted gray shift stepped out of the building and stood behind the man. "Don't forget the revival meeting in Russellville," she said.

"What's the news, John?" Wiley asked. "How are you, Dagmar?"

Sadie presumed Dagmar was the woman's name.

"Too many little ones, but we're fine," she said.

"Turned religious, have you, John?" Micajah asked.

"The wife…" John said, shaking his head.

Six children, ranging in age from perhaps four to twelve, came out of the cabin door to cluster around Dagmar's skirts and stare at the strangers. Sadie couldn't determine the sex of several of them. They were cute if extraordinarily dirty, especially a small girl with shiny blonde hair and pale blue eyes.

"I see you have some children of your own," Dagmar said, smiling.

Tooly cut her off. "Children, back inside," he said curtly. He hadn't taken his hand off his pistol. "You too, Dagmar."

The shutter of a window in the upper floor opened and two more, somewhat older, children looked out. Waving her skirts at the little ones, Dagmar shooed them in through the door.

"Are you going to invite us in, John?" Micajah asked.

"Several posses have come through asking about you folks," John said. "That fellow, Balinger, the old Indian fighter, he led one party of maybe fifty men."

Micajah's head tilted as he listened, and he looked at Tooly from under his brow, clearly unhappy with the man's words.

Tooly seemed to know Big Harpe wasn't pleased, and his voice took on a querulous tone. "I've never known anyone to upset the hornet's nest the way you two have. For old time's sake, I'm hoping you're gonna understand that I—I've got to protect my own. They come back here and find out I gave you comfort, they'll burn me out."

"If we have to leave," Wiley said, "you know we'll come back. What do you think *we'll* do to you?"

Tooly pulled his pistol from his belt and pointed the weapon at Wiley. Sadie and Bett backed away.

"I—I can't think about that now," he said. Sweat ran down his face though the air was cool. "I built a home here for my family because folks hereabouts don't care much I was Tory. Balinger, he knows we ran together. I don't know how, but he does."

"Are you not proud of your history with us, Tooly?" Wiley asked.

"It's not that, and you know it."

"I suppose a share of what the governor is offering for us would do you some good." Wiley added a derisive chuckle to his words.

A widening of Tooly's eyes betrayed his knowledge of the bounty.

"What will you tell the next posse that stops here?"

Micajah's lip pulled back from his teeth.

"I, uh, well…I'll say I don't know anything about you."

The man's hesitation was his doom. Micajah turned suddenly to his right, as if he'd seen something. When Tooly glanced in that direction, Big Harpe knocked the pistol out of the way and crashed into him. The pistol fired harmlessly into the air. Then Micajah's tomahawk was in his hand. The weapon rose and fell, crushing the face of the screaming Tooly. Screams also emerged from the cabin, cries of "John" and "Daddy."

Bett cried out and ran.

Rooted to the ground, Sadie watched Tooly's thick, red blood burble up out of his exposed nasal cavities and shattered upper jaw as he writhed and gasped for air. His eyes crossed as if trying to find his missing nose.

The tomahawk rose and fell again, and Tooly became still.

Sadie's own blood sang in her veins with the strange vigor she felt when the brothers killed. Despite the restless energy, she was numb, for she couldn't allow herself to feel anything for the victim, the loss of life. He would have helped those trying to capture or kill the Harpes. Micajah had been right to kill him.

The voice of Suesanna's infant rose to join those crying inside the cabin.

Micajah sat down next to the corpse and leaned heavily against the outer wall of the cabin. He didn't stop Wiley from entering the dwelling.

Suesanna clutched at Sadie's arm and quickly guided her toward the forest where they found Bett cowering within the trees, rocking her infant.

The cries within the cabin grew louder for a time, then died down quickly.

30
No Place in the World

"I will not go in there," Suesanna said to Micajah, after he and Wiley had spent time clearing out the cabin, "and I won't take my sister and Sadie in there either."

Micajah struck her, and she fell to the ground. She remained where she'd fallen, curled up on her side, looking at him. Bett and Sadie watched from a distance among the boles of maple trees.

"We've got work to do," Little Harpe said, tugging on Big Harpe's sleeve. Micajah made as if to strike him too. Wiley dashed out of the way.

The big man stared at Suesanna for a moment, then said, "There's no place for us in this world, not anymore." He shrugged and walked off with Wiley.

"What did he mean?" Sadie asked.

"He's giving up," Suesanna said with great weariness. "He's given in to what Wiley wants."

"What does Wiley want?"

"To return to the war years, when cruelty knew no bounds and the Harpes did as they pleased. Killing a whole family is not new, but it's been a long time. Micajah had hope for a different life. I think he's given that up now."

"That's why he let Wiley…?"

"Yes."

"No," Sadie said to Suesanna. "We can't let that happen. We'll find a place, I know we will. The wilderness is large. He won't allow Wiley to destroy us. The killing must stop. I'll talk to Micajah."

Suesanna had no response. She began setting up a camp in the forest.

With her back against a tree trunk, Bett had sat through the conversation silently, breastfeeding both her infant and Suesanna's.

Sadie found Micajah behind the cabin, wringing the necks of chickens while Wiley collected eggs from a rickety coop. The big man glanced up at her approach, then quickly returned his eyes to his work.

Sadie had rarely asked him for anything, and then only in passing. She found she didn't possess words she believed would get his attention. She stood watching him for a moment, unable to open her mouth.

Finally, he looked up again. He appeared weary and troubled. Seeing in his gaze the tenderness he held for her encouraged Sadie. "W-would you c-come with me?" she asked, and held out a trembling hand.

Micajah released the chicken he held. The bird squawked and ran away as he slowly stood.

Wiley was still busy with the chicken coop.

Sadie looked up at the big man's face and saw no anger. She turned, led him around to the front of the cabin, and stopped beside the open door. The sickening smell of blood came to her from inside. Although she wanted to lead him to another spot, she didn't want to look indecisive.

"I—I," she began, and her throat closed so tightly on her words, she thought she might gag. She wanted to say to him that they should be rid of Wiley, change their names, and find a place to live where no one knew them, but how could she? How could she ask him to abandon his own brother? She became dizzy and swayed where she stood.

Micajah put one of his great hands on her shoulder to steady her and looked her in the eye.

Finally Sadie squeezed out, "Wiley is—" She couldn't go on. Tears of frustration slid down her cheeks.

Micajah drew her in and hugged her gently. "I know," he said.

Sadie's pulse quickened at the thought that he intuitively understood what she wanted to say. Did he love her enough to consider her wishes over those of his brother? She had no way of knowing. Her efforts to speak to him had come to nothing, however, and she could only hope for the best.

～ ～ ～

She was awake the next morning when Micajah rose before everyone else. Sadie watched him quietly approach Little Harpe, who lay on his bedroll with his left arm outstretched.

Micajah saw her watching him. He looked her in the eye and nodded, right before putting his full weight behind stepping on his brother's forearm. Wiley's screams of pain followed the sound of cracking bones.

Everyone awoke in an instant. Both infants began to wail.

Micajah jumped back as if horrified that he'd hurt Wiley. "I'm sorry, brother," he said. "I didn't see your arm there."

Suesanna hurried to try to help, but could only cradle Wiley's head while he cried out.

Sadie could not discern through the pained expression on his face whether he knew Big Harpe had stepped on him intentionally. She was pleased to see that Micajah understood the danger Wiley posed and had done what he could, short of killing his own brother, to remove the threat. Being left-handed, Little Harpe wouldn't be doing much killing for some time to come. Even so, his desire would mount, and she feared how he might express his frustration.

Sadie knew then that her child must endure existence as a bastard because she would never wed the brutal lunatic, Wiley Harpe. She could only wonder how her life with Micajah might continue.

31
Running

The Harpe party spent another day ransacking the Tooly property and making preparations to leave. Suesanna made a wooden splint from parts of a broken chair she found in John Tooly's work shed and tied the contraption in place to immobilize Wiley's left forearm. Micajah hauled a chest of Dagmar's sewing supplies out of the cabin so Suesanna could look through the contents without having to go inside the bloody dwelling. She found in the chest a swath of blue calico with a print of pretty yellow flowers on it. She fashioned a sling from the cloth to support Wiley's splinted arm.

He seemed to accept the idea that his brother had stepped on him accidentally. That didn't stop him from cursing Micajah as tarnal clumsy and a jo-fired prick.

The Harpe party loaded what they had plundered from the cabin and outbuildings onto a bay nag and a tan quarter horse that had belonged to the Tooly family, and set out in the early morning, heading east. They were all dressed in fresh, clean clothing—part of the plunder—and looked the part of an ordinary frontier family moving along the road with sober purpose.

Wiley had looked all over the Tooly property for drink to deaden the pain of his broken arm. He hadn't found any. His complaints of suffering, combined with the crying of Suesanna's son, set Micajah on edge, and he threatened to twist Wiley's broken arm if he didn't shut up.

Just before nightfall, they came upon a cabin set off the road a few hundred yards. Micajah approached and hailed the cabin. The door opened and a small unarmed man stood in the entrance, peering out into the gathering dusk.

Sadie heard an urgent voice speaking within, but couldn't make out what was said.

Micajah approached the man. "Good sir, we are the Walker family and we're on our way to a revival meeting. If you'd be so kind, we would like your permission to set up our camp for the night beside your cabin. I promise you we will not disturb the peace of your home and will be gone at earliest light."

Sadie was surprised to hear Micajah speak so pleasantly.

"Of course, Mr. Walker," the man said, "anything to help my fellow man become closer to God. I am Howard Thompkins."

"I am Michael Walker." Micajah said, then he gestured toward his companions one at a time. "This is my wife, Sue, my brother, William, his wife, Elizabeth, and her sister, Sally."

"If you mean the revival meeting in Russellville on the ninth of June, you'd better hurry, for that is tomorrow."

The ninth of June was Sadie's birthday. She was surprised to hear that was the next day's date, and found herself smiling.

"Yes, tomorrow we'll hurry. Thank you kindly, sir, for your hospitality." Micajah began to turn away.

"I would be most honored if you and your family would come in and have some cider," Thompkins said. "My nephew and I were just sitting down to enjoy a cup."

"Yes," Wiley said eagerly.

"That would be a godsend," Micajah answered.

The nephew, another small fellow, perhaps twenty years of age, with short blonde hair and a shiny face full of pink blebs, watched Micajah and Wiley warily as they entered, but warmed quickly when he saw Bett and Sadie.

"This is my nephew, Richard Blevens, my sister Sarah's son. He believes I shouldn't answer the door so readily without a weapon in my hands."

The young man looked somewhat embarrassed. He bowed slightly, glancing quickly several times at the women.

Wiley plopped down into a chair at a table.

"You must forgive my brother," Micajah said. "As you see, he suffers from a broken arm. I'm sure he looks forward to the drink to help ease his pain."

"Yes," Thompkins said, turning to Wiley. "Please, Mr. Walker, make yourself comfortable. We'll get that cider served right away. It is a particularly strong batch."

Wiley smiled miserably.

Blevens set cups on the table, pulled out a large ceramic jug, and poured a generous amount of pungent cider into each one.

Wiley clutched awkwardly at a cup and downed the contents in one draught.

"Pour him another," Thompkins said. "We can't have our friend suffering."

"*Thank* you," Wiley said as Blevens refilled his cup. He downed the drink immediately and Blevens poured him another.

"Please have a seat," Thompkins said.

The Harpes, Bett, and Sadie sat around the table and sipped their cider while Micajah talked religion with Thompkins.

Again, Micajah surprised Sadie. She hadn't considered that he might have religious knowledge. He put on a good act, she thought. The conversation made her uncomfortable, however, reminding her of her father, so she asked to be excused and for directions to the privy. Thompkins lit a candle within a small metal and glass lamp, handed it to Sadie, and told her she would find an outhouse fifty paces beyond the rear of the cabin. As she walked out the door, she hoped that when she came back, the new friends of the Harpes would still be among the living and they'd have a new and better topic of discussion.

She found the outhouse easily enough and relieved herself. Upon her return, Sadie was grateful to find that both Thompkins and Blevens were still alive, and the subject had indeed changed. The nephew was cooking hoecakes on a griddle placed over hot coals. Beans had been served in additional cups.

"I apologize for the lack of meat with supper," Thompkins said. "I have no powder to go hunting."

"We can't have that," Wiley said drunkenly. "There are dangerous men wanderin' the countryside."

Micajah's eyes grew wide.

"Perhaps you've heard of 'em," Wiley continued.

Desperately, Sadie reached within herself for something to say to change the subject. She didn't want Wiley to give Micajah a reason to leave no witnesses.

"They are the Harpes and—"

"Yes, powder!" she said a bit too loudly, but effectively cutting Wiley off.

Everyone was looking at her.

She quickly turned to Micajah. "Michael, we can help Mr. Thompkins. Please give him a portion of what you carry in your horn."

Thompkins looked a bit startled.

"I—I'm sorry," Sadie said, thinking fast. "I speak too loudly when

I've had drink. Please forgive me."

"Of course," Thompkins said. He turned back to Wiley. "Now, what were you saying about dangerous—"

"She's right," Micajah interrupted. He stood to retrieve his powder horn which he'd hung on a peg beside the door. "May I have another cup?" he asked Blevens.

The young man placed one on the table. As Micajah filled the mug with powder from his horn, he looked at Wiley. "That's enough talk of bad men, brother. You'll frighten the women again."

"We don't want that," Blevens said, and his uncle nodded in agreement.

~ ~ ~

The evening had been pleasant except for the frequent sobbing fits of the teething baby boy and the frequent furtive glances Blevens gave to Sadie. She could see the longing in his eyes, and she worried Micajah might see the desire too. Wiley had fallen asleep in his chair, undisturbed by the crying jags. After another hour of quiet talk, the Harpe party exited the cabin, assembled their camp, and turned in for the night.

Sadie lay down on one side of Micajah. Suesanna and her sleeping baby lay down on the other side.

Sadie was so relieved that the folks in the cabin had not been murdered, she found herself looking forward to the next day. How long since she'd felt that way? She didn't know. Tomorrow, she would become seventeen years old. Perhaps she was receiving a birthday present of some small happiness.

Was anger, hatred, and pain draining out of the world, Sadie wondered. She didn't for a moment believe that were true, but found the idea a pleasant fancy to ponder while falling asleep.

~ ~ ~

As the sky began to lighten toward the east, the Harpe party set out again.

Sadie's good mood persisted, and, as the sun rose, she felt its warmth in the humid air surround and embrace her. Life was changing for the better. She would believe that, and what began as notion would come true. The posses would all go home. The Harpes would find a place where they were not known, where they could settle down and have a good, prosperous life. She was certain Micajah wanted the same. Somehow, he'd make her wishes come true.

Clearly, though, Suesanna's infant didn't agree—he was crying again. The older woman hung back from the group, sometimes as far as one hundred yards. Sadie assumed she lagged behind so Micajah wouldn't become irritated with the infant's crying.

Bett's little girl periodically fussed too. "She's colicky," her friend said.

Micajah glared at the tiny girl a couple of times, as if he might frighten the child into silence.

A good ten miles had passed beneath their feet when Suesanna, huffing and puffing, came running up. "Dogs, horses," was all she had the breath to say.

Everyone scrambled off the trail toward the north.

"We have to cut through the forest," Micajah said.

As the Harpe party moved into the dense forest, Sadie heard the sounds of horses, dogs, and men approaching back on the trail, and then the sounds began to diminish. They seemed to pass by the spot where the Harpe party had entered the forest. Looking back, Sadie tripped on vines within the underbrush. Bett helped her to rise. Picking up their feet, they hurried after the others. Micajah and Suesanna struggled to pull the horses forward through the underbrush. At least the infants were quiet.

"We must leave the horses behind," Micajah said. "Gather what you need."

They quickly went through the supplies the horses carried and loaded into their packs food, weapons, and accoutrements, then moved on. The animals tried to follow, but the viny underbrush presented too many encumbrances, and they couldn't keep up.

With time, the Harpe party came upon a stream. Micajah led the way down into the creek bed and they all walked along in the water for at least half an hour. The cool water felt good on Sadie's sore feet. The stream deepened and broadened, then cascaded over several short falls, and finally disappeared into an opening in the exposed rock face of a hillside.

Micajah fashioned a couple of torches from green wood, tree bark, and some cord he'd scrounged at the Tooly place. Once lit, they provided the illumination needed to explore inside the cave beyond the entrance. The infant boy's crying echoed eerily within the stone chambers as the Harpe party walked through the gravelly creek bed. As they explored, they found several entrances as the creek wandered in and out of the rocky hillside.

"There's good flint here," Suesanna said as they stood in the creek outside one of the entrances. "The Indians came here to make tools, see." She pointed out a myriad of flint shards littering the ground.

"What if they come back?" Sadie asked.

"They might, but not to make stone tools. This is old. They have rifles now."

Dogs barked in the distance.

"They're coming," Micajah said. "let's climb to the top." He pointed up the rock face, and then led the party toward the west.

As they all ran along in the creek bed, the sisters' infants were jostled so severely within their slings that they both began to cry.

"Shut them up!" Micajah said.

"Then I will have to stop," Suesanna huffed out as she ran.

"Not until we reach the top," he demanded.

A sloping side of the hill met the level of the creek a couple hundred yards further on. A path led up the edge of the hill along the top of the rock face. The way was easier than crashing through the forest. As they left the creek bed and began to climb, Sadie wanted to look out to see if the posse was near.

"Don't get too close to the edge," Suesanna warned. "They might see you."

Sadie noticed Wiley had fallen behind. The broken arm had taken more out of him than his ability to kill—his spirit was dampened.

They were halfway to the top when Bett's infant wailed like never before.

Micajah lunged at Bett. "Quiet your bairn now," he said, "or I'll have to!"

Bett stopped suddenly and sat, exhausted. Suesanna stopped with her, panting. Wiley sat down next to Bett, moaning and leaning against her. Sadie held her bulging abdomen and with one hand, rubbed her sore back with the other.

"Move up the trail," Micajah cried.

"No, we must rest." Suesanna shook her head, glared at Big Harpe. She rocked her boy, she whispered in his ear, she hummed a tune. She bent forward and swung him gently in his sling.

Bett tried all the same things, having less success. Suesanna's boy had quieted some, enough that Sadie could hear the dogs barking again. She couldn't tell if the animals were closer.

Sadie was grateful for the pause, but she could find no rest.

Big Harpe paced, rubbing his head, his permanent scowl more fearsome than ever.

Bett's girl wailed as if her toes were on fire.

"Up! Up!" Micajah said.

They got to their feet and moved upward at a walk. Bett's child became quieter, yet still occasionally sent out a great yowl.

Sadie tripped on a root and stumbled toward the edge, but caught herself before going over. She avoided falling on her belly, landing instead on her left hip. Below, she saw the men on horseback and the dogs near the falls. She recognized Balinger leading the posse of forty or fifty men. They weren't looking in her direction. Instead, they poked around the cave entrances aimlessly. The sound of the waterfalls and the barking of the dogs had perhaps masked the sound of the crying infants. That would not last—when far enough from the falls, Balinger and his men would surely hear unless the children were silenced.

Sadie picked herself up and joined the others at the top of the bluff. Micajah was trying to get them to follow the path that went down the backside of the hill. Wiley lay on the ground, hugging his splinted arm and moaning in pain, while Bett and Suesanna continued to try to quiet their children.

Micajah stumbled from one mother to the next, his hands flexing from claws to fists. "Hush!" he said to Suesanna's child, his frustration turning the word into a deep, malignant utterance. He struck at the infant with his fist, but the child's mother swung the baby out of Big Harpe's reach and the blow landed on Suesanna's shoulder.

"They will hear," he said. "They'll find us!"

Bett's little girl sent out a wail to wake the dead, and Micajah shook with rage. He snatched the infant from her sling, grabbed the girl's ankles and swung her with great force.

Sadie turned away, yet could not stop herself from hearing the girl's head strike the tree trunk. When finally she turned back, she found Micajah gagging Bett's screaming face with the palm of one of his hands. Though her face seemed to cry out, no sound emerged. Within moments, she had become unconscious.

Miraculously, Suesanna's infant had stopped crying too. Then Sadie discovered the reason; the woman had her hand over the child's mouth and nose. No light shone from his little eyes. Both Quinton and Virginia were gone.

Sadie turned and ran down the slope, away from the rock face and the posse beyond, away from the Harpes, her friend and the dead infants. Her abdomen rocked awkwardly and she stumbled, lost a shoe, but still she ran on, her bare foot scraped and cut painfully. Her sore muscles and the ache in her back were all that chased after her. She ran until she was no longer aware of the pain, until she lost awareness of her abdomen, her feet, her breath. Then, briefly, she knew she lay upon the rough ground. Sadie caught a glimpse of tree trunks rising on all sides and flecks of blue sky flashing through the rustling green leaves above before darkness closed around her.

32
Frontier Justice

"Bide a moment, Ericson. I won't be long."

Sadie heard the voice and saw a man standing over her. Beyond, several men on horseback waited impatiently. When the man bent down, she recognized him as Howard Thompkins' nephew, Richard Blevens. His shiny face full of blebs was too close.

"You must come with us," he said, helping her sit up.

How does he come to be here? she wondered. Disoriented, her thinking muddled, Sadie shook her head. Forest surrounded her. She remembered her flight, and—

"No!" she screamed, and struggled against Blevens.

Not the sweet babies!

She didn't want to remember, but couldn't help it. Micajah and Suesanna had taken the infants' lives as if they were nothing.

Such cruelty! Unnamed and unloved, the little ones were gone.

The failure to name them suggested Suesanna and Bett had known what would happen. Even Wiley had talked about losing children because Big Harpe found them "vexing." Foolishly, Sadie hadn't wanted to believe Micajah capable of such savagery, and she certainly had never seen that in Suesanna.

Indeed, the babes' mothers had not named them to avoid becoming too attached. Sadie would be cursed to remember them forevermore as Quinton and Virginia.

And what of Bett? Had Micajah killed her too?

Sadie tried to curl into a ball on the ground. Blevens lifted her.

"We can't leave you here." He got her on her feet, led her to a horse, and struggled to help her up onto the beast.

The other men on horseback huffed their disgust at his efforts.

"Leave her," said one in an odd green cap.

"No, Ericson," Blevens said, "she must come with us." He lifted her to her feet, mounted his horse, and drew her up to sit sidesaddle while he rode pillion. He gripped the cantle in one hand, the reins in the other.

Ericson and the others moved on and Blevens followed. With the young man's arms around her, Sadie stayed in the saddle, though she sagged forward sobbing. The horse increased its pace, matching that of the others, and the party rode eastward at a canter.

As they went, Sadie began to worry about Bett. Was her friend lying somewhere, barely alive, abandoned in the wilderness? Riding away with Blevens, could Sadie find her way back to help Bett?

She wiped away her tears and found her voice. "Will you help me find my friend—" What had been the name the Harpes gave Bett the night before? "—Elizabeth?"

"My uncle stayed with her and the other woman, uh…Sue," Blevens said.

"Is she alive?"

"Both are alive."

She was relieved to hear about her friend. Even so, she feared facing Bett in the future; Sadie blamed herself for the death of the baby girl. She hated Micajah for what he'd done, but his murder of the infant would not have occurred if Sadie hadn't deceived Bett into staying with the Harpes.

Her thoughts turned to Micajah and, to her horror, Sadie knew she loved him still.

What have I given to him? What has he taken from me?

Now was not the time to sort her feelings. Sadie worried about his safety.

She remembered how the Harpes had introduced themselves the night before. "What of the Walker men, Michael and William?"

"Mr. Balinger and his men are catching up with them even now, I'd imagine."

"Balinger!" she said without thinking. but Blevens didn't respond. "Will you help me find them before he does?"

"We are headed for them now," he said. "When we catch up with Mr. Balinger—"

"No!" Sadie said again, and she tried to slide off the saddle. Blevens gripped her around the waist and held her in place.

"You'll harm yourself!" As he struggled with her, his horse slowed to a walk and the others continued without them.

"You're with the posse?" Sadie asked, breathlessly.

"Yes."

"The Harpes did you no harm."

"So, indeed, they are the Harpes!"

Sadie pressed her lips tightly together. Had she given them away? Regardless, the posse was after them. Since Blevens was trying to catch up with the posse, riding with him was, for the present, the shortest route to the Harpes. She settled down as the horse resumed a canter.

Blevens and Sadie caught up with Ericson and the other riders just as they caught up with the main body of the posse. Balinger was a hundred yards away. He sat astride his horse atop a sharp prominence rising among the trees that allowed him a view of the small valley beyond. Blevens and his party moved closer to Balinger as he turned and gave instructions to his men. "Walton, take your men around the eastern rim of the valley. "Mclean, you take the western rim."

The two groups of about fifteen men each set out in opposite directions.

As Blevens and his group of riders came closer, Balinger guided his mount off the prominence. He caught sight of Sadie and said curtly, "Hello Miss Rice."

"I thought your name was Walker," Blevens said, but she had no response.

Beside Balinger rode Robert Brassl. He simply glared at Sadie. When he turned away she saw the bulge of a bandage under his shirt on the right shoulder.

"Ericson," Balinger said, addressing the man in the green cap, "it's good you caught up. I'll need you. If you come with me, you might get a chance to show off your marksmanship."

Sadie was certain the Harpes would not get themselves shot. Still, they were up against so many, she feared they wouldn't get away. She reminded herself that the brothers were good at breaking out of confinement.

Balinger looked uphill to his right. "You still see them, Sweet?" he yelled.

A figure standing at the rocky edge of the ridge top pointed to a spot out in the valley and shouted, "Yes, they're, moving on foot."

"Follow me, men," Balinger said, and the riders, including Blevens and Sadie, moved forward.

Reaching the bottom of the valley, Sadie saw the men ahead pointing up the far slope. Shortly, she was able to see Big and Little Harpe moving through the trees over three hundred yards away. She thought back to the morning, so long ago, after she'd slept in the tree and awoke to find a hunting party coming for her wolves. Much as she'd said to the wolves then, she whispered now to the Harpes, "Run!"

Ahead, while pointing toward the retreating figures, Balinger spoke to Ericson, who had dismounted. As Sadie and Blevens came closer, she heard the tail end of what Balinger had to say, "—the big one before he gets to those rocks."

Ericson steadied himself against a tree and raised his rifle. He sited for a moment, pulled the trigger, and held steady as the rifle did its work with a flash, plume of smoke, and sharp crack of sound.

"Missed!" he said.

"Use mine," Blevens yelled, pulling his rifle from a scabbard depending from the right side of the saddle. "It's charged with that big man's powder."

"No!" Sadie cried, clawing at the weapon's frizzen and flint, but Ericson had a grip on the stock and pulled the rifle free.

"He gave my uncle a cup of his own supply last night, and I loaded my weapon with it this morning."

Ericson quickly inspected the firearm, then set the cock to the firing position. He leaned against the tree, raised the rifle, and sited.

"Shot driven by his powder ought to find him," Blevens continued.

"Hush," Balinger said.

In the interminable moments that ensued, Sadie watched the Harpes running through the forest about four hundred yards away, picking up their feet to avoid the encumbering underbrush. Wiley veered off to the left and disappeared from view. Micajah was hidden behind a tree trunk for a time, and Sadie had hoped he would get away too. Then he reappeared, still running, and Ericson fired. Immediately following the blast, Micajah dropped from view.

He hid just in time, Sadie told herself.

"I hit him," Ericson said.

Robert Brassl whooped a cheer as he and Balinger moved forward swiftly.

"No!" Sadie wouldn't have it. She had been the one to insist that Micajah provide the powder! "He's too fast. He is too strong. He's—"

Sadie realized no one was listening. She swallowed hard to stop the flow of words, but refused to look in the direction Micajah had taken. Still, she was headed that way—Sadie had no choice as Blevens guided his mount to follow the others.

She saw men heading in the direction Wiley had taken, and found herself hoping they'd catch him. He'd abandoned his brother when help was most needed. Wiley Harpe deserved whatever he got.

Looking over Blevens' shoulder, she watched Ericson stow his gear, mount his horse, and follow. She hated him, his confidence, his silly green hat, his ugly gray spotted mount. He would not go far in life, especially after Micajah got away and Ericson was left to look foolish.

A hubbub of voices rose up around her as they caught up with the others. Men were dismounting. Others, still on horseback, came quickly down the slopes on both sides.

"We've got him now," Brassl said, and he let out a great yelp of joy.

Sadie heard Micajah's voice and swung around to look.

"Get back," Big Harpe said. He lay facedown among the underbrush with a bloody hole between his shoulder blades, while Brassl danced around him hooting and hollering.

Sadie slid out from under Blevens' arms and off the saddle, hit the ground feet first, and fell hard on her backside. Getting up, she ran toward Micajah. Balinger grabbed her by the arms and held her ten feet away from the big man.

Several of the posse members trained their rifles on Micajah.

He struggled on the ground, his arms moving weakly. His head, neck, and shoulders were the only part of him that appeared to have any strength. He gasped for breath. Arching his neck, twisting his head this way and that, and working his shoulders, he seemed to make an effort to wriggle away. He grabbed the trunk of a bush in his teeth and pulled himself forward an inch or two, the muscles in his neck bulging from the effort, but Sadie could see he wouldn't get away. Fresh tears fell down her cheeks.

Brassl kicked him in the side, and Micajah made no response.

"Stop," Sadie cried, struggling against Balinger.

"He can't move!" Brassl said. "His spine is broken."

"Enough," Balinger said. "Give him some peace."

"Why?" Brassl asked.

Others joined him in questioning, outrage evident in their murmuring.

"We must carry him to Russellville and justice," Balinger said.

"He killed my brother without a thought." Brassl gave Micajah another savage kick.

"Can't you see he's hurt?" Sadie cried.

Brassl spun on her. "Don't listen to that woman." His words were flung with such force that the spittle that emerged with them reached her, spattering her face. "She watched him crush Jim's skull."

Members of the posse shouted and screamed. Sadie couldn't make out their words, but there was no mistaking the hatred in their tone.

"We all need to remain calm," Balinger said.

Sadie knew from the way he spoke that his heart wasn't behind his words.

The posse members' response grew more belligerent. Several glared at Balinger and spat on the ground.

Blevens appeared beside Sadie, glanced at her awkwardly.

"Give *him* some peace?" Brassl asked in a mocking tone. "Here's the bloody peace I'll give him." He turned to a big blonde fellow on the other side of Micajah. "Help me prop him up."

They grabbed Micajah under the arms, turned him over, dragged him a few yards to the bole of an oak, and jammed him up against it. His head struck with enough force that he seemed addled for a moment.

Sadie tried to turn and face Balinger. "Do something to stop them," she said.

"I've seen this enough to know there's no stopping it."

"You must!"

"Nor do I want to. This is frontier justice, miss. He brought it on himself."

"He's disturbed the peaceful lives of everyone here!" Brassl cried.

The posse roared their agreement. As he pulled out a long, broad knife, they howled their approval.

"You should turn away," Balinger said.

Micajah had caught sight of Sadie and she couldn't look away, even as Brassl reached down, and in one quick motion, cut off Big Harpe's left ear. Blood gushed from him, Sadie screamed, and the posse cheered. Micajah took no notice of the loss, kept his eyes on her.

The posse cheered as Brassl took off Big Harpe's right ear. Again, Micajah made no notice. The look in his eyes—she couldn't decide whether the expression was one of tenderness or merely gawking animal desire—was the same as when he first saw Sadie a year ago.

His nose came off next, and blood fell down his face and into his shirt. The posse yelped and howled. Sadie was sickened, but didn't turn away. Micajah had never before looked so much the part of the demonic presence he represented for these people.

Brassl took away a large portion of Micajah's scalp. Still, the big man stared at Sadie as if she were an oasis of calm beauty within a world of ugliness and pain. The intensity of that gaze became frightening, and she finally glanced away.

When she looked back, his eyes were squinted slightly and he pressed his mouth into a hard line. After a year with the man, she'd gotten good enough at reading his moods that she knew he was disappointed she had looked away. He felt betrayed. If he weren't immobilized by his wounds, he would show her his displeasure.

With that realization, she felt her expression change to one of fear and disgust, which he noticed. Micajah became more frightening than ever. The man was no wolf with the innocent, simple needs of such a beast. No, his savagery emerged from a calculus of greed and anger. Sadie saw the baby-killer glaring hard at her.

How could she have loved such a monster?

"Sharpen your blade, butcher," Big Harpe said to Brassl, "and be done with it! There's nothing for me here. Never has been."

He intended to harm Sadie with his words. She knew he'd never loved her.

Brassl pulled Micajah's head forward and began cutting at the back of his neck.

"Faster," Big Harpe growled. "Who taught you to butcher? I've given better service to swine."

Brassl slid the knife around to the front of Micajah's neck and, pressing hard against the flesh, drew the blade quickly across the throat. The vessels gushed open, spraying gouts of brilliant red through the air.

One last angry glance at Sadie and Micajah Harpe was done. His eyes rolled up and back, and Brassl allowed the head to fall forward.

Big Harpe was gone, and Sadie felt nothing but relief.

Blevens, beside her, had turned aside to vomit.

Brassl repositioned the knife under Big Harpe's chin and began to saw. With a great effort, he worked and twisted, jabbed and poked while the posse cheered him on. When the head came free of the shoulders, he held up the terrible, bloody visage and shrieked with laughter. The posse joined him with great guffaws, whooping cries, and demonic howls.

Sadie hated them all.

Balinger turned her around, and she allowed him to lead her away, though she hated him too.

Sadie would hate almost everyone for the next thirty-five years, but most of all, she'd hate herself.

33
Harpe's Head

The date of Micajah's death was June 9. Sadie never celebrated her birthday again.

The posse left Micajah's body in the forest so the wild animals would scatter his parts. His head was placed in a sack that Brassl slung on his saddle.

Those who had chased after Wiley rejoined the posse with the news that Little Harpe had gotten away.

Moving back the way they'd come, the posse gathered up Howard Thompkins, Suesanna, and Bett. Thompkins and the sisters had buried the infants on the hill where they had died, in a spot overlooking the cave and creek below. Balinger was given to believe by the sisters that Big Harpe had killed both infants, and Sadie had no interest in informing them otherwise.

Coming out of the forest onto an established trail, the posse stopped at the first crossroads they found. Brassl and several others worked to strip an oak branch that hung over the road. Once the small growth was removed from the end, the wood was sharpened to a point. Brassl stuck Micajah's head onto the limb. The branch entered through the base of the skull and exited through the mouth so that the head appeared to scream while a wooden tongue jutted forth.

"That ought to serve as a warning," Brassl said.

Sadie didn't recognize Micajah in the lifeless, ruined face, darkened with black blood. Looking at the head she wasn't moved to pity. She felt little, and wondered if she would have strong emotion ever again.

Satisfied with their work, the posse moved on. Sadie rode with Blevens until he and Thompkins turned off to return to their home. In parting, Blevens gave Sadie a hopeful look and said, "If you are released from the jail, you could come to me."

She had no response. Thankfully, he did not linger waiting for one.

Once he was gone, she rode with Suesanna on the same mount. Sadie truly did not want to touch the woman, but had no choice. They didn't speak to each other throughout the trip. Bett would not speak or look at Sadie.

The long road to Russellville took three days. Balinger posted guards to keep watch on his three prisoners at night. Sadie wasn't in a mood to flee. Nor, apparently, were the sisters.

Arriving in Russellville, the three women were held in a single cell within another log jail to await a hearing and, eventually, a trial at the courthouse across the town square. Sadie's betrayal of Bett and inability to forgive Suesanna for the murder of the infant thickened the interminable silence endured within the cell. The sisters no doubt had their own reasons for not speaking to one another.

Predictably, after the hearing the women were held for trial. The wait would be two months.

Considering that she might hang for her participation in the Harpes' crimes gave Sadie little trepidation at first. Death, she thought, might be a welcome release from the darkness that gathered within her: The memories of her role in so many deaths; recurring nightmares in which she still walked the trail with Micajah, fearful of what lay beyond each bend in the road; her creeping hatred of each and every human soul she met; and her disinterest in nearly every aspect of daily life. Food was bland. She found no pleasure in reading to pass the time. Color had drained from the world. Sadie felt dead inside.

~ ~ ~

One day, Daniel Early appeared at the jail and asked to speak with her. They were allowed to meet in an empty cell. Sadie found herself curious about why he had come, which was striking, since she had not felt anything similar since before the death of Micajah Harpe.

"I have a new post as constable in the sheriff's office in Russellville," he said. "I hope you don't mind if I visit you from time to time."

Sadie found herself thinking of him as a good, kind-hearted man. Much like her curiosity, the reaction was also uncharacteristic for her of late. Her impression fit the man, for he'd tried to help the women of the Harpe party merely to satisfy the dictates of his heart. In Stanford, he'd had a romantic interest in her, but he never let that show in his face or manner. His eyes did not reflect carnal hunger, and he treated her as if he believed she had a brain in her head. He could clearly see that Sadie was pregnant, and surely he knew the child was the bastard of one of the

Harpes. No doubt that knowledge had quashed his romantic desires and yet he was still good enough to see her.

"I will gladly receive you when you come calling," she said with little feeling. She realized her words had come out rather flat and that he deserved better. Sadie produced a smile of sorts. The one he returned to her looked a bit sad.

Early looked in on the sisters, said his goodbyes, and left. He came back a couple times a week. Upon Suesanna's request, he found spinning work for her to do. Soon, two walking wheels were in the jail, and both sisters were earning an income. Sadie was placed in a separate cell when she exhibited a bad reaction to the wool with which the women worked. Early brought in a treadle wheel for Sadie to use, and she earned an income spinning flax. She was relieved to be on her own and to have something to occupy her time.

Early organized liberty from the jail for the women under his close supervision. During outings to market, the women found clothing and other small comforts to purchase.

In September, the trial of the Harpe women ended in acquittal for all three. Early met with Sadie at the jail and took her to a small tavern for a meal. They had barely sat down when he said, "Please forgive me for speaking bluntly, but I have nearly waited too long as you may be leaving soon."

"I have no plans," Sadie said. "We had word from our attorney some time back that we weren't to suffer the wrath of the court. That left me troubled, for I've made no plans for life beyond my present confinement. I've come to the conclusion that I'm not the best one to make decisions for myself."

"Perhaps then you will value my assistance."

Sadie wondered if he had found further work for her. Perhaps something within a local household, a family in need of someone to do small work.

"You will give birth any day now," he continued, "and the child will need a father. I've had feelings for you ever since we met in Stanford."

Sadie stared at him. He didn't make any sense.

"Please marry me before it's too late. Your child will suffer as a bastard, but at least I will be there to provide defense. I took the position with the sheriff's office here with the hope that you would grant my wish."

Sadie had entertained and dismissed the idea that he was playing an elaborate joke, and found herself accepting the impossible—that he truly cared enough for her that he would offer her everything he had.

Still staring at him, new calculations began. If she left Russellville, her past would follow. Run through the rumor mill, stories of her would only be worse when they caught up with her, wherever she went. If she stayed in Russellville as the wife of a constable for the court that acquitted her, rumor could only go so far before meeting up with the truth.

Considering how she felt about almost everyone else, she was surprised to realize that she was comfortable in his presence.

"No," she said, "I cannot make this decision. I find myself considering the advantages and disadvantages without the benefit of feeling. I do not love you."

"After what you've been through, I can understand how you might have difficulty knowing yourself. But I will be devoted to you whether you love me or not. I said I would offer my assistance in making decisions. Please allow me to make this one for you."

She had nothing else in the world, and so she manufactured a small hope; if Early, a good man, desired Sadie, there must be something good inside her, even if she couldn't feel it. She thought briefly of the infant she carried, yet dismissed that because she knew she could not feel anything for the child of the Harpes. Perhaps, in time, she would return to life.

In response to Early, Sadie merely nodded her head.

～ ～ ～

Five years later, Wiley Harpe delivered a criminal's head to the law in Natchez, Mississippi, intending to collect a bounty for the wanted man. The head belonged to his one-time friend, the leader of the pirates at Cave Inn Rock, a notorious outlaw named Mason. A law officer in Natchez, who had been with the posse that caught Big Harpe, recognized Little Harpe when he attempted to collect the bounty. Wiley was arrested, tried for his crimes, and hanged.

Sadie never spoke to her friend again. Bett returned to Knoxville, Tennessee, where she married a man named Hofstettler and had many children. Suesanna stayed in Kentucky and worked on a plantation, spinning and weaving. She never remarried.

Micajah's head eventually disappeared from the crossroads that had come to be known as Harpe's Head. Rumor held that a local woman had taken the remains to treat her ailing son after learning from a healer that the bone of a murderer's skull ground to powder and administered by mouth was a cure for fits.

Daniel Early was a good man to the end. He never asked her about her experiences with the Harpes. He allowed Sadie her emotional distance without complaint. He saw the birth of Sadie's daughter, Minerva, and was a good father to the child, a good provider and an interesting companion for fifteen years. About the time Sadie thought she might have developed feelings for the man, when she began to wonder if he was the shapeless man she had dreamed she would one day fall in love with, he was gunned down while trying to settle a dispute at a local tavern.

Minerva grew up and married Doyle Tenbrook, a hardworking to-bacco and pig farmer. Sadie had been a member of the household ever since.

Despite the stirrings of emotion she'd experienced late in her marriage to Early, Sadie would not feel anything for anyone, including Minerva, until her grandson, Timothy, was born.

34
Rising
Russellville, Kentucky
1835

Timothy was the embodiment of all that Sadie had gambled for when she'd married Daniel Early—she'd taken a chance on living with the hope that, despite all the evidence of the year she'd spent with the Harpes, *life* itself was indeed *good*; that human beings, for all their destructive tendencies, were essentially good, and that, given time, she would come to feel the truth of that again.

As the grandson of either Micajah or Wiley Harpe, if Timothy were to have had no qualms about stealing pies, Sadie might have thought, *the apple doesn't fall far from the tree*, and hoped he didn't become a bolder thief. She might then have gone on about her business without the painful remembrance of her earlier life.

Sadie had suffered a grievous wound, however, one that had not healed in thirty-five years. Keeping her distance from others had protected the injury, but because she loved Timothy, she was vulnerable to his feelings. With the depth of his despair over the theft, she could see that he wasn't in imminent danger of turning bad like the Harpes. Although his emotion had dredged up some of Sadie's worst memories, she had not avoided those recollections entirely over the years. So what about her recent experience with the boy had pulled the scab off her wound? Why had she harmed him?

Sadie resented the ease with which her grandson took responsibility for his own actions. She understood that that came, in part, from his religious training. *Reverend Hunley has put the fear in adults and children alike*, she thought bitterly. She knew the shackles of that fear quite well. She'd had more cause to rebel against the church's teachings than Timothy did, and had thrown off those fetters at an early age.

Her grandson didn't choose the forces that shaped him. Deciding that she loved him all the more for his guileless nature, Sadie suspected her anger toward Timothy was in response to seeing the loss of his innocence. Once the naiveté was gone, she feared the inevitable: that the void would fill with the ugly, mindful calculations of an adult. He might see no advantage in his tenderness toward her. Indeed, he could seek favor among those who still looked upon her with disdain. Timothy's and Sadie's love for one another would end.

Many years had passed since the people of Russellville had openly looked at her with suspicion, contempt, or fear. Even the children told fewer tales about her. She avoided most gatherings and stayed home much of the time. Perhaps her age and gentle demeanor had persuaded folks that she was no threat.

Still, she remembered the stares of hypocrites. The worst had come from those who would eventually become known as the most sinful: Minister Bouchard of the Baptist Church, charged with polygamy twenty-five years ago; the mortician, Mr. Rollo, caught selling his clients' bodies to medical men in Nashville; and the well-to-do Looney sisters, considered the height of society in Russellville, who poisoned their mother to hasten their inheritance. Sadie had endured their glaring scorn at church, at market, in the town square, at seasonal gatherings and celebrations. Most of all, she'd hated the hypocrites for reminding her that she could never fully forgive herself. They were long gone from Russellville, though, and she remained.

Perhaps she feared that if Timothy could not pardon himself, he might become one of them. He knew only that his grandfather was a murderer. Nothing more on the subject was discussed within the family. When Timothy brought home stories told by other children, Doyle convinced him the tales were too tall to be believed. Even so, his acute awareness of others' suspicions about his grandmother perhaps contributed to his fearful scrupulousness.

Sadie rolled over. Her straw mattress was hopelessly lumpy. After two days resting in bed, only rising to relieve herself in the chamber pot, to sip water, and nibble at the food Minerva brought her, Sadie's ribs on both sides hurt and both hips ached. Settling into a more comfortable position, her thoughts returned to Timothy's confession at the bridge over Wooten's Creek.

On the bridge, he had seen Sadie's distress as bad memories

welled up inside her. His brow had furrowed, his eyes had narrowed, and she'd read the expression as contempt and anger. Although she'd denied the truth all Timothy's life, Sadie knew that his eyes, his expressions, were much like those of Micajah. The last time she'd looked at the big man, he'd given her a look similar to what Timothy displayed on the bridge, one that she'd read the same way.

Sadie had lashed out at the boy, knocking him down and then falling herself. Following his expression and her actions, however, had come the boy's words: "Are you all right, Grandma?" As he helped her up, she could see that he couldn't imagine his grandmother had intended him harm.

My shame crafted the contempt and placed it in his eye!

If she had misinterpreted Timothy's expression, that begged the question: On the day of Big Harpe's death, had she misread his features too? For most of her life, she'd carried in her mind that look on Micajah's face as anger and contempt, but now she could see that both the boy's and the man's expressions were, in truth, concern.

Micajah didn't want to die alone and unloved. He thought she had turned away for good. As he was wont to do when he didn't get his way, he'd lashed out with the weapon he had available, and on that day, all he had left were cruel words. Indeed, she *had* glanced away, but only briefly, then she'd kept her eyes on him until the end. Still, he was right, for even as he died, in part because of his last words, she'd turned away from him within her heart. Sadie had hated Big Harpe for lo these many years, while hiding from herself her love for the man. He was horrible, driven by forces within that she would never truly understand, and he deserved what he got. Now, though, after so long, she found herself willing to admit that they had loved each other.

He was the shapeless man she'd hoped to one day fall in love with, and while the notion horrified her, she found the idea strangely comforting as well.

Sadie didn't want to be alone either. She would find and love Timothy, who clearly loved her in return. Perhaps he had gotten over his burden of conscience. If not, she must see him through it. She would do whatever it took to deserve his affection.

Sadie found herself rising from her bed.

On the bridge, the boy had asked, "How can I make it right when I knew it was wrong?"

As small as Timothy's crime might seem to Sadie, she knew he saw the misdeed as large.

Perhaps there was no answer to his question, but she'd had enough experience with deep personal doubt that she would find something to say to him that might help. She had to have the courage to try.

End

About the Author

Alan M. Clark, fine arts painter, illustrator, and author hails from Tennessee, where he grew up in a house full of human bones and old medical books. At present, he lives in Eugene, Oregon with his wife, Melody. In his 33 year freelance career, he has created illustrations for hundreds of books, including works of fiction of various genres, nonfiction, textbooks, young adult fiction, and children's books. He is the author of seventeen books, including eleven novels, a lavishly illustrated novella, four collections of fiction, and a nonfiction full-color book of his artwork. The World Fantasy Award and four Chesley Awards are among the honors he's received for his work. Mr. Clark's company, IFD Publishing, has released forty-four books, including hardcovers, paperbacks, ebooks, and audio books. IFD Publishing's authors include F. Paul Wilson, Elizabeth Engstrom, and Jeremy Robert Johnson. www.alanmclark.com

Connect with the Author Online.
You can email the author or find out more about him through the following websites:
http://www.ifdpublishing.com
http://www.smashwords.com/profile/view/IFDPublishing

IFD Publishing Paperbacks

Novels:

Death is a Star, by Christina Lay
Baggage Check, by Elizabeth Engstrom
Bull's Labyrinth, by Eric Witchey
The Surgeon's Mate: A Dismemoir, by Alan M. Clark
Siren Promised, by Jeremy Robert Johnson and Alan M. Clark
Say Anything but Your Prayers, by Alan M. Clark
Candyland, by Elizabeth Engstrom
Apologies to the Cat's Meat Man, by Alan M. Clark

Collections:

Professor Witchey's Miracle Mood Cure, by Eric Witchey

Nonfiction:

How to Write a Sizzling Sex Scene, by Elizabeth Engstrom

IFD Publishing EBooks

(You can find the following titles at most distribution points for all ereading platforms.)

Novels:

Bull's Labyrinth, by Eric Witchey
The Surgeon's Mate: A Dismemoir, by Alan M. Clark
York's Moon, by Elizabeth Engstrom
Beyond the Serpent's Heart, by Eric Witchey
Lizzie Borden, by Elizabeth Engstrom
A Parliament of Crows, by Alan M. Clark
Lizard Wine, by Elizabeth Engstrom
Northwoods Chronicles: A Novel in Short Stories, by Elizabeth Engstrom
Siren Promised, by Alan M. Clark and Jeremy Robert Johnson
To Kill a Common Loon, by Mitch Luckett
The Man in the Loon, by Mitch Luckett
Jack the Ripper Victim Series: Of Thimble and Threat by Alan M. Clark
Jack the Ripper Victim Series: The Double Event (includes two novels from the series: *Of Thimble and Threat* and *Say Anything But Your Prayers*) by Alan M. Clark
Candyland, by Elizabeth Engstrom
The Blood of Father Time: Book 1, The New Cut, by Alan M. Clark, Stephen C. Merritt & Lorelei Shannon
The Blood of Father Time: Book 2, The Mystic Clan's Grand Plot, by Alan M. Clark, Stephen C. Merritt & Lorelei Shannon

How I Met My Alien Bitch Lover: Book 1 from the Sunny World Inquisition Daily Letter Archives, by Eric Witchey
Baggage Check, by Elizabeth Engstrom
Death is a Star, by Christina Lay
D. D. Murphry, Secret Policeman, by Alan M. Clark and Elizabeth Massie
Black Leather, by Elizabeth Engstrom

Novelettes:
The Tao of Flynn, by Eric Witchey
To Build a Boat, Listen to Trees, by Eric Witchey

Children's Illustrated:
The Christmas Thingy, by F. Paul Wilson. Illustrated by Alan M. Clark

Collections:
Suspicions, by Elizabeth Engstrom
Professor Witchey's Miracle Mood Cure, by Eric Witchey

Short Fiction:
"Brittle Bones and Old Rope," by Alan M. Clark
"Crosley," by Elizabeth Engstrom
"The Apple Sniper," by Eric Witchey

Nonfiction:
How to Write a Sizzling Sex Scene by Elizabeth Engstrom

IFD Publishing Audio Books

Novels:
The Door That Faced West by Alan M. Clark, read by Charles Hinckley
Jack the Ripper Victim Series: Of Thimble and Threat by Alan M. Clark, read by Alicia Rose
Jack the Ripper Victim Series: Say Anything But Your Prayers by Alan M. Clark, read by Alicia Rose
Jack the Ripper Victim Series: The Double Event by Alan M. Clark, read by Alicia Rose (includes two novels from the series: *Of Thimble and Threat* and *Say Anything But Your Prayers*)
A Parliament of Crows by Alan M. Clark, read by Laura Jennings
A Brutal Chill in August by Alan M. Clark, read by Alicia Rose
The Surgeon's Mate: A Dismemoir by Alan M. Clark, read by Alan M. Clark
Apologies to the Cat's Meat Man by Alan M. Clark, read by Alicia Rose